"Connor—

He snorted derisiv[...] know it."

"Look closer, Connor. She *is* yours." Mallory shoved Liddy's photo under his nose. "She's six now. She's ill. I swear I wouldn't be here otherwise. I...we...*she* needs your help, Connor."

It was only after Connor stopped to examine Liddy's baby picture that Mallory began to relax. "I named her Lydia Beatrice," she ventured. "I, uh, everyone calls her Liddy Bea."

"This isn't some practical joke, is it? This child really exists. And she's mine." Connor's shell-shocked eyes rose from the photo at last. He stared at Mallory, who had once again retreated into the shadows.

Something moved deep inside her. Finally, mercifully, she was able to place herself in Connor's shoes. "I shouldn't have sprung this on you with no advance warning. I'm sorry." Her hand fluttered. "Liddy Bea is ill, Connor. Her kidneys have stopped functioning." Fumbling, she extracted a manila envelope from her bag. "Her doctor's office prepared a report for you."

He took the report, and as he skimmed it, she backed slowly away from him.

A moment later, the report in one hand, Liddy's baby picture in the other, he stalked toward her. "You waltz in here after seven years of...of nothing, announce I fathered a child, and oh, by the way, she needs one of your kidneys, Connor. That's a hell of a monkey wrench to throw in a man's life, Mallory."

Dear Reader,

In an earlier career of mine, I had the privilege of working for a doctor who led the race in the pediatric kidney transplant program. Although there have been great medical strides in the dialysis programs since those first forays into the field, the desperate need for organ donors has changed little. Doctors and patients still have to beg for lifesaving organs. And yes, even though transplants are easier than they once were, problems do still occur, even when it seems that all factors point to the perfect donor.

This story is dedicated to a sorority sister and good friend who has had one failed transplant. She's now near the top of the national donor list, but her "perfect" match hasn't shown up. The problems facing people in the long waiting list are not as simply solved as I've made them for the sake of a happy ending. Yet I hope Mallory, Connor and Liddy Bea's situation adds in some small way to public awareness of the constant need for organ donors.

I also want to give special thanks, always, to my editor, Paula Eykelhof, for continuing to let me write stories that are close to my heart.

Roz Denny Fox

P.S. I love hearing from readers. Write me at: P.O. Box 17480-101, Tucson, AZ 85731. Or you can reach me by e-mail: rdfox@worldnet.att.net.

Books by Roz Denny Fox

HARLEQUIN SUPERROMANCE

The Seven Year Secret
Roz Denny Fox

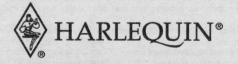

HARLEQUIN®

TORONTO • NEW YORK • LONDON
AMSTERDAM • PARIS • SYDNEY • HAMBURG
STOCKHOLM • ATHENS • TOKYO • MILAN • MADRID
PRAGUE • WARSAW • BUDAPEST • AUCKLAND

ISBN 0-373-71069-0

THE SEVEN YEAR SECRET

Copyright © 2002 by Rosaline Fox.

Visit us at www.eHarlequin.com

Printed in U.S.A.

The Seven Year Secret

CHAPTER ONE

A LIGHT TAP AT THE DOOR of Liddy's hospital room drew Mallory Forrest's attention. Her daughter's doctor, Fredric Dahl, motioned for her to come out.

Liddy Bea had fallen asleep. Mallory hated leaving without telling the fretful six-year-old where she'd be. But Tallahassee's leading pediatric nephrologist was a very busy man. Dropping a kiss on Liddy's cheek, Mallory slipped out, closing the door softly behind her.

Dr. Dahl strode briskly toward a small conference room near the bustling nursing center. Mallory's heart quickened, and fear clawed at her stomach as she followed him. Busy doctors didn't use conference rooms to impart good news.

Fredric pulled out a chair for Mallory. He leaned against one corner of the table, all the while clutching a thick metal hospital binder. Liddy Bea's chart. Mallory knew from its size. It pained her to think of the number of times Liddy had been hospitalized in her short life. To avoid Dahl's unsettling frown, Mallory concentrated on smoothing wrinkles from the suit she'd worn that morning for work.

Fredric spoke gently, though ever blunt. "It's as we feared. Liddy's rejecting the kidney you donated. I need you to authorize its removal, Mallory." He drew a paper from the chart and slid it across the table. "The organ is dying. Any delay taking it out means we risk gangrene setting in.''

''How is that possible?'' Mallory ignored the gold pen he extended. She wrapped her arms around her midsection and tucked her hands under her elbows to slow their shaking. ''Can't you switch Liddy's antirejection medication again? Surely there's something new on the market. Something different we can try?'' Tears spilled from beneath Mallory's eyelids. ''She was doing so well. Why? Why her?''

''Now, now, Mallory. We knew it wasn't a perfect transplant. It's those rogue antibodies of Liddy's I told you we're dealing with. And you weren't an absolute match.''

''But I *should* be, shouldn't I? I'm her mother. Oh, it's not fair! She doesn't deserve to have her new life snatched away.''

''It won't help to beat yourself up over this setback. We weighed all the consequences eight months ago and took the risk. Liddy Bea will go back on hemo, or peritoneal dialysis. I'll relist her immediately in the national donor computer.''

''But the list is so long…overwhelming. And if transplants from complete strangers work, why did she reject my kidney?'' Mallory tried but failed to keep hysteria from erupting as panic built inside her. ''If only Mark—''

''Your brother's out of the question. The malaria he contracted in the military makes him unacceptable. And we both know your dad's heart condition rules him out. I know how tough it is to accept, Mallory, but you simply have to face the fact that you've exhausted your family options. The national list is our best hope now.''

Mallory tore at a tissue Fredric had thoughtfully

pulled for her from a nearby box. She focused on the white bits coming apart in her nervous fingers. "We haven't totally scraped the bottom of the family barrel. There's…Liddy's father."

Uncrossing his ankles, Fredric came to his feet. "The senator—Brad—er, your dad informed me quite succinctly at the outset that Liddy's father is out of the picture. If you're planning to start a family feud…well, it's awkward for me. Your father gave me the opportunity to head kidney studies at the university, and also to supervise Forrest Memorial Hospital's transplant program. I'm forever in his debt—but for Liddy, I'd be happy to step aside and call in someone else, if you'd like."

"No, you're the best, Fredric. Dad wanted the best for his only grandchild," Mallory said sharply. "He'll agree this is our only choice, given what's happened."

"I hope so. He didn't mince words when he closed the subject of Liddy's father."

"Dad never minces words. Nor do I. Liddy's my child. It's my decision. And her father's, assuming he'll listen…" Mallory snatched the pen from the doctor's limp fingers and scribbled her name at the bottom of the surgery authorization form.

Dahl accepted the paper she shoved back. "I recall Brad mentioning your…uh…former husband lived out of the country. On a remote atoll in the Pacific, I believe. That'll pose a huge logistics problem, Mallory."

"Connor's stateside again. And he's not my ex. We were never married. In fact, he's unaware he fathered a child. Believe me, Fredric, if I could see another donor on the horizon, I'd let things stand. But I'll go to any lengths to ensure Liddy's health and happiness."

After an uncomfortable silence, she ventured in a less

certain voice, "When is Liddy scheduled for surgery? I'll have to run downstairs and arrange with Alec for more time away from work. Poor Alec. It's only mid-May. I feel like I've barely gotten back into the swing after taking those months off to give Liddy Bea a kidney."

Dahl leaned over and patted her shoulder. "From what I hear, Dr. Robinson and his staff would make any accommodation to keep you. Our esteemed administrator has said repeatedly how lucky we are to have you heading our fund-raisers."

Mallory dredged up a thin smile. "I always thought he only offered me the PR job because I'd more or less become a fixture at the hospital during Mom's illness. It coincided with my pregnancy, and I dashed out of her room so many times to throw up, Alec stopped to find out what was going on."

"Your family's suffered more than its share of medical setbacks. Odd how it sometimes works that way. But the illnesses aren't related. Although, your dad's arteriosclerotic heart disease has likely been exacerbated by worrying about your mother and Liddy and you. Not to mention all his responsibilities as a state senator."

"Dad's heart condition is exacerbated by the rich food he eats, the nightly brandy he drinks and those dreadful cigars he refuses to give up."

This time Dahl's chuckle was dry. "Your diagnosis may be closer to the mark than mine. Tough old codgers like Brad can be set in their ways. That's why I wonder if you ought to reconsider contacting Liddy Bea's father."

"If anyone understands doing whatever it takes to help the people we love, it'll be Dad. I haven't seen or heard from Connor O'Rourke in almost seven years. But if there's a chance in a million that one of his kidneys will lengthen Liddy Bea's life, I'll crawl to Miami on my hands and knees to beg.''

The slightly stooped, balding physician stared at her gravely. ''I know you will, Mallory. I know you will.'' He passed a hand over his sparse hair. ''Lord knows, I want a perfect donor for Lydia, too. Yet I have to weigh that against worry over what you might be walking into. I've been involved with this business of begging for donor organs for twenty years. I've witnessed verbal squabbles, fistfights and actual bloodshed. I've seen parents divorce and families so torn apart they never speak to one another again. You, Mark and Bradford are rare in that any one of you would have given Lydia a kidney.''

Mallory stuffed the mutilated tissue into her pocket and stood to brush the remaining lint from her skirt. ''Once upon a time, the man who fathered Liddy Bea had a tender heart buried under a tough outer shell. Surely it's still there. Connor may hate *me* for not telling him he has a child, but he wouldn't let his anger extend to his daughter.'' Although the hand she placed on the doorknob wasn't steady, Mallory hauled in a deep breath and squared her shoulders before leaving the conference room.

''Liddy's surgery is at four o'clock.'' Lowering his voice, Dahl fell in step with Mallory as they walked back along the cheerily lit hall. ''We'll insert a new cannula and start dialysis immediately. Peritoneal, if the abdominal wall is in good shape. So there's no dire urgency about confronting her biological dad. I want Liddy recovered from this surgery before attempting another implant. Perhaps a donor will turn up on the national list by then.''

Mallory stopped outside Liddy's room. "Every piece of literature you've given me says blood relatives are the preferable donors."

Dr. Dahl twisted his lips. "True. But if I set aside the fact that I'm a doctor and view it instead from the perspective of a friend and a father of three—well, I'm worried you'll be opening a can of worms. Fathers today demand and get parental rights in the courts."

Mallory stared at Dahl from cloudy blue eyes, all the while twisting a strand of hair around her index finger. "I must be more exhausted than I thought. I don't understand what you're implying."

"Maybe nothing. Maybe everything. Put yourself in Mr. O'Rourke's shoes. Liddy is a bright, charming child. And you've had her all to yourself for six years."

A burst of light exploded inside Mallory's head, leaving her slightly woozy. She groped the doorknob to Liddy's room for support. "You think Connor may decide it's time to…share custody?"

"It's a possibility."

"Then it's a possibility I'll have to deal with." She inhaled quickly. "Liddy Bea was barely two when her kidneys first failed. For the next year and a half, she underwent hemodialysis. I sat there holding her night after night, listening to her sob in pain as one after another her veins collapsed or got horribly infected around the shunt. I rocked her throughout the long, dark hours when it seemed all either of us could do was cry. If only you knew how I prayed for a match on the national donor list—but…there were none. I thought giving her one of my kidneys, even though it wasn't a hundred percent match, would be better than nothing. For eight months it was. For eight glorious months, she was normal. Happy. So, Fredric…I'd make a pact with the devil to see her that way again.''

Out of breath from her impassioned speech, Mallory wrenched open Liddy's door, inadvertently banging it against the wall. The child's translucent eyelids fluttered twice, revealing gray irises so like Connor O'Rourke's. The gray eyes focused on Mallory, and a huge smile blossomed on Liddy's face.

"Is it morning, Mommy? Are you here to take me home?''

Mallory steeled herself against the pain of telling Liddy Bea she'd be losing the kidney and going back on dialysis.

Bradford Forrest's timely arrival gave Mallory a reprieve. The senator always entered a room as if he owned it. And considering the amount of money he'd donated over the years to the private hospital he'd been instrumental in seeing built, he probably *did* own a fair portion. Florida's senior statesman remained a suave, handsome man, if one overlooked his tendency toward portliness.

Because Mallory loved him, she overlooked many of his faults. Friends and acquaintances were prone to say that her thick brown hair and direct blue eyes came from Brad, even though his hair was shot with silver now. The same folks joked that it was fortunate his daughter's slender build and sweet disposition came from Bradford's beloved wife. Beatrice had died just the day of Liddy's birth, and he'd never truly recovered.

Recently reelected for a fifth term, Bradford was a powerful and influential force in Tallahassee and in many parts of the state. This man who made others quake turned to mush in the presence of his only grandchild. Like now, he drew a huge stuffed bunny from behind his back and plopped it on Liddy's bed.

"Grandpapa!" The girl's face lit up as her arms circled the toy. "Thank you! I'll call her Flopsie Rabbit. Are you going to give me and Mommy a ride home? And will you and Davis drive me to school tomorrow?"

It was well-known that Liddy Bea loved riding to school in her grandfather's chauffeured limousine, and that he often rearranged his busy schedule to accommodate her. He kept the limo's bar stocked with her favorite juices, since hydration was of the utmost importance with her condition.

Senator Forrest was a man always in charge of any situation. This might be the first time he'd ever been at a loss for words. He flashed Mallory a helpless glance and mumbled, "I...uh...came because Fredric's office left...ah...a message with my secretary."

Mallory understood. Dr. Dahl, who'd become a good friend of the family, hadn't wanted her to go through Liddy's impending surgery alone. They'd moved out of their own apartment and in with her father a few weeks before the first transplant, and ever since then, the three Forrests had functioned as a more traditional family might. Just now, Mallory appreciated having her dad's strength to draw on.

Pushing the huge rabbit aside to sit on the edge of Liddy's bed, she cradled the child's smaller, warmer hand between her cold ones. "Liddy Bea, baby...the kidney Mommy gave you isn't working right." Mallory's breathing grew labored. "It's, uh, what's been making you sick lately. Dr. Dahl has to take it out."

Liddy blinked away tears, her stoicism another O'Rourke trait. At birth, Liddy Bea had appeared so like him, Mallory was moved to name her baby after Con-

nor's mother and hers. Even if he wasn't around to set
eyes on his child, Mallory determined then and there that
Lydia Beatrice would forever be a composite of both
Forrest and O'Rourke. If only she'd informed Connor
then that he had a daughter. Maybe...

"Will...it...hurt?"

Bradford wheeled to face the window overlooking the
pediatric nursing station. He rammed his hands deep in
the pockets of an expertly tailored jacket. Mallory
couldn't help noticing how the stalwart shoulders bent.
Perhaps she should've sent her dad off on some fool's
errand. He'd weathered his wife's premature death, his
daughter's unplanned pregnancy and his granddaughter's
kidney failure. Was it any wonder the man's heart had
weakened?

While Mallory was solicitous of all her dad had been
through, she'd made a point of never lying to her child.

"It'll hurt some. About like it did when Mommy gave
you the kidney. But anytime you feel pain, tell me. Or
if I'm not here, push this bell and the nurse will give
you something to make you feel better."

"Will I be able to go to school tomorrow?"

"No. We'll have to ask Dr. Dahl if you'll get to finish
out this year. Liddy, do you remember the tube you used
to have in your arm, then in your leg? You may have
another of those for a while. Until we can find you another kidney."

The little face puckered. "I didn't like those things.
Why can't we find 'nother kidney today?"

Yes, why? Mallory wanted to rage and shout. "That's
what Dr. Dahl, Mommy and Grandpapa are going to do.
Search until we find the perfect kidney."

"Okay. But hurry, please. I hafta get back to school,

'cause my teacher said we get a vacation party on the last day.''

"I'll hurry my fastest. And I'll ask Dr. Dahl if I can take you to the party."

Bradford fumbled for his handkerchief, found it and blew his nose. He turned slowly, discreetly blotting his eyes. "Listen, sugar pie. If Fredric says no, I'll bring the party to our house when you're better. I'll hire the clowns we had for your last birthday. And we'll have cake and all the ice cream you kids can eat. And—"

"Dad." Mallory interrupted, cautioning him with a glance.

"What? Are clowns too extravagant? I commissioned a three-ring circus for *your* tenth birthday, missy."

"A circus? Oh, goody." Liddy clapped her hands.

Mallory rolled her eyes. "Dad! You promised not to overindulge Liddy Bea if we moved in with you."

The practiced southern statesman didn't look the least bit contrite.

"Liddy, play with your bunny a minute," Mallory said. "Mommy and Grandpapa are going to walk down the hall for a soda."

"Can I have grape juice?"

"Oh, baby, I don't think Dr. Dahl wants you to eat or drink anything until after the surgery." Mallory leaned over and kissed Liddy's nose before sliding off the bed, raising the side rail and locking it in place.

Liddy buried her face in the rabbit's soft fur, but she didn't cry or beg for juice as another child might. She accepted her mother's decision.

The senator waited until they were out of earshot before speaking. "If you're going to nag me about offering to throw a party for Liddy's class, you may as well save your breath. What good is all the damn money I have if

I can't spend it on the people I love? I'd hire all the characters in Disney World and fly them here if I thought it'd give her pleasure.'' His drawl was never more pronounced than when he was passionate about something. The same impassioned manner had won him prestige as a lawyer and later convinced junior legislators to vote his way. However, his daughter had never quaked before him.

"I know you mean well, Dad, and that you love Liddy Bea to bits. But I want her to value things money can't buy. I want her friends to value her for who she is and not worry that they might have to compete with the Forrest fortune."

His eyes narrowed as he held open the door to the room with the soda machines. He forged ahead and shoved in money, then smacked a selection button. "You're not talking about Liddy Bea now, are you? We're back to what happened with you and O'Rourke."

"It's all tied together. And yes, I need to talk to you about Connor," she said, accepting the cola and closing her eyes as she rolled the cold can across her suddenly hot forehead. "He's back in the States. In Miami."

Brad turned around to get his own soda, effectively hiding the guilty flush that climbed his neck. "I know. So I take it he's finally contacted you?"

"No." Mallory wasn't nearly as effective at concealing her pain. "I read an article on him in one of your business magazines while I was recovering from my part of the surgery. Connor's become a leading expert in baroclinic instability relative to cyclostrophic and thermal winds." She rattled the words off with ease. "A gadget he's invented might facilitate early detection of hurricanes. They're testing it at Miami's weather cen-

ter.'' Mallory's voice held a tinge of pride, even as she
studiously avoided the scrutiny in her father's eyes.

Brad took a deep pull from his soda. ''I assume
there's a point to this recap of O'Rourke's success? By
the way, I read the article. I also happened to walk into
your room the day of his TV interview. You were so
engrossed you didn't realize I was there. I went back to
my study to see the remainder of the program. Must say
I was impressed by everything he's accomplished.''

That tidbit stopped Mallory cold. She'd been impressed, too. She'd also foolishly waited, expecting Connor to phone her. He could easily have done so, had he
wanted. After all, *she* wasn't the one who'd left home
to flit all over the globe. Yet, even now, she couldn't
bring herself to discuss the barrage of emotions seeing
Connor had evoked. Her first thought was that Connor
had matured well. As the interview progressed and she
heard his voice, observed the intensity in his gray eyes,
all her old feelings for him had flooded back. After the
show, she'd been oh-so-tempted to phone him—to unburden her conscience. Her next reaction had been *who
was she kidding?* With Connor, it was out of sight, out
of mind. She owed him nothing.

Her fingers tightened on the soda can. ''I'm flying to
Miami to see Connor. I wanted you to know so you
could arrange to spend extra time at the hospital with
Liddy. I'll wait until she's out of the woods, of course.
Then I'll fly down one day and back the next.'' She
didn't want to accost Connor at work. Evening, at his
home, would be better. Mallory skewered her father with
the ''Forrest look.'' ''Will you use your clout to get me
his home address?''

Bradford heaved a sigh. ''I've been expecting something like this.''

"You have?" She gaped. "It only occurred to me today. So, you aren't going to try and talk me out of it?"

"I can see your mind's already made up. But…is it wise? Isn't O'Rourke a stone better left unturned?"

"I'm assuming he has two functioning kidneys. Maybe I sound mercenary, but his child needs one. And the rest of her family has been ruled out."

"I don't think you're mercenary, Mallory. In fact, I've toyed with the thought of contacting Connor myself. But it wasn't my place. I'm frankly worried about how he'll react. He could get nasty, or even deny that Liddy's his."

Mallory crushed her can, hardly aware of what she was doing. "I guess I've always had more faith in Connor than you or Mother did. She hated him, you know? Or rather, she looked down on him. Mom couldn't handle the fact that Lydia O'Rourke worked as a maid to support herself and Connor after his dad ran off. Mom could be such a snob."

"That's enough, Mallory. Make peace with Connor for Liddy's sake. Leave your mother out of it. Whatever Beatrice did, she did out of love for you. I won't let you speak ill of her." Spinning on the heels of his polished wingtips, Brad stomped out of the room. He pitched his soda can in a wastebasket outside the door. Then he waited for Mallory.

"I'll go make a few calls," he said tiredly. "See if I can turn up a current address on O'Rourke. Tell Liddy I'll be back before they give her the anesthetic. Her surgery's at four, right?" He shot a cuff to check his watch. "It's two-fifteen. That allows me time to twist a few arms."

Mallory hugged him. "Thanks. I may not always

sound like it, but I appreciate everything you've done for me and Liddy Bea. You're our rock. And just because I felt Mom treated Connor unfairly doesn't mean I love her less. It's certainly not her fault he went off to the South Pacific chasing storms. I made a conscious decision not to tell him I was pregnant, so I wouldn't stand in the way of his big dream. It's taken a while, but I can finally accept that I never meant to him what he meant to me. What I won't do is take the easy way out now. Not if there's even a remote possibility he can help Liddy Bea.''

Brad's brow furrowed. ''I could hire someone to tell him. Then you wouldn't even have to speak to him.''

''I should've tracked him down when Liddy Bea was born. It would have been the right thing to do. If Mother hadn't been so ill…if she hadn't suddenly died…'' Mallory gnawed at the inside of her mouth. ''Time seemed to drift away from me, and…well, I rationalized that if he didn't care about me, he didn't deserve to…'' Her voice faltered, her throat too tight to go on. The truth was, Connor had hurt her terribly by forgetting she existed.

Her dad's shoulders slumped. ''All hell will break loose, but it can't be helped. I told Beatrice that someday…'' The senator pulled himself up short, turned and stalked heavily off, shaking his head as he went.

Mallory stared after him. He seemed to shuffle down the hall. Her father, who did everything decisively. He'd suffered so much with her mother's death. And Mallory hadn't been as cooperative as she might have been. Her dad had begged her to live at home and assume the many social duties Beatrice had once performed so perfectly. But Mallory craved a life of her own, and she'd been determined to raise Liddy without the Forrest money—

money she blamed, at least partially, for Connor's lengthy silence. Yet after Liddy Bea got ill, she'd gravitated again toward her family.

When Liddy was an infant, Dr. Robinson had offered Mallory the job in the hospital's public relations department; it had been an answer to a prayer. Life was idyllic until Liddy Bea took sick. Thinking of Alec prodded Mallory to action. She had to make arrangements for another leave. Or perhaps it'd be better for the hospital if she just quit this time.

Robinson didn't agree when she went to see him. "We muddled along without anyone to do fund-raising until you fell into our lap, Mallory. There's nothing crucial in the works until our winter dance. And you've already booked the site. Fredric will find Lydia a kidney soon. For now, take whatever time you need." Alec checked to see that no one was watching, then kissed Mallory's cheek.

"Thanks." She drew back so the kiss barely grazed her face. "Once Liddy Bea's out of the hospital, I'll finish building the database for the ball invitations. I can do that at home, while we wait for a donor."

Sliding an arm around her shoulders, Alec escorted Mallory from his private office. Concentrating on the ball helped take her mind off the impending surgery and a larger concern—visiting Connor. Mallory wasn't sure why she hadn't mentioned her plans to Alec. Maybe because she suspected he, too, would disapprove.

LIDDY'S SURGERY WENT WELL. By nine that evening, Mallory marveled at how quickly the child bounced back. Her own recovery as a donor had been slow. Liddy also had an optimistic outlook, a willingness to assume the best, something for which Mallory was extremely grateful.

The doctor elected to keep Liddy hospitalized a few days to monitor her for infection and to set up her dialysis schedule, but he told Mallory there was no valid reason to stay with Liddy around the clock. Which was why, Friday noon, she found herself on a Miami-bound commuter plane.

It was still officially spring, yet the air in Tallahassee was already summer-muggy. She actually looked forward to the coastal breezes. Mallory wasn't sure, though, whether she looked forward to meeting Connor again, or dreaded it. At one time, she'd loved him more deeply and completely than she'd ever loved another human being. He, on the other hand, had been the one to drag his feet in their relationship. Despite that, she'd never dreamed he'd go off and forget all about her.

In fact, she thought she'd scaled all his barriers the year he entered grad school at Florida State University. She'd collected her public relations degree and moved into his apartment to devote herself to making him happy. That was the first time he'd used the word *love* in connection with her name. He'd even said he didn't think he could live without her. But he'd certainly managed to do just that.

The eve of his master's graduation, Mallory had news of her own—which she held back, planning to surprise him after they'd enjoyed his favorite meal of fat Gulf shrimp and tarragon rice, topped by skewers of mushrooms and tomatoes. If she closed her eyes, she could almost smell the Cajun spices—could feel the sultry air in the tiny apartment.

Connor, it so happened, arrived home with an MS and his own exciting news. A plum job offer—on a remote atoll in the South Pacific, complete with an opportunity to get his Ph.D. via correspondence. Courtesy of a Tallahassee manufacturer, and in conjunction with the national weather service, he was awarded a chance to realize his dream of developing an early-detection system for hurricanes.

Excited for him, Mallory suggested she accompany him as far as Hawaii. ''I'll find a job, then when you have breaks, I'll be waiting there for you,'' she'd said.

Although she'd tried hard to wipe out his answer, it came back as clearly now as the night he'd broken her heart. ''You stay here. Marry one of those up-and-coming lawyers your folks keep parading past you. It'll take me years to finish my work. You're a distraction, Mallory. A huge distraction. This is the opportunity of a lifetime, and I can't afford to blow it.''

She'd given in to tears. Connor had relented marginally, saying they'd keep in touch by mail. And she had written once or twice. Until her mother's illness worsened, and pregnancy sapped her own flagging energy. In all those nine months before Liddy Bea was born, Mallory never received so much as a word from Connor.

Beatrice Forrest died the day Mallory left the hospital with her new baby. After that, her life changed drastically, and she'd lost the courage to write him again. But she'd kept tabs on him occasionally by checking the national hurricane site on the Internet.

Sipping lime water provided by the stewardess, Mallory checked the creased blue paper on which her dad had scribbled Connor's address. When the hour came to actually face him, she hoped the words would flow and her tears would not.

The plane landed on time. Her dad had ordered a car service to take her to the Biltmore, an elegant old hotel

that rose like a terra-cotta wedding cake from the middle
of residential Coral Gables. The driver said he'd return
at six-thirty to drive her to Connor's. Mallory knew
without asking that the man had orders to wait outside
the apartment while she went in and said her piece. She
didn't doubt that he might also drag her out if she didn't
leave in a reasonable period of time.

Nervously Mallory showered off the dust of travel.
She dressed in a no-nonsense pin-striped suit. One
glimpse in the floor-length mirror, and she stripped out
of it again. She wanted to appear mature and profes-
sional. But pride demanded she look feminine, too. Connor, never stingy with compliments, had always liked
her in blue. In a weak moment, she'd packed such a
dress. A sleeveless sapphire silk with a flared skirt,
banded by a straw belt. She had shoes and an oversize
bag to match. The last thing she did was spritz her throat
and wrists with her trademark perfume. If nothing else,
the familiar scent bolstered her courage.

At the preappointed hour, her driver wove unerringly
through thickening traffic, arriving outside Connor's
apartment building in record time. "There's nowhere to
park, miss. Shall I circle the block until something opens
up?"

"Yes, please." Mallory found speaking difficult because her throat had gone dry. "I don't expect this to
take long." She figured on giving Connor her canned
spiel. Then she'd hand over Dr. Dahl's business card,
plus his typed report, and leave Connor to work things
out for himself. If he hadn't changed, it was how he
operated best. Facts before action.

Mallory thanked providence that his apartment was at
ground level. Her weak knees would never propel her
up a set of stairs. Blocking out the boisterous laughter

and loud music pulsing through his open window, she rapped loudly enough to be heard over the din.

A casually dressed man with sun-bleached blond hair juggled two frosty glasses of beer in one hand as he opened the door. His wolf whistle and shouted "Greg, she's here!" had Mallory stepping back. A second man appeared. Grabbing her arm, he pulled her inside. Mallory squeaked out a protest as, against her will, she entered what was clearly a keg party made up of fifteen to twenty males.

"We thought you'd be wearing a skimpy sequined cop uniform," the man clutching Mallory confided with a wink. "I guess the costume and handcuffs are in this bag." Releasing her arm, he began pawing through her straw purse.

Mallory yanked it back. A tug-of-war ensued, which upended her bag. Photos of Liddy Bea at various ages, which Mallory had included to show Connor if all else failed, fell out and slid across a slick tile floor.

"Stop!" Dropping to her knees, she scrambled to gather up the pictures before the oaf with the beer spilled it on them. Her heart hammered madly. "I'm afraid you've confused me with someone else. I'm looking for Connor O'Rourke."

"This is his place." The man holding the beer did splash foam on Mallory's bare arm. "Oops. Sorry. I'm Paul Caldwell. That's Greg Dugan. We contracted with your agency for you to come here and do your cop routine."

Still on her knees, Mallory stared up at him, uncomprehending.

"Jeez, you know—where you handcuff Connor to a chair and then do a little…uh…bump-and-grind number. Hey, it's for his bachelor party! Connor's getting hitched.'' The beer drinker enunciated slowly this time, as if Mallory were addle-brained.

Indeed she was. She'd envisioned Connor O'Rourke in a whole lot of ways over the past seven years. On the verge of marriage was not one of them.

She went hot, then cold, then hot again. Her fingers groped for the baby picture of Liddy Bea.

She hardly noticed that another broad hand had reached over her shoulder to scrape the photo off the floor. Nevertheless, Mallory froze as a voice she remembered too well rained down on her head. ''Paul? Greg? What's going on? Who is this woman? I thought we agreed there'd be no females at this party.''

Mallory couldn't say how she found the courage to stand and face the man she'd come to see. But she did. And she managed to pluck Liddy's picture from his suddenly slack fingers. Clearly the advantage of surprise was on her side.

''Mal…lo…ry?'' Her name fell from Connor's lips in three distinct syllables.

In spite of all the time that had passed and all the rehearsing she'd done, Mallory couldn't speak. She couldn't do anything but swallow repeatedly and stand before him like a statue, watching the play of dark shadows cross features she'd never forgotten.

A jumble of heat and fury contorted Connor's angular face as Greg and Paul lamely attempted to explain the surprise they'd arranged. He silenced them with a slice of his hand. ''I don't know what the hell kind of sick joke you and these idiots are pulling, but I'm not amused, Mallory. Not in the least. You have a hell of a nerve coming here, tonight of all nights.''

As his friends stepped back, the real performer rushed up the steps. She wore a very minuscule rendition of a cop uniform. So minuscule, the well-endowed woman hardly had room for the badge she'd pinned above one ample breast.

Paul and Greg ran to greet her. Mallory felt Connor's cool hand propelling her toward the door. His jaw was locked in place. Figuring she had maybe two seconds at best to make him listen, she dug in her heels.

"Connor, you have to give me a minute."

The instant he glanced down at her, Mallory shoved Liddy's photo under his nose. "We have a child, you and I. She's six now. She's ill, I swear I wouldn't be here otherwise. I...we...*she* needs your help, Connor." Her plea was uttered in spurts.

He snorted derisively. "That's a damned lie and you know it."

"Look closer, Connor. She *is* yours."

At that moment the CD player suddenly stopped. All movement in the room beyond ceased. A hush descended as a now-uneasy group of guys waited for Connor's response. Regardless of his obvious fury, he couldn't seem to tear his eyes away from the five-by-seven glossy print wavering in Mallory's unsteady hand. A single second went by before he tightened his grip on Mallory's wrist. Lips tightly compressed, he practically slung her into a nearby room. In the process of shutting them both inside, he glared at the men huddled around the exotic dancer. "Paul. Greg. When I come out, I want everyone gone. Not just out by the pool, either. Gone, as in goodbye!"

Mallory felt her knees knock as Connor's rage swirled over her. Why, oh why hadn't she heeded Fredric Dahl's warnings? And her dad's? She should never have come here.

CHAPTER TWO

MALLORY HAD THOUGHT SHE'D steeled herself for this encounter with her child's father. The only man who'd ever touched her heart. In reality, being closeted in a small room with him, knowing he was on the brink of marrying another woman, was Mallory's worst nightmare. Or perhaps it was watching him pace the perimeter of his study, gazing in outrage and denial at Liddy's photo, that broke Mallory's heart and turned her stomach inside out.

Why didn't he say something? Anything? Although, Connor O'Rourke had never been a wordy man. In the past she'd been content to spend hours with him, often without a single comment passing between them. Now, as she tracked his tense, jerky movements, she found his silence hell on her nerves.

It was only after Connor stopped in front of an oak desk in the center of the room to examine Liddy's baby picture under the light that Mallory's rubbery legs felt strong enough to let her join him. She'd carefully selected pictures of Liddy taken at birth, two years, four and six. "I named her Lydia Beatrice," Mallory ventured as Connor glanced at the new offerings. "I, uh, everyone calls her Liddy Bea."

"This isn't some practical joke Paul and Greg conjured up, is it? This child really exists. And she's mine." Connor's shell-shocked eyes lifted at last from the photo he tenderly caressed. He stared at Mallory, who had once again retreated into the shadows.

Something moved deep inside her. Finally, mercifully, she was able to do as Dr. Dahl suggested earlier—place herself in Connor's shoes. "I shouldn't have sprung this on you with no advance warning. I'm sorry." Her hand fluttered. "Liddy Bea is ill, Connor. Her kidneys have stopped functioning."

Fumbling, Mallory extracted a manila envelope from her handbag. "Her doctor's office prepared a report for you. It explains her condition more clearly than I can."

She thought he wasn't going to take the envelope, but eventually he did "Considering the shock I've given you…" Mallory tossed back a lock of hair. "I'm sure you'll want to study the facts and probably ask Dr. Dahl some questions before you agree to be tested. I've attached his card with office and home numbers. Meanwhile, I won't intrude on your evening any longer. I have a car waiting." She slipped by him and began collecting the photos.

"Leave them." Connor's hand collided with hers as they both attempted to rake in the pictures. He'd already skimmed the doctor's report and found it difficult to comprehend. He rubbed his temple with his free hand.

She backed away slowly. The pictures had been removed from her album. But Connor deserved to have a set. With the exception of the recent school photo, all had been taken by a Tallahassee studio. She could get copies. Feeling the doorknob press into her back, Mallory reached behind her and twisted it. The outer room, which had bubbled with sound, now lay quiet as a tomb.

"Where are you going?" Connor's ragged voice halted her retreat. "Lord, Mallory. What in hell am I supposed to think—to *do*—here?"

"The report is self-explanatory, Connor. Read it, think about it, call Dr. Dahl." She shrugged nervously. "No point in wearing out my welcome. There's really no need for us to deal with each other again. I imagine you'll want to meet Liddy Bea. I can leave authorization with the nursing staff at Forrest Memorial if you visit while she's there. Or…other arrangements can be made. From here on, though, any contact you have will not be with me but with Dr. Dahl or his staff. That should ease your mind a lot."

"Really?" He stalked toward her, the report in one hand, Liddy Bea's baby picture in the other. He shook them both under her nose. "You waltz in here after seven years of…of…nothing, announce I fathered a child, and oh, by the way, she needs one of your kidneys, Connor. Then you flit merrily out again. That's a hell of a monkey wrench to throw in a man's life, Mallory." His lips twisted harshly.

She took in each feature of his rugged, anguished face before saying quietly, "You have a right to be angry with me, Connor. But it won't change the fact that we had a child together. Nor will it alter Liddy's situation. I'm not going to fight with you. I will get down on my knees and apologize if that's what you need from me. There's nothing I won't do for Liddy Bea. Nothing." Her quavery voice broke.

A muscle in Connor's jaw jumped twice, and his face contorted in pain. He turned away from Mallory and made his way back to the desk, where he dropped the items he held. Flattening both palms on his desk, he braced himself with his back toward her. "I have arrangements to make, people to consult before I can go to Tallahassee," he said, sounding raw.

Mallory noted how the muscles in his shoulders

bunched beneath his knit shirt. She resisted a strong impulse to cross to him and massage away his tension. The feeling came as a shock, considering he'd gone off seven years ago and never looked back once to see how she'd survived the breakup. Or even *if* she'd survived.

But she no longer had the right to console him in any fashion. The right now belonged to his fiancée. Merely thinking about Connor's engagement almost crushed the breath from Mallory's lungs.

Whirling, she ran from the room, damned if she'd let him see a single one of the tears that blinded her.

CONNOR SENSED THE MOMENT Mallory left. It was more than an absence of a perfume called Desire, a scent he never failed to associate with her. One he'd missed so terribly that first year he'd been stuck on a solitary outpost, he'd wandered up to a department store perfume counter on his first R and R to Honolulu, just for a whiff of the bergamot-and-magnolia mixture. A whiff he'd never, ever assumed would lodge in his nostrils for so many years.

He lifted his hands then slammed them down on the desktop, hoping the subsequent pain would eject him from this pointless reverie. Needless to say, it didn't.

"Dammit to hell!" He'd finally made a new life for himself. One that didn't include lingering memories of Mallory Forrest. He had found a new love. Claire Dupree, who was at home with her best friends in the midst of a bridal shower.

Claire's shower. For their wedding, scheduled the day after tomorrow!

"Lord." Groaning, Connor lifted the picture of a child fashioned in his image. "How in hell does a guy break *this* kind of news to his fiancée?"

Staggering around the desk, he dropped into a swivel chair. Pulling the most recent of the photos toward him, he traced dark-lashed gray eyes, an off-kilter smile and a slightly narrow yet stubborn jaw. The O'Rourke jaw. Connor couldn't refute the evidence staring him in the face. And Lord help him, deep down, unmistakable pleasure seeped upward until it squeezed his heart.

He had a child. A daughter Mallory had named after his mother. Why had she done that? It seemed out of character for someone who hadn't seen fit to answer any of his damned letters, who'd ignored every one of his pleas for forgiveness.

Connor rocked gently in his chair as the anguish surfaced, displacing even his outrage at Mallory. His mom, Lydia O'Rourke, had lost her life in a storm the folks in the weather-reporting business had failed to class as a hurricane. She would never experience the joy of meeting her first grandchild.

The telephone sitting near Connor's right hand jingled loudly, making him jump. He fumbled it to his ear, scrabbling to gather up the baby pictures the cord had knocked askew.

He shut his eyes. *Claire.* He wished he could ward off the questions that would undoubtedly come.

"Hi," she said cheerily. "I know you didn't expect to hear from me until we met at the church on Sunday. But Paul just came by the house to pick up Lauren. He acted really odd. He said your bachelor party broke up early, but he wouldn't say why. In fact, he was so insistent I ask you, it frightened me. Of course, I realize I'm suffering prewedding nerves." She gave a short laugh. "Janine and my other bridesmaids said I wouldn't feel better until I phoned you. So here I am."

Connor felt the pressure of her unspoken need to have

him alleviate her fears. He ran a hand through his hair, not having a clue where to begin. He'd known Claire for almost a year. In their early, getting-to-know-you phase, he'd mentioned that there'd once been someone special in his past. *Hadn't he?* Still silent, he tried to recall those initial conversations.

"Connor? Say something. You're really frightening me."

"We have to talk," he said abruptly. "But not over the phone. Can you get away if I come by in…say, twenty minutes?"

"I guess so," Claire said a little shakily. "It'll be after nine o'clock, though. You have to have me home by midnight. Not that I'll turn into a pumpkin," she murmured, stabbing weakly at humor. "But if the groom sees the bride the day before the wedding, it's supposed to be bad luck for a marriage…." Her voice trailed off.

"We'll go for coffee at that burger place just off Twenty-seventh, okay? I could use a cup of strong Cajun coffee about now."

"Did you overindulge tonight? I know you didn't really want a bachelor party."

"No," he said stiffly. "But I'll admit we made a fair dent in the keg Paul brought. If you'd rather not go for coffee, Claire, I can do without."

"Coffee's fine. And twenty minutes will give me time to tell the hangers-on goodbye, and hide away all the lacy lingerie I received at the shower," she said, giving a feeble rendition of a sultry growl.

"That's right. I forgot you had a—what did you call it?—personal shower."

The woman at the other end of the line sighed. "Honestly, Connor, aren't you intrigued enough to sound at least a little excited about the lingerie I got?"

"Sorry, I guess my mind's not the sharpest it's ever been. Knowing Janine, Lauren and Abby, I suspect what they bought won't leave much to a man's imagination." This time, his drawl could be considered closer to normal.

"No. My friends aren't what you'd describe as conventional."

"That's a fact."

"You sound as if you disapprove of them."

"Because I agreed with you? Look, Claire, I've explained that I'm not myself tonight. And for whatever reason, you seem oversensitive. Perhaps it'd be best if we saved the rest of this conversation for when we're sitting face-to-face."

"One question first," she said abruptly. "Connor, why haven't we slept together yet?"

"What?" he said too loudly as a strange wave of guilt washed over him. If Claire had asked that question even last week, he wouldn't have known why he'd continued to resist their spending an entire night together. Unfortunately, it was no longer a mystery. Miami, and indeed all of Florida, was tied to his prior history with Mallory Forrest. Plain and simple, his memories of her in and around this city held him back from making love with Claire.

Unable to see Connor's guilty look of alarm, his fiancée charged ahead. "I don't consider myself promiscuous by any means. But during the shower, when it was only us girls talking, the subject of sexual compatibility surfaced. I didn't tell anyone we haven't…ah…done the deed. They'd never believe it. So…I'm willing to toss out my superstitions if you'll forgo convention. Let's be wicked and book into one of the beach hotels tonight. Janine said couples who do are more relaxed at the wedding ceremony.

They aren't so anxious to dash off to start their honeymoon. What do you say, Connor?''

He couldn't say anything. His conscience played havoc with his mind. In the end, he didn't have to make lame excuses. Claire, typically accommodating, let him off the hook. ''Okay. I won't ask you to sacrifice your principles because I let Janine and the others override my good sense. I'll be waiting on the porch in twenty minutes. I can tell something's really bugging you. Just one last thing. Remember—together, we can overcome anything. That's what people in love do.'' She blew kisses into the phone, as had been her habit since he'd given her an engagement ring three months ago.

Connor heard the soft click when Claire replaced the receiver. Still, he continued to hold the buzzing instrument to his ear.

Had he ever believed that a nebulous emotion like love could conquer any and all adversity? No. He placed his faith in the logic of science. Yet he did love Claire, didn't he?

Throughout his five-and-a-half-year hiatus on an atoll in the Pacific, he'd been too engrossed in his work to want a substitute for Mallory. The restlessness, the feeling that something was missing in his life, didn't emerge until after he returned to Florida. Co-workers said that since he'd been out of the social circuit for so long, he needed a woman. He'd decided they were right.

Not counting the years he'd been with Mallory—for two of those they'd even lived together—he'd been pretty much a loner. Maybe that was why on the day he flipped the calendar and turned up his thirty-third birthday, he'd judged it was high time he settled down and started a family.

In areas where there were major weather centers, meteorologists formed tight-knit communities. Claire, an operational weather-support person and part-time forecaster, fit in his world. Short and blond, she looked nothing like Mallory Forrest, who was tall, willowy and brunette. Somehow, he and Claire hit it off. For eight months, they'd dated exclusively. And why not? From day one, she'd bent over backward to please him.

In that aspect, Connor realized, Claire was like Mallory. Was that why he'd proposed marriage so fast? Hanging up the phone, he planted his elbows on the desk, buried his face in his hands and rubbed away a fine tension that tightened the skin around his mouth. Damn, if he didn't love Claire for herself, he was a class-A asshole.

Figuring he'd better leave if he was meeting Claire in twenty minutes, he tucked the pictures of his daughter and the report about her condition into an envelope to take along, then dug out his car keys. He would lay this newest development in his life on the table and let Claire decide if she still wanted to hook up with a guy who had a shady past.

As usual, Claire was ready. And, also as usual, she looked immaculate. That always amazed Connor about her. Her pale hair never had a strand out of place. Her blouses matched whatever else she wore, whether skirt or pants. Her makeup and nail polish were perfectly applied.

Connor complimented her appearance as he helped her into the front seat. She linked her hands tightly atop her purse, frowning worriedly.

He hauled in a deep breath, walked around the car and climbed back into the driver's seat. Guessing it was going to be a silent ride, Connor selected one of Claire's favorite tapes, popping it into the player before entering into traffic. The soft piano strains of "On My Own," a tune from *Les Miserables,* floated from the back speakers.

"Balmy night," Connor remarked, thinking the weather a safe topic.

Claire nodded but kept her eyes ahead as she twisted her engagement ring around and around her finger.

"Sorry I was a few minutes late. I didn't allow for weekend traffic."

"Connor, if you aren't going to tell me why we need this impromptu talk, just hush. Please." Claire unclasped her hands and massaged her neck. "If I'd known we were going to do this, I wouldn't have had so much of the champagne Lauren brought."

"If you hadn't phoned me, Claire, I wouldn't have bothered you until morning."

"No. No." She let her hands fall. "I have a hunch it's something we need to settle tonight."

Connor battled a sick feeling in his stomach. He probably should've asked Mallory more questions, particularly as he didn't have any idea why she'd never informed him she was pregnant in the first place. But maybe the details didn't matter. Claire was right; they needed to hash out the primary issue tonight.

He breathed a sigh of relief when he saw the neon sign of the café looming up on his right. Connor parked in a lot behind the building, glad to see it was sparsely populated. By ten-thirty or so, after the movie houses let out, his favorite local hangout would get crowded. He'd counted on business being slow at this hour.

"If the back-corner booth is available, let's take it," he said, locking the car after helping Claire out. "Or any booth that offers privacy."

Again she said nothing. Not that Connor blamed her. Paul shouldn't have shot his mouth off. And yet it certainly saved him having to dive headlong into deep water.

The back booth was vacant. Connor waited until the waitress had delivered water and two cups of black coffee before he eased the envelope from his jacket. He set it unopened on the table between them, studying Claire with a troubled expression.

"I'm not going to like this, am I?" she finally whispered.

He shook his head, his own pain rising. "I don't even know where to begin," he said, turning his coffee cup around in its saucer several times.

Claire ran a forefinger along the rim of hers. Neither of them seemed inclined to test the dark, steamy brew, although both of them loved chicory coffee. "At the beginning is probably best," she said reluctantly.

Connor shifted one hip, slumping sideways a little. "There's this woman I used to be best friends with. Mallory Forrest. She, uh, we met here in Miami at a science camp when I was a junior and she was a sophomore in high school. We both lived in Tallahassee. She attended an exclusive private school. I went to public." His voice faded, as Connor recollected that long-ago first encounter. Mallory, the beautiful dynamo who outclassed everyone at that camp, and forever after.

Noting Claire's stony expression, Connor cleared his throat. "Given the disparity in our backgrounds, that camp should have been the beginning and end of our friendship. Her dad was a prominent attorney. A year or so later, Bradford Forrest was elected to the state senate. He's still there. Mallory's mom headed the state's volunteer hurricane-relief program. It was through Mallory that I got involved in relief work. I told you my mother died, and we lost most of what we owned in a hurricane the year I was a senior. Disaster insurance on mobile homes was too expensive, and after the hurricane, my application for government relief got bogged down in the system. Mallory found out. She tracked me down in the aftermath. I don't really know how she did everything she did. Like helping me arrange a funeral. Wangling me a place to stay, and later, a full-tuition scholarship to FSU. At the time, Mallory believed in me more than I did. She was convinced I could invent a system for early detection of hurricanes even though I wasn't nearly as sure about my abilities. I…uh…always felt in awe of her, but one step behind, too, if you know what I mean.''

Connor saw the light dawn in Claire's eyes.

''You're going to tell me this woman suddenly appeared again, aren't you? That she…she…wants you back.''

Wanting to save Claire as much pain as possible, he decided to bypass everything that had happened between him and Mallory at college and during his grad-school years. Though his hands were far from steady, he pulled open the envelope flap and dumped out the pictures and the report Mallory had brought him. ''She doesn't want me back, Claire. She came to tell me I'd fathered a child. Her child.''

Claire turned chalk-white. ''Obviously she's lying. Why, you spent almost six years alone, for all intents and purpose, on a remote island.''

He nodded miserably. ''My rationale, exactly. But this little girl—named Lydia after my mother, by the way— is six now. There's no mistaking she's mine, Claire. These baby pictures could be me at the same age.''

Claire pressed her lips together tight, then poked gingerly through the photos until she came to the report. "What's this? Proof of some kind? A demand for child support? What precisely does this woman want from you, Connor?"

"A kidney," he said, straightening again. He lifted the cup of now-cold coffee to his lips and took a healthy swig, grimacing as he did so.

"This is hardly the time to crack jokes," Claire snapped.

"I'm not joking. Read the paper. It's from a Tallahassee doctor. A detailed explanation of my daughter's condition, and the subsequent need for me to be tested as a possible organ donor."

"Why you, Connor? Why can't her mother give her a kidney?"

Connor rolled his head around his shoulders, failing to relieve the tight muscles in his neck and back. "The report says Mallory did give one of her kidneys eight months ago. Lydia's body started rejecting the organ last month. Recently that kidney had to be removed."

Claire picked up and read the report. Once she reached the end, she folded it neatly and glanced past him, fiddling with her cup. "It's a unique way to get a man back, I have to admit."

Connor stirred, angry at Claire for the first time since they'd met. It was the most cutting thing he'd ever heard her say. "This isn't about my renewing a relationship with Mallory. In fact, the last thing she said before she left was that I'd deal exclusively with Dr. Dahl, who wrote the report. Mallory said there'd be no reason for my path and hers to cross again. For all I know, she may be married."

Claire stared at him. "You didn't ask? Come on, Connor, what did you talk about after she broke up your bachelor party? She did, didn't she? Break it up? That's why Paul was so rattled.''

"Yes. Although Paul was already rattled because he mistook Mallory for an exotic dancer he and Greg hired to perform at the party.''

"A stripper?''

Connor shrugged. "I can't say. The party didn't progress that far. The dancer showed up as I was trying to throw Mallory out.''

"Really? You were going to throw her out?''

"Yes. Before she shoved one of those baby pictures into my hands and announced in front of everyone that she and I had a child together.''

Claire fingered the report. "According to this, the mother's dad and brother have been ruled out as potential donors. It doesn't mention her mom. You said she headed up the state's hurricane-relief volunteers.''

"Beatrice. Yeah. There was never any love lost between us. She wanted Mallory to marry an up-and-coming lawyer. She referred to me as *that storm-chaser*. Bea looked on me as a stray her daughter had rescued from the slums. I can't tell you why she's not a candidate. Her name only came up in passing today, when Mallory told me she named Lydia after both our mothers. Lydia Beatrice. She said everyone calls her Liddy Bea.''

"This is really happening, isn't it,'' Claire declared unhappily. "You have a child with another woman.''

Connor reached across the table and tried to take her hand, but she deflected him so fast, she bumped her cup and spilled coffee all over. "I'm sorry,'' he said earnestly, using his napkin to soak it up while he moved Lydia's pictures out of harm's way. "I'd give anything for us not to be having this conversation. But, frankly, I doubt the news comes as any greater shock to you than it did to me. I haven't seen or heard from Mallory Forrest since the night before I left Florida, headed for that remote island.'' He thought it was probably wisest not to mention that he'd tried desperately—and unsuccessfully—to contact Mallory.

''Did you fight over your going away? Is that why you split up?''

A perplexed frown settled between his eyebrows. ''No. Maybe. I don't know. She seemed happy I'd gotten the grant. Honestly, Claire, seven years is a long time to recall a specific conversation.'' Connor didn't see any need to describe his and Mallory's final parting. She'd cooked his favorite meal to celebrate the fact that he'd received his master's. At the ceremony, a courier had brought him news of the grant.

What he hadn't told Claire was that Mallory had wanted to go live in Hawaii. He informed her it'd be a bad idea to pack in what she had in Florida and trek halfway around the world on the off chance he'd see her a couple of times a year when or if he got breaks. She'd burst into tears and stormed out. A week later, after he realized how terribly he missed her, he'd written Mallory a letter, telling her he'd changed his mind. But she didn't write back. In fact, she didn't answer a single one of his letters. He'd poured out his heart in them, talking about love and marriage and the future. It was plain to see she hadn't spent any time pining away for him.

''I don't know, Connor. This all seems so ludicrous. So unreal. Like something out of a daytime soap.''

The waitress came by with a pot of hot coffee. ''Oh, my. Didn't your coffee taste right?'' she asked.

''I'm afraid we let it get cold.'' Connor slid their cups

to the edge of the table. "Would it be an imposition to have you dump these and pour fresh?"

"Not at all. I would've come by earlier, but you two seemed engrossed."

"Thank you" was Connor's only comment. Claire said nothing. However, she was the first to sip from the new coffee when it arrived.

"What are your intentions toward this child?" she ventured, during a moment when Connor seemed content to let silence reign.

"Intentions? What do you mean? This is all brand-new to me, Claire. I haven't made any concrete plans. But I don't see how I can ignore the situation, do you?"

"No. No, of course not. She's an innocent, regardless of what went on between you and her mother."

"Nothing *went on* between us—not what you're implying when you use that tone, Claire. We were best friends who drifted into a…a…well, when I began work on my master's, Mallory got a job at a PR firm near the campus. We shared an apartment. In the beginning, it was to save money…."

"You lived with that woman?" Claire's voice rose. "And we're engaged, yet we've never spent a whole night together? Boy, do I feel like a fool, bragging to my friends about what a perfect gentleman you are."

Connor swore under his breath. "I like to think I *am* a gentleman, Claire. I asked you to be my wife. Doesn't that count for something?"

"I don't know anymore. Right now I'm confused, Connor. I've built this image of you in my mind. Now I find out you're not that person."

"I'm exactly the same man you've been dating since we met. This all happened in another life. Which doesn't alter the fact that I have obligations toward a child I unknowingly helped bring into this world.''

Claire looked completely unhappy as she murmured, ''You make it sound so logical. I don't want to lose you, Connor. But neither am I ready to go into marriage with this hanging over our heads.''

He forced her to connect with his eyes. ''What's your solution, then?''

''I think we should postpone the wedding.''

''All right. That shouldn't be a monumental task, since we planned such a small gathering. I'll phone half our guest list tomorrow. What excuse shall we give people?''

''Much as I dislike being the subject of gossip, Paul and Greg and half the guys we work with were at your bachelor party and heard this woman... Mallory,'' she said, choking out the name. ''Don't you figure we owe our friends the truth?''

''I do, yes. But I'll say whatever you want, to save you embarrassment.''

''It's too late for that, Connor. I do have one request, however.''

''If I can grant it, you know I will.''

''Like I said, at the moment I'm not sure of anything where you're concerned. What I'd like to do is go with you to Tallahassee. You're planning to consult this doctor in person, I assume.''

''I...uh...yes. I'll take the tests. Mallory indicated she'd arrange with the hospital for me to visit Liddy. I have to see her, Claire.''

''Am I welcome?''

Connor felt the tension shrouding her question. He shouldn't have hesitated, but he felt caught in a vise without fully knowing why. ''Sure. No problem. We'll ask this Dr. Dahl whether or not we should both visit Lydia. I'll need a few days to set up an appointment.''

''Will you make the flight arrangements, or shall I?''

''I'll do it. This is my—'' he didn't want to call his daughter a problem or a mistake, so he settled on a more neutral word ''—my responsibility.''

''All right. If you don't mind, I'd like to go home now. You can come over around eleven tomorrow. That'll give me a chance to warn my parents and also the minister before we begin phoning guests.''

''I repeat, I'm so sorry, Claire.''

She rose without a word. While he paid the bill, she walked out to the car.

If possible, the ride back to her cottage was more strained than the trip to the café had been. Both of them remained locked in private misery. Neither took the initiative of switching on the music that had previously softened the strain.

''Don't bother getting out,'' Claire said, when Connor stopped in front of her house. He did, anyway, and walked her to the door as was his habit. He bent to kiss her good-night, but she turned her head so that his lips only grazed her hair. Claire hurried inside, leaving him standing on a pitch-black porch.

Burying his hands in his pants pockets, Connor wandered slowly back to his car. He couldn't blame Claire for how she felt. He'd hit her with a hell of a mess. But he'd told the truth when he said it was as great a shock to him.

CHAPTER THREE

"DO I LOOK ALL RIGHT?"

Connor shifted his eyes from a blueprint he'd pulled from his briefcase to Claire, who sat next to him on the commuter plane. "Great. You always look great."

She fussed with a silk scarf nailed to the lapel of her suit by a brooch. Connor recognized it as the art deco pin he'd given her for her birthday. A gold cloud, crossed by a diamond-studded lightning bolt. He'd seen it in the window of a jewelry store and had hoped that Claire would appreciate the significance. "Hey, you're wearing the pin."

"Yes. So if any of your old friends in Tallahassee remark on it, I can point out your generosity." Her fingers traced the sparkling stones. "What type of gifts did you used to buy Mallory?"

Connor's brows drew in. "None. I could rarely spare a dime in those days."

"Oh." She leaned close and slid her arm through Connor's.

He eyed her sideways. "Claire, this trip isn't about Mallory. It has to do with a sick child who didn't ask to come into this world. A child I helped create. That's as hard for me to comprehend as it is for you."

"I doubt that," she murmured. "My mother, Lauren and Janine all took pretty pointed shots at your obvious switch in principles. They asked how you could claim to love me and never try to get me into bed when it's obvious you had unprotected sex with another woman. Lauren said maybe we should both get blood tests.''

''Do we have to discuss this in public?'' Connor flushed and glanced around surreptitiously. ''And we never had unprotected sex,'' he whispered. ''Something must have happened.''

''Obviously!'' Claire arched a penciled eyebrow. ''Or maybe it's not your kid at all.''

''You never saw baby pictures of me, Claire, because all my family albums were lost in the hurricane. Most of what we owned was lost. But if you get to see Liddy, the resemblance will be as plain to you as it is to me.''

''Maybe.'' Claire pulled away, and Connor buried his nose in his work again.

Ten or so minutes passed before she nudged him. ''I forgot to ask what hotel you booked us into. I should tell the station where I can be reached.''

''The two motels I contacted were completely booked. It's Florida State University's graduation, one of the hotel clerks told me. He said most of the better accommodations were already full.''

''Well, what are we going to do?''

''He also said there are always cancellations. And apparently hotels usually keep rooms in reserve for drop-ins. It'll be okay, Claire. I didn't have time to do an extensive search, but we can check some places when we arrive. Someone will have a couple of free rooms.''

''Two? Not just one?''

''Claire, if you're questioning my commitment, sleeping together will only muddy the waters even more. Let's get this ordeal behind us, then we'll sit down and work through any remaining doubts before we reschedule the wedding.''

"Why are you always so damned logical, Connor? Haven't you ever done anything on pure impulse?"

A period in his life when Mallory had drawn him into some pretty wacky, spur-of-the-moment outings flashed past Connor's eyes. Images he quickly erased. "Not for a long time," he said in all seriousness. "What you see is what you get, Claire. I hope you understand this is who you'd be marrying."

She turned to stare out the window. "I thought I knew you." She swung back. "Surely you realize that the curve you threw me two nights before my wedding—a day I've dreamed about since I was fourteen—would upset any woman? I don't think I'm being unreasonable, Connor."

"No. I just think you're forgetting that the same curveball came out of left field and hit me, too."

The plane took a decided dip. The stewardess announced their descent into Tallahassee, noting they were half an hour late. Connor returned the blueprint to his briefcase and placed the case under the seat in front of him. It wasn't lost on him, however, that Claire neither agreed nor disagreed with his statement.

Collecting both their bags from the overhead bin, Connor stepped aside and let her lead the way off the plane.

"So what's the plan?" she asked, seeming not to notice that he juggled her suitcase, cosmetic case, his duffel bag and a briefcase, while her hands were free.

With difficulty, he glanced at his watch. "My appointment with Dr. Dahl starts in twenty minutes. He's sandwiched me in between a speech he had to give at the U and an afternoon surgery. We'll have to go directly to his office instead of phoning hotels from here."

"Go to the clinic with our bags? We'll look like a couple of vagabonds."

"Just me. I'm wearing jeans. You look like a million bucks, as usual. Come on," he said, motioning over her head to one of the waiting cabdrivers.

Once he'd given the driver the address and they'd settled into the back seat, Connor took Claire's hand. "It'll be fine. We won't see a soul who knows us or who'll likely ever see us again. I'll ask the clinic receptionist if you can use their phone book along with my cell phone to locate rooms. Cost is no object," he added, having learned early on that Claire liked everything first-class.

"Really?" She perked up at that. "Okay, but you may be sorry. I may find an indecently expensive resort. I mean, if the doctor's able to schedule your tests for tomorrow, I'd rather sit by a pool than hang out in some hospital waiting room."

"Can they do blood tests on demand?"

"You mean you might have to come back a second time?"

"Possibly. I'm operating in the dark, too, Claire. I've never met anyone who's donated an organ. Well, except for Mallory, who gave Liddy a kidney. I should have questioned her more, I guess."

"That's all right, Connor. I'm sure the doctor will have all the information you need in order to make an informed decision."

He smiled. Not his best effort. He'd managed to avoid hospitals since his mother died in one during emergency surgery, but even the thought of voluntarily allowing a surgeon to cut out a vital organ left Connor feeling edgy. Oh, he'd get over it, he supposed. *No "supposed" about it. This was his child. He'd get over it.*

What he'd have a harder time getting past, he feared, was the fact that Mallory had kept from him the news that she'd borne his baby. Anytime he thought about that, his blood boiled.

The cab swung into a circular drive, stopping under a brick portico. A profusion of greenery and blooming flowers flanked glass doors. "This is a clinic," the driver said in accented English. "You take your bags inside?"

Claire jammed an elbow in Connor's side. "See? He thinks we're tacky."

Connor peeled off the fare plus a generous tip. "We'll be going to a hotel after we're done. I'll request your cab number."

The driver smiled and nodded happily.

Connor manhandled the bags inside, discreetly depositing them behind a huge potted fern. There was only one other patron in the posh waiting room, a woman who had her nose stuck in a book. She didn't glance up.

Claire took a seat. She pawed through magazines spread out on a glass-topped table. Connor approached a bank of windows. One slid open to reveal an elegant woman with smooth, coffee-colored skin. "Dr. O'Rourke, I presume?"

"Connor, please. I hope I didn't keep Dr. Dahl waiting. Our plane was late."

She smiled. "When aren't they? Or other forms of transport, for that matter? The doctor's with someone else—a last-minute meeting. If you'll fill out this paperwork," she said, handing Connor a clipboard with a sheaf of documents, "we'll have you hooked up with Dr. Dahl in no time."

Connor felt a door breeze open behind the receptionist and heard the jovial rumble of male voices.

"I believe he's concluded his business," the receptionist murmured. "You'll have to write faster than I anticipated."

In spite of her warning, Connor ignored the clipboard he held. "Due to FSU's graduation, I wasn't able to book a hotel," he said. "I was told to check for possible cancellations when I arrived. I wonder if you can spare a phone book? Claire, my fiancée, will call around while I see the doctor."

A door situated on Connor's left flew open. A booming voice exclaimed, "Connor? Connor O'Rourke? Fredric said you had an appointment, but what's this about a fiancée? Mallory didn't mention you were engaged." Bradford Forrest's dark eyes canvassed the room. "Is that the little lady? Come, introduce us."

Connor was too stunned at seeing Mallory's father to act on his demand.

And Claire, although she rose, bristled at being called a *little lady.* She was petite compared to the bulk of Senator Forrest, however. Also compared to Connor, who topped six-two in his stocking feet.

Even Bradford Forrest, bear of a man that he was, had to reach up to clap Connor's shoulder. "You've filled out since I last saw you, my boy. That was when? At Mallory's graduation?"

"Yes, sir," Connor said, recovering. "Claire, meet Senator Forrest." At one time, Connor had been plenty intimidated by Mallory's folks. Now he felt on a more equal footing with the senator, who'd aged.

Brad headed for Claire, saying to Connor, "I read good things about you in the *Florida Business Review.* You've done all right for yourself. Let me say how grateful I am that you've consented to set aside important work in Miami to come here for Liddy Bea's sake. Gotta say, I did my damnedest to talk Mallory out of contacting you. To be perfectly honest, I expected you to dodge responsibility.''

Connor stiffened at that. ''You and Mrs. Forrest always had a mistakenly low opinion of me, Senator.'' Connor's earlier congenial manner downshifted noticeably.

Bradford shrugged. ''I was too busy back then to get to know Mark or Mallory's friends. And Beatrice, rest her soul, loved them both to distraction. Some say she spoiled them. Really, she wanted the best life had to offer for our kids.''

Connor laid a hand on Claire's arm. His bluster faded a bit. ''I didn't know you'd lost your wife. I'm sorry.''

''Bea went rather quickly after being diagnosed with a neuroblastoma. Under a year. We...the family has weathered some rough patches, what with the discovery of Liddy Bea's polycystic kidneys, and now her latest downward spiral.''

''And Mark? How's he?''

''Still career navy, stationed at Pensacola. He pops in and out. Not often enough, considering he keeps an apartment in town and a boat docked down on the Wakulla. But here we are discussing old times, leaving a beautiful woman in the dark.''

Claire edged closer to Connor, appearing to look on the senator with somewhat more favor after his last remark.

The receptionist glided up to the trio, who had yet to complete introductions. The woman passed Connor a thick telephone book. ''I've marked the lodgings section with a paper clip. I hope you can find something. I saw on TV that FSU is graduating record numbers this semester.''

''What's this?'' Brad growled. ''You two need a place

to stay? Nonsense. I insist you stay with me. The old place has twelve bedrooms, eight of which have private baths. When Beatrice was alive, most of 'em were full every weekend.'' He shook his head sadly. "Every year at tax time, I say I'm going to downsize. But the house holds so many good memories of Bea.... I know, I know—you wouldn't think I'd be a sentimental old fool. Don't tell anyone who sits on my senate subcommittees, or I'll deny every word.''

Everyone laughed, except Claire. She was trying to catch Connor's eye.

"Anyhow, I won't take no for an answer.'' Brad gestured to the receptionist. "Here, Rhonda, Connor doesn't need the phone book. He and Claire will be my guests for as long as Fredric needs Connor in town.''

The senator relieved Connor of the book and replaced it with a business card he extracted from his jacket pocket. "Ring the second number after you're finished here. My driver will bring the car around.''

Claire, standing fully behind the senator, shook her head vigorously at Connor.

"Senator, this is very kind of you,'' Connor began. "But we really can't impose.''

Claire relaxed, until Dr. Dahl opened the door to say gruffly, "What's the delay, Rhonda? Where's O'Rourke? I'm due in surgery at Forrest Memorial in fifty minutes.''

"Sorry, Fredric.'' Bradford stepped out to where Dahl could see him. "I'm afraid I detained them. Connor's going to be staying at Forrest House. That way, he'll have my car at his disposal if and when you need him. I'm on my way to the hospital to look in on Liddy Bea. Shall I swing past surgery and tell them you'll be late?''

"Yes, thanks, Brad. Tell them to delay preop for fifteen minutes."

Connor, not fully comprehending how disgruntled Claire was, turned toward the doctor. "Dr. Dahl, our plane landed late. I haven't even begun to fill out your paperwork. If rescheduling my appointment is more convenient, I'll take these with me. That'll give us a chance to locate lodging. There's really no need to put Senator Forrest out."

"Put me out? On the contrary. In fact, if Claire doesn't mind my stealing you away for an hour or so, I'd like to discuss the work you're doing on early hurricane detection. Look, I'll phone my housekeeper right now and have Marta prepare a room." He proceeded to pull out his cell phone and do just that.

Dr. Dahl moved into the waiting room. Smiling, he grasped Connor's elbow. "What Brad really wants to learn is who dropped the ball and let you go to Miami's weather center instead of ours. I guess, technically speaking, I should be referring to you as Dr. O'Rourke, should I not?"

"No, please. Only in a work environment do I use Dr."

"Well, it's your choice. Come, then, Connor, we'll fill in your chart as we go. Today is going to be nothing more than me explaining what's entailed in donating a kidney, should your tests be positive. I'll talk a little about the tests themselves, and answer your questions. Have you visited Liddy Bea yet?"

"No." Connor glanced uneasily back at Claire, whom he'd left more or less on her own to deal with the senator. "Mallory said she'd arrange with the hospital to give me access. I, uh, planned to ask what's appropriate to say—about who I am. And also, if possible, I'd like my fiancée to meet Lydia. The news that I had a daughter came as a shock to us both. Our wedding was scheduled for this past Sunday. We, uh, postponed the ceremony.''

Sympathy and understanding entered the doctor's eyes. ''It speaks well for you and your fiancée that you're here. I told Mallory it'd be best for now if Liddy Bea thinks you're an old friend of her mother's. If I'd known you were engaged, we could have included your fiancée in today's appointment. I'll give you literature to take back to her.''

''She's here. That's Claire with the senator. Claire Dupree.'' Connor left the doctor and crossed the reception area to retrieve their luggage.

Dr. Dahl walked over and greeted Claire. ''Please, you two come to my office. And Brad,'' he added, ''since they'd both like to visit Liddy, will you clear that with Mallory? Is it possible to have Davis collect them at the hospital? Oh, I see they have luggage.'' He stared at the items now grouped at Connor's feet. ''It'd free them considerably, Brad, if you sent their bags with Davis now.''

No sooner had the suggestion been made than it happened. Bradford Forrest stepped to the door and wiggled two fingers. A man in a dark blue uniform materialized to whisk away Connor and Claire's bags.

Connor knew that if *he* felt steamrollered, Claire must be feeling it twice as much. But he had no time to make amends. Rhonda, Dahl's receptionist, handed the doctor a message as she ushered Claire into the clinic's inner sanctum.

Gazing helplessly toward the entry where Bradford, his driver and the bags had now vanished, Connor had little recourse but to fall in behind the women.

Rhonda directed them to roomy leather chairs that flanked a large mahogany desk. She left, returning a moment later with two frosty glasses of fruit juice. Claire sat and drank from hers. Connor wiped the condensation off his glass as he made a slow circuit of the room, closely eyeing the framed certificates on the wall. A low whistle escaped his lips. "Dr. Dahl has impressive degrees, including a fellowship in the Academy of Pediatric Nephrology."

"Sorry for the delay." Dahl breezed into the room. "I had to phone the hospital and change medications for a patient experiencing a lot of pain."

Connor quickly went and sat next to Claire. As Dahl launched into a description of kidney transplants, the implications of the news Mallory had brought him a few days ago well and truly sank in. At a nearby hospital lay a child who was *his*. She, too, had undoubtedly endured a lot of pain. The thought humbled Connor, and also renewed his anger at Mallory. *His child.* He should have been there for her in times of crisis.

Half an hour later, the doctor's detailed interview wound to a close. He handed Claire and Connor packets containing diagrams and brochures. "You both have that dazed expression, which tells me I've nattered on too long. Basically, everything I've discussed is covered in the packet. You'll want to study the material and discuss the impact such a surgery will have on your lives. I'm sure questions will arise. I or my staff will answer them as forthrightly as possible."

"Thanks," Connor said, getting to his feet. "Perhaps after I visit my daughter, all of this will make perfect sense."

Claire leafed through the pages. She pulled out one that bore the letterhead of the clinic's legal counsel. It absolved staff in cases where complications developed as a result of the surgery. "What, exactly, is Connor's legal obligation to give this child one of his kidneys?"

Dahl stroked his chin. "Probably none at the moment, since Liddy's mother withheld news of her birth. If Connor walks away, Mallory has the right to petition the court and ask a judge to order paternity tests. Once paternity's established, it would be up to a judge to rule whether or not to force Connor to take the next steps. I'm obliged to tell you that in my twenty-plus years in the field, I've never known a judge to force anyone to give up an organ involuntarily."

"You said she's on dialysis," Connor said. "How long can she live on that?"

"Well, under normal circumstances, a patient can exist until we find a donor from the national donor list. However, Liddy's had a great deal of trouble with veins collapsing around her cannula. Those have resulted in numerous infections."

"Still, you're saying she's not in imminent danger of dying without Connor's kidney?" This came from Claire.

"I can tell you that with an operating kidney, Liddy's quality of life will dramatically improve. I wouldn't presume to predict anyone's life span. Any one of us could walk out of here today and be wiped out by a drunk driver." The doctor drew back his sleeve, exposing his watch. "If either of you think of other questions, I'll answer them en route to the hospital. I must say, I'd hoped you were committed to the idea of being a donor, Connor."

Connor folded his papers and stepped aside to let the doctor pass. "I flew here from Miami to be tested, Doctor. What more do you need in the way of a commitment?''

Dahl's steps slowed. A smile lit his careworn features. The smile faded as Claire grabbed Connor's arm. ''I, um, think you're agreeing far too hastily. This affects both of us, Connor. As the doctor said, we need to discuss the pros and cons.''

''What cons? The pro's a given. The quality of Liddy's life improves.''

Claire pursed her lips. ''Shouldn't we fully explore all the ramifications to *you?* In private,'' she stressed, opening the door through which Rhonda had led them earlier.

''We'll use the back entrance if you're riding with me,'' Dr. Dahl said.

''That's another thing,'' Claire murmured. ''Will we be able to talk freely at the senator's? Clearly, it's in his best interests to convince you to have the surgery, Connor.''

Now Connor frowned. ''As our bags are there, and since the senator's inconvenienced his entire household on our behalf, we have to accept his hospitality for tonight. Tomorrow, I'll make other arrangements. Surely not everyone who came for the graduation will stay on once the ceremony's over.''

Fredric Dahl stripped off his white medical coat and donned a suit jacket. After informing his office staff where they could reach him for the next few hours, he escorted Connor and Claire out to his roomy Mercedes. ''Forrest House is like a small hotel,'' he told Claire, once he had the air-conditioning cooling the car's interior. ''Were you ever at the mansion?'' Dahl asked Connor.

''Inside? Once. For Mallory's sixteenth birthday party. I'd been living out of my car. Wrinkled as I was,

I didn't make a very good impression on Mrs. Forrest. Mallory soon realized her mother and I mixed like oil and water.''

"Why on earth were you living out of your car?" Dahl seemed truly horrified.

Connor explained briefly about losing his mother and his home to a devastating hurricane. "I bounced back and forth between friends during the last half of my junior year. Finally a few parents caught on to the fact that I was more or less homeless. They wanted to notify the authorities. I'd known kids in bad foster situations, so I didn't want any part of it. I swore my buddies to secrecy and got fairly adept at living in the old Chevy. Until Mallory heard about it. She talked a family friend into giving me a job as his part-time gardener. The job came with quarters over his garage. I lived there until I got my initial degree from FSU.'' He broke off guiltily, remembering again how much he owed Mallory.

"Who'd have thought gardening would provide enough money for tuition.''

"It didn't,'' Connor admitted. "Again thanks to Mallory, a local organization awarded me a full scholarship to the meteorology program.''

"A lot of people have fallen prey to Mallory's silver tongue. You probably know she's the PR department's fund-raiser at Forrest Memorial. According to our chief administrator, her fund-raising is single-handedly responsible for all the perks we've enjoyed these past five years. We're lucky Dr. Robinson discovered her haunting the hospital halls when Bea Forrest was so ill. Alec now says it's the best move he ever made. He calls Mallory our fund-raising goddess.''

Connor noticed that Claire grew stonier with each new mention of Mallory's name. While he might like to hear more about what Mallory had done in the years since they'd parted—mostly to understand why she'd felt a need to hide the birth of their daughter from him—he also realized how inconsiderate it was to constantly throw Mallory's name in Claire's face.

"Why don't you tell us a little about Liddy Bea, Dr. Dahl? Is she well enough to play with toys? I didn't think to bring a gift, but I'm sure the hospital has a shop."

"Ah. You know the way to that child's heart." The doctor grinned. "Brad's constantly trying to lavish toys on her, but Mallory has managed to rein him in. She's raised a delightful child. Liddy Bea is bright, and funny and articulate beyond her years. I'm warning you—she'll steal your heart."

Connor caught himself smiling, until he glanced across at Claire and sobered. "I'm not aiming to compete with her grandfather. I was just thinking of a small icebreaker, maybe a stuffed animal. Something soft and cuddly."

"Our gift shop stocks a nice selection. I don't think you can go wrong with books or huggables. We don't try to keep our pediatric rooms clutter-free. Children do better in a homey atmosphere." Dahl swung into a drive that wound through a parklike setting of well-tended flower beds. Brick walkways crisscrossed lush green lawns. Every now and then they passed statuary of elves and fairies, strategically tucked beneath cypresses and palms.

"Practicing at this hospital doesn't look like hardship duty," Connor murmured.

"It's privately endowed. Generously so by men like the senator. But Forrest Memorial is also a top-notch teaching facility. Unlike other private hospitals, we take indigent cases. And anyone admitted here receives the best medicine has to offer.''

"So, having Liddy in and out of here hasn't strapped Mallory financially?'' Connor asked the question of Fredric Dahl, but Claire jumped in with an answer.

"Are you kidding, Connor? Read the plaque. The name of the place is Forrest Memorial. Daddy endows it. I'm sure he got Mallory her cushy job. I'd ask if the word *nepotism* rings a bell, but isn't that a foregone conclusion?''

Connor disliked these jabs Claire was making. Dr. Dahl mildly rebuked her. "Bradford may exert influence when it comes to building additions and hiring doctors. He doesn't meddle in support staff. He didn't want Mallory to work. In the end, he couldn't stop her. As for the service his family gets, they pay full freight. Mallory's only perk is the decent insurance package all hospital employees receive. She's refused government benefits for Liddy because she said there are patients in far greater need. You're mistaken if you think this has been easy on her.''

Connor thought it was fortunate they'd reached the parking space marked with Dr. Dahl's name. He'd plainly been dreaming when he hoped Claire wouldn't be jealous of Mallory. It was a side of Claire he'd rarely seen. There'd been the occasional glimpse, but never enough to instill serious doubt. Nervous though he was at the prospect of meeting his daughter for the first time, he could do little but squeeze Claire's knee reassuringly. "We won't stay long, this visit,'' he said, hoping to set her mind at ease. "Lydia doesn't know me, and I don't know her.''

"Then what's the point in coming?'' Claire demanded.

Dr. Dahl exited the car and opened Claire's door, while Connor scrambled out his side.

"Please don't argue like this in front of Liddy Bea," Dahl cautioned. "She's recovering nicely from last week's surgery. Being only six, she may not totally comprehend the significance of what it means to have lost her donor kidney. All the same, her emotions are fragile."

Connor clasped Claire's hand. "This situation has us all stressed. Claire and I will be mindful of what we say, won't we, darling?"

She blinked several times. When she opened her eyes, they were filmy. Still, she nodded. "I *am* upset. I'll let Connor do the talking."

That seemed to satisfy Dr. Dahl. He escorted the couple to the lobby. After pointing out the gift shop, he gave them Lydia's floor and room number. "Connor, nice meeting you. Understand, my hands are tied until you phone my office and give the go-ahead to schedule preliminary tests."

"Claire and I will talk tonight. I'll phone your office tomorrow."

"Good. Enjoy your visit with Liddy Bea. She's a normal six-year-old in every way except for her nonfunctional kidneys. Oh, and she's a regular authority when it comes to Blue's Clues, and Hello Kitty."

When Connor was obviously stumped by that, Dahl laughed. "Blue is a cartoon dog. Hello Kitty is a cat logo that appears on almost every type of little-girl merchandise imaginable. Liddy Bea loves books and videos, too."

"Thanks," Connor called as the doctor quickened his pace and left them.

Claire entered the gift shop first. She picked up a

white bear sprouting angel wings and a glittery halo. Its hard body was hidden by layers of a frothy net covered in glitter.

Connor reached for a floppy-eared pink elephant. "Squeeze this," he told Claire. "He's huggable, don't you think?"

"Okay if she was three. First-graders are more sophisticated. Angels are the in thing, Connor. I recommend buying this."

He continued to eye the elephant he put back on the shelf.

"Trust me. My cousin Pam has a daughter who's seven. Her room is filled with angel junk."

"What do I know about little girls?" Taking the angel bear to the counter, Connor paid for it and asked the cashier to remove the price. "We're delivering this to someone upstairs."

Purchase complete, they walked to the elevator and rode upstairs. The closer they came to Liddy's room, the more Connor hung back. Eventually they reached her half-shut door. "Show time," he muttered, taking a deep breath. Pinning on a nervous smile, he stepped into his daughter's room.

A pixielike child with russet Shirley Temple curls reclined on a bed framed by a battery of beeping monitors. She gazed at him from eyes exactly like the ones that stared back at him each morning from his bathroom mirror. Connor's stomach heaved, and something seemed to tear inside his chest. He wanted to burn this image into his brain—and then run like hell.

Instead, he moved closer to the bed. Up to now, he'd thought his most important contribution to mankind was his hurricane-detection system. How wrong he was. This beautiful child made every other accomplishment pale in significance. She looked part imp, part angel, with an unruly mop of dark curls bobbing around a swollen face. Dr. Dahl had warned them Liddy would appear puffy from having returned to steroids. To Connor, she looked absolutely perfect.

The child stared openly back at him, her lips quirked in a slightly crooked smile also reminiscent of his own. The coy way she cocked her head reminded him of a younger Mallory. As his child's features coalesced before him, Connor's memory flew back to the day he'd first met Liddy Bea's mother.

Suddenly, another thought crowded in, refueling his anger at her for keeping his daughter a secret from him for six long years of her life—and nearly seven of his. He'd never hear Liddy's first coo. Never see her crawl, or take that all-important first step. He'd missed her first words. So many milestones gone. Lost to him forever. And why? Why had Mallory cut him out?

Liddy rose on one elbow. Her other arm was taped to an IV drip. "Hi. I'm Lydia Beatrice Forrest. I don't know you, so you've probably got the wrong room. I can ring a nurse. She'll help you find where you want to be."

Connor rallied. "Thanks. Actually, uh…we came to see you. I'm Connor and this is Claire. I'm an…old friend of your mom's. I've been away a long time, but I'm back visiting Tallahassee. Your grandpa said you could probably use some company. So here we are," he finished, sounding as if he'd run a fast mile.

The child's eyes sparkled. "Oh, good. I love comp'ny." She settled back.

"The bear," Claire muttered, jabbing Connor.

"Oh, yeah. I almost forgot." He produced the bear,

which Liddy instantly shied away from. "Go ahead, take it. Claire picked it out."

Liddy frowned and shook her head until her curls danced. "Angels took my grandmas to heaven. Don't want no angel coming for me." The child's own eyes brightened with tears as she tried to crowd into the far corner of her bed.

"It's just a toy," Claire exclaimed.

"That's okay, honey," Connor quickly consoled the child. "We'll give this bear to the playroom," he promised, handing the toy to Claire. "Anyway, it looks to me as if you have stuffed animals aplenty to bring you cheer and good luck."

"Stuffed animals aren't for luck, silly." Liddy giggled and brushed at the tears lingering on her dark lashes. She pointed to a small figurine of a fat pink elephant sitting centerstage on her windowsill. "Ellie's my good-luck charm. She's really Mommy's," Liddy confided in a whisper. "I only got her 'cause I had surgery." An oversize sigh escaped. "Ellie watches over me, but I can't touch her. She's special."

Connor followed her finger to the glass figurine. Memories suddenly overwhelmed him, dumping him headlong into a long-ago afternoon when Mallory discovered that very elephant in the window of a beach shop. She had no money or credit card with her, which was unusual. But, oh, how she'd coveted that odd little piece.

The next day he'd cut class and hitchhiked back to buy it—all the while fearing it'd be gone. It wasn't. But buying it had taken every cent he had to his name, with not one red penny left for wrap. So he'd wrapped it himself, in newsprint, for Mallory's sixteenth birthday. Even now, heat crept up his neck as he recalled his later embarrassment. His badly wrapped gift had looked worse than tacky sitting among the expensive things Mallory's other friends had brought to her party.

"I can't believe Mallory saved this," he blurted. "I gave it...uh, I mean, your mom's had this since she was sixteen." Extending an unsteady finger, Connor stroked the cool glass.

Liddy Bea sat up straighter, her eyes suddenly alight with interest. "Did you know my daddy?" she whispered. "Mommy said Ellie's the only present my daddy ever gave her, 'cept for me. Isn't that silly? Nobody can *give* somebody a girl."

Claire inhaled sharply.

Connor caught himself seconds before he slipped and said that he and Liddy's daddy were one and the same. Luckily, a nurse popped her head into the room just then. "Visiting hours are over," she announced. "You can come back this evening."

Thoroughly rattled, Connor uttered a hasty goodbye. Fast though it was, he still had to jog down the hall to catch Claire. "Hey! I thought we'd leave this bear at the desk. Claire, what's your rush?" he called, puzzled that she continued walking rapidly in the direction of the elevator. Once there, she jammed the button several times.

"As if you don't know," she hissed when he reached her. "You lied to me. On the plane, when I asked what gifts you'd given Mallory, you said nothing. That elephant sure looks like *something* to me. Now I see why you wanted to buy the stuffed one. It's some kind of family good-luck symbol, isn't it?"

Silently, the elevator door opened. Claire wedged herself into the only space left on the packed car. Without warning, she threw the angel bear at Connor. It bounced off his chest as the doors slid closed.

Connor juggled the toy to keep it from striking the floor. "Honest, I didn't remember buying the elephant," he shouted—too late for explanations. He felt a sharp ache behind his eyes. Floundering momentarily, Connor turned to stare back at Liddy's room, which was a wash of light and warmth. The unexplained pain receded, and at once his world righted itself. Granted, Claire had a lot to contend with just now. In time, they'd be able to agree on the course of action that was best for everyone.

CHAPTER FOUR

ON AN EVEN KEEL AGAIN, Connor found the stairs. He clattered down the first flight in pursuit of Claire. He couldn't get mad at her. Poor Claire was caught in a mess of his making. His and Mallory's. Lord knew his feelings for Mallory still ran hot and cold. One minute old memories—good memories—let him go soft on her. Then he'd think about her deception, and he'd be as angry as a man could be.

Claire was the innocent here. Her only fault lay in falling for a guy who had a shady past she knew nothing about. Hell, *he* hadn't known about it himself.

As he burst from the stairwell into the lobby, Connor saw Claire pacing near an occupied public phone. Relieved to see her, he loped across the room, still holding the angel bear.

Slowed by the tense set of her shoulders, he automatically gentled his tone. "Claire?"

"That man," she burst out. "The senator's driver. He's waiting for us outside. I know they took our bags, but how can you put me in a position of staying in a house with your former mistress?"

"Mistress? Mallory wasn't my..." Connor's brows dived together. "No, Claire—our relationship wasn't like that."

"Then how was it? You admit you two lived together." Her lower lip protruded. "What *should* I think,

Connor? Am I supposed to just accept these little surprises?''

"Listen...Mallory and I were teenage friends who grew closer during a horrible time in my life. She helped pull me through. Looking back, I think we saw each other differently. Oh, hell, I'm not doing a good job of explaining, am I?''

"Maybe I should go home to Miami now and let you work this out.''

Heaving the stuffed toy into a vacant lobby chair, Connor took Claire's arm and herded her toward the revolving door. "Please stay. You heard what Dr. Dahl said about how huge the Forrest home is. Let's go there, at least accept their hospitality long enough to freshen up. We'll probably have the house to ourselves for a few hours. Once we're rested, it'll be easier to discuss things rationally.''

"And what will your Mallory be doing throughout our rational discussion?'' Claire sniped, balking at the door.

"She's not *my* Mallory. Anyway, Dr. Dahl said she works. Here at the hospital.'' Glancing at his watch, Connor saw that it was five, normally quitting time. "Even if she's finished for the day, I imagine she'd go to her own home rather than her dad's.''

Seemingly mollified by that prospect, Claire shook off Connor's hand and exited the hospital under her own steam. He stopped a passing nurse and asked her to donate the angel bear to one of the children's play areas.

Outside, Brad Forrest's driver bounded from the limousine to whip open the back door. "The senator asked me to let you know he has a cocktail party that started at four-thirty. I'll pick him up at seven, in time for dinner at eight. Meanwhile, Marta—she runs the house—will make you comfortable.''

"Thank you. And your name is?" Connor asked politely before he slid in next to Claire.

"Davis, sir. I've been with the senator since he was first elected."

"Well, Davis. Thanks for waiting. It's been a tough trip for us, but you probably know the situation."

"Yes, sir," the old man murmured, gently closing Connor's door.

"The ride across town ought to be relatively short," Connor informed Claire. Then, because the sliding window between them and Davis remained ajar, he didn't bring up anything personal. Instead, he drew Claire's attention to remembered landmarks as they drove past. "Look, there's the old capitol. Over there's the new one. Clyde's is a locally famous bar. By day," he said, grinning, "state legislators conduct high-level meetings there. After hours, college students swarm the place."

He rattled on with such fondness for the sights that Claire finally interrupted. "You miss Tallahassee, don't you."

Connor, who still had his nose pressed to the side window, turned to stare at her. "I haven't thought much about it. The culture's more Old South here than in Miami. I like that. Remember, I was born and raised here. But there are good memories, and bad." A muscle in his jaw jumped as he studied the landscape over her shoulder. "Ah—there's the cemetery where my mother is buried."

"Really?" Claire spun to see it.

"Yes. I'd like to bring flowers, maybe tomorrow. It's been a while since I've visited. Too long." He craned his neck to keep the wrought-iron fence in view.

"Mrs. Forrest's buried there, too." Davis glanced at Connor in the rearview mirror. "The senator takes white roses by her grave every Monday, rain or shine. White roses were the missus's favorite.''

"Then you'll be able to direct me to a florist. I'm afraid that when I lived here before, I never had money for extras—like flowers.''

Claire gave a little snort. "Only hand-blown glass elephants. And that's a pretty ritzy cemetery.''

"Meaning what? There's a difference in cemeteries?''

From Claire's dry expression, Connor figured there must be. "I…uh, didn't purchase the plot.'' He paled under his robust tan. "I guess I was too out of it at the time to notice. Mallory took charge. She handled the entire funeral.''

"She was how old? Sixteen? Obviously her parents made the arrangements.''

"No. I'm absolutely sure she got no help from them. She did it all by herself.''

"I forgot. St. Mallory.''

Connor gnawed on his upper lip, deciding silence was the safest bet. Which was okay, because Davis slowed and turned into a driveway facing a massive set of iron gates. One gate swung open when he pressed a button under the dash.

Forrest House, an antebellum, white-columned structure, commanded the entire top of a grassy knoll. Stately magnolias and spreading live oaks flanked the residence. The postcard picture it presented was grand enough to draw a gasp from Claire.

"Intimidating, isn't it?'' Connor muttered.

"Impressive,'' she said in a small voice. "Oh, my, is that a pool near those cabanas off to the left? Um…maybe we shouldn't be too hasty about finding another place, Connor. This is like a five-star resort.''

"What about privacy?'' Connor twisted in his seat,

realizing belatedly that Davis had circled a bronze sculpture of towering pine trees and stopped at the bottom of marble steps leading to an even more imposing set of carved wooden doors. Troublesome memories assailed him. Connor helped Claire out of the car this time, and Davis drove on to a detached seven-car garage situated at the end of the cobbled terrace.

"Place looks deserted," Connor observed, trailing Claire up the broad steps.

"Just ring the bell," she said, still attempting to take in all the sights around the parklike grounds. "Surely the senator's staff is home. Davis said the housekeeper would take care of us. I can't recall her name. Do you remember?"

Connor shook his head as he pressed the bell. Suddenly, he wished he'd heeded Claire's first preference and found another place to stay.

INSIDE HER FATHER'S HOUSE, Mallory, who'd entered moments before, having indulged in a rare after-work swim, heard the door chimes. "I can tell you're busy cooking something delicious, Marta, judging by that wonderful smell. I'll get the door. Are you or Dad expecting anyone?" she called into the kitchen, her voice muffled as she toweled her wet hair.

Marta responded from the depths of the commercial-size kitchen. But her words didn't penetrate the fleecy towel.

Concerned more with the water tracks she was leaving on the black marble entry floor than with who might be calling on her dad, Mallory hurriedly yanked open the heavy door, expecting at most to direct a deliveryman elsewhere.

It'd be impossible to judge who was more shocked by

her sudden appearance in a skimpy bikini—Mallory, Connor or Claire, whose breath escaped audibly. "I thought you said she had her own place," Claire muttered in an accusing voice.

"Mallory?" Connor sounded incredulous. And Mallory's hands shook so hard, she had trouble dragging the wet towel off her head. She made a fumbled attempt to cover the greater expanse of flesh left open to the scrutiny of her unwelcome guests.

"What are you doing here?" she managed to ask at last. "I skipped my after-work visit with Liddy Bea. Because D-Dad left a message at my office saying you were in town and would be stopping by to see her this afternoon."

"I take it he didn't tell you he'd invited Claire and me to stay at Forrest House?" Connor, jarred by Mallory's thin frame, shifted his eyes from her the instant Claire's fingernails dug into his arm. Yet it hammered inside his head that Mallory had lost too much weight. Though always leanly built, she'd never looked as gaunt as she did now. Her skin used to be perpetually tanned. One of the first things that attracted Connor—and everyone else—to Mallory had been her all-American-girl looks. Looks that were secondary to her limitless energy. Today, however, she appeared tired. Drawn.

Claire? Blinking, Mallory forced her eyes off Connor to focus on the cool-eyed blonde clinging to his arm. She understood, even before formal introductions were made, that this was Connor's bride-to-be. Or, for all Mallory knew, they could be married already. Feeling her head begin to swim and her grip on the door handle weaken, she fought against losing the remnants of her self-control.

Fortunately, Marta burst out of the kitchen carrying a

silver tray filled with a pitcher of lemonade and frosty glasses. "Senator Brad said we should make the O'Rourkes feel at home, Miss Mallory. I'll set these cold drinks on the courtyard table, if you'll show them to the blue suite on your way up to change."

"We'll need two rooms," Connor interjected smoothly. "Claire and I aren't married. We're just engaged."

Claire, who'd miraculously managed to recover her voice, squeezed Connor's arm. "Come on, darling. I'm sure we're dealing with two modern women here." Her cat-that-swallowed-the-canary smile sent a clear message to Mallory. A message underscored by the flash of her diamond engagement ring, as Claire deliberately tightened her possessive hold on Connor's arm. "It's so like him, to worry about my reputation," she murmured in an aside to Marta. "On the drive here, we discussed our need for privacy. But with one room, we'd have all we need."

Connor shifted away from Claire's possessive hold, too late for Mallory to see. She busily knotted the towel around her breasts while leading the way up a circular staircase.

Marta missed nothing. "Senator Brad didn't specify the number of rooms. We have plenty. I'll leave this tray here on the hall table. It'll take me two shakes of a lamb's tail to move Ms. Claire's suitcase from the blue room to the violet one. You'll love the violet room," she informed Claire, motioning her guests left at the top landing.

Mallory seemed to have disappeared.

"Miss Beatrice, rest her soul, decorated the violet room herself. She reserved it for special guests. Wait till you see the sitting room that opens onto a private veranda,'' Marta murmured. She popped quickly into the blue bedroom and sorted Claire's bags from Connor's. Then she rejoined Claire.

Claire glared over her shoulder at Connor, who lagged behind the others. But Marta turned a corner at the end of the long hall, hiding him from view. She dragged Claire into a suite about as far from Connor's as a body could get and remain in the same house.

''Oh, this is really nice,'' Claire exclaimed, once she took a moment to inspect the antique furnishings. ''But couldn't you give Connor and me connecting rooms?''

Marta, involved in opening violet-sprigged brocade drapes, could have missed hearing Claire's request. ''Dinner's at eight,'' she announced. ''Senator Brad prefers informal meals except on Sundays. I'll go move the lemonade to the courtyard.''

Marta peered at a watch worn on a thick gold chain looped around her neck. ''You'll have time for a shower before dinner. Or a swim. If you didn't bring a suit, Miss Mallory stocks a variety of styles and sizes in the pool house.''

Claire again attempted to ask for a room closer to Connor but failed to get her wish out before Marta sped from the room.

Slowly massaging her temples, Claire wrenched open her suitcase, found her travel kit and shook out two analgesic tablets. She stalked into the adjoining bath in search of water with which to take the pills, and stopped short, gazing raptly at a pale lavender Jacuzzi tucked into a secluded corner of the room.

Which was precisely where Connor found her some thirty minutes later. ''Claire?'' He opened her bedroom door after receiving no response to his knock. As Claire's suitcase lay open on the bed and the clothing she'd had on was strewn about, he knew this was the right room. Drawn by faint strains of music and a mysterious rumble, Connor opened a second door. A blast of steam hit him full in the face.

Once the vapor dissipated, he saw why Claire hadn't heard his knock. Cuban music pulsed from a built-in CD player. A bottle of wine and a crystal glass she'd unearthed from somewhere danced on a table attached to a bubbling Jacuzzi. Up to her neck in suds, Claire had her eyes closed tight.

He would've backed out of the room and left her to her enjoyment had she not lazily opened one eye. "Hey!" She raised the glass, half filled with dark-red wine. "You'll find another glass on the top shelf in that white cupboard." Her instructions were slightly blurred.

Connor took a second look at the wine bottle and judged there probably wasn't enough left in it to fill a second glass. "I've been downstairs with the lemonade, waiting for you. I made a fair dent in that pitcher." He patted his flat stomach.

Claire's gaze followed the path of his hand. Her eyes, already bright from the wine she'd consumed, grew slumberous. "Lemonade is for children, Connor. If I must dine with your former lover, I deserve, uh, *need* something stronger."

"I thought we were going to use the time before dinner to discuss what we learned from Dr. Dahl."

"So come over here, big guy, and we'll discuss." Claire waggled her wineglass and gave him a naughty grin.

Conner smiled indulgently. "Finish your soak, Claire. Dress in something casual, and I'll meet you downstairs. The inner courtyard is directly to the right of the main entry. You can't miss it."

"Can't we talk later? Oh, all right," she snapped. "I'll be down shortly. At least top off my glass before you go." She held it unsteadily.

Connor decided she didn't need more wine. Stepping farther into the room, he felt overpowered by the heavy rose scent rising from her tub. Trying not to breathe, he snatched a glass from the cupboard, then reached for the bottle, only to be tipped off balance when Claire lunged up and grabbed his shirtfront with wet, soapy hands.

"Lose the clothes and join me," she said huskily, scant seconds before she mashed her mouth over his.

Connor couldn't catch his breath. And both his hands were otherwise occupied. One held tight to the wine bottle, the other to the glass he was afraid might shatter all over Claire and the tub.

It was a brief struggle. One that ended with the front of Connor's clean shirt soaked through and Claire ultimately getting the message that he wasn't kissing her back. Releasing him with a sigh, she slid into the tub again. The resultant splash drenched his khaki pants.

"I've already showered, for Pete's sake." He retreated a safe distance. "What on earth has gotten into you, Claire?"

"Into *me?* I've got a flash for you, bud. I'm the woman you're supposed to love."

His irritation muted by a stab of guilt, Connor took his time returning the wine bottle and empty glass to the table where Claire set hers down with a thwack. He could no longer deny that something was eroding his feelings for her.

As his guilt increased, Connor swung aside and grabbed a towel to blot up the water on his shirt. "I know all I've done these past few days is apologize, Claire. Maybe it's being in Tallahassee again. Or maybe it's the jolt I got walking into Liddy Bea's hospital room—and confronting the fact that I really do have a child." Connor stopped pacing. "I need some space. Things *have* happened to change me from the man who put that ring on your finger. But…that scene just now…isn't you, either, Claire."

She sank farther under the water. "My robe's hanging on the back of the bathroom door," she said quietly. "Will you hand it to me before you go, Connor? I'll dress and come downstairs. Will…Mallory be there?"

"She wasn't when I came to see what was keeping you. I haven't laid eyes on her since we walked in. Claire, I told you that's history. Don't be jealous of Mallory."

"Of course I'm jealous of her," Claire snapped, ripping the robe from his hands. Standing, she belted it swiftly around her. "You two share a child. Not only that, she crooks her little finger and you come running." Claire's motions were jerky as she shut off the Jacuzzi motor and let the water out of the tub.

"That's not how it happened. You sound as if you think she invited me here for a romantic tryst. Can't you see that dealing with me is the last thing she wants?"

"Yeah, sure. She wants you, all right." Claire brushed past him, marching into the bedroom. Connor followed more slowly. His own anger at Mallory, which he thought he'd successfully extinguished, roared back, darker and more crushing than before. Not only had she stolen something vital from him by keeping Liddy Bea a secret, she seemed bent on destroying his hope of finding happiness with Claire.

"I don't know what it'll take to convince you that Mallory decided to deal me out of her life a long time ago. Nothing can ignite a spark that doesn't exist."

"Men can be so obtuse." Claire reached the bed and dug through her suitcase. "I saw the look that came into her eyes when she discovered you standing at her door."

"Me, too. She was mad as hell at her father for inviting us. I'm part of a past she'd prefer didn't ever resurface." Walking up behind Claire, Connor stroked lightly up and down her robed sleeves. "Let's not argue. I know you have concerns about some of the information Dr. Dahl gave us. I left my copy downstairs. Dress, and come down. We'll talk. If there's stuff we don't understand, I'll make a list and phone Dahl. We'll keep asking questions until you feel reassured."

"Okay." Claire pulled out of his loose grip. "I do have questions, Connor. Including a couple I'm not sure anyone can reassure me about."

A knot formed again in the pit of Connor's stomach. He backed away, attempting to offer a comforting smile. He suspected it'd come out more of a grimace.

It didn't help to round the corner and come face-to-face with Mallory, who suddenly exited the room directly across from the one he'd been given. At first, all Connor could imagine was how Claire would feel if she saw how close his room was to Mallory's. Then he decided that was silly. They were all going to have to find a way to get along. For the sake of Liddy Bea. Because now that he'd found his daughter, he didn't intend to let her disappear from his life. And therein lay what was perhaps the biggest obstacle between him and Claire.

Mallory glanced at him, then quickly away. She didn't remark on the wet handprints on Connor's shirt or the water splotches on his pants, but she didn't have to. Her elevated eyebrow made her opinion abundantly clear. Of course, she knew exactly where he'd been.

But dammit, Connor didn't feel he owed her any explanation. Staring at her stonily, he fell back a step to let her precede him down the winding stairs.

"You shouldn't have insisted Marta make up two rooms," Mallory said. "As Claire pointed out, we're all adults." Mallory hoped she sounded more matter-of-fact than she felt. Her stomach had tensed the instant she saw the state of Connor's clothes. It probably served her right for keeping the man on a pedestal all these years. The Connor she'd known and loved would never have flaunted an afternoon romp across the sheets—or in the Jacuzzi. She remembered that when the two of them had succumbed to the overpowering tug of youthful hormones, he'd gone to great lengths to keep what went on between them private and personal.

Gnashing her teeth, Mallory grabbed her purse from the hall table and marched straight to the front door. As she yanked it open she surprised her father coming in.

He glanced at his watch. "Where are you going? Marta will be serving dinner in an hour. I see you know we have guests." Bradford acknowledged Connor, who still stood on the staircase, with a nod.

"*You* have guests, Father." Mallory attempted to skirt him.

Marta stuck her head out of the kitchen. "I thought I heard voices. Senator Brad," she exclaimed, wiping her hands on her apron. "I'm glad you're home early. The roast cooked faster than I anticipated. I'm afraid you'll have to forgo cocktails before dinner, unless you want overdone meat. Oh, Miss Mallory, you're not leaving, are you? I set the table for four."

"I'm sorry, Marta. I decided since Dad has guests tonight, I'd go on back to the hospital and have a second tray sent up to Liddy Bea's room."

"And leave me to entertain alone?" Bradford caught

her elbow. "Your mother taught you better manners. Liddy Bea won't miss you," he said. "Fredric gave her two new Disney videos, and you know how engrossed that child gets when the TV's on. Now, occupy Connor and Claire while I shower off the scent of Marge Livingstone's perfume."

Before Mallory could respond, Brad wrinkled his nose. "If there's anything I can't abide, it's a woman who bathes in perfume. Ever since Beatrice passed away, Marge has felt it incumbent upon her to drag me around the room at all her parties until she finds another lonely soul to hook up with me. By then, my jacket reeks of...what *is* that stuff she douses herself in?" he muttered, shoving his jacket sleeve under Mallory's nose.

She drew back. "Phew! I don't know. Ghastly would be a good name. Pepe Le Pew has nothing on you, Dad," she teased, finally unleashing a genuine smile.

"That's what I mean. I can't sit down to dinner without first sealing this suit in a laundry bag. Mallory, please run down to the cellar and select a wine to go with the roast Marta slaved over all afternoon."

Mallory capitulated ungraciously. She flung her car keys and purse back onto the hall table. She swept past her father and Connor without another word.

"Bring up a bottle of my favorite after-dinner brandy, too, will you?" her father called. "Connor promised to tell me all about his invention. I need to figure how much money it'll cost the state to adequately protect Florida's coastline. Especially the Panhandle."

From his position on the lower stair, Connor gave a start. "Aren't you rushing things, Senator? I'm still field-testing my system. High as my hopes are for this last modification, it's still too early to speak in terms of appropriations."

Brad waved a hand, flashing a diamond pinkie ring. "My boy, it's never too early to lay groundwork in matters where one day you'll need government funding. That's the main fault I see with scientific grants. The science community refuses to share their findings with the people ultimately responsible for buying and producing their bright ideas."

Connor's lips edged up in a smile. "Because we won't be pressured to produce by politicians. I saw some great systems scrapped too early by hovering backers demanding results. I want to save lives. For that reason, I don't want eager-beaver politicians jumping the gun, forcing me to react before I know all the components operate. If that happens, it's not the politicians who lose credibility. It's the scientist whose funding gets lopped off."

"Nice speech, my boy. But you strike me as a man who'll land on his feet after any setback. I hope you're smart enough to realize grant money doesn't get extended indefinitely. Not without showing the public some results."

Connor chewed on Bradford's last remark.

Already partway down the hall, Mallory, oddly enough, sprang to Connor's aid. "What are you saying, Dad? Is someone at the state level threatening to pull the plug on Connor's grant?"

"Aren't my field tests funded by the national tropical-prediction center? I'm at the center in Miami but my funding is independent of theirs."

"Look, I never intended this topic to get out of hand. Especially not without first relaxing over dinner and drinks. Anyway, I'm facing a more pressing issue. Namely that Marta will kill me if I dink around and let her roast dry to shoe leather."

"Senator Brad is right. Shoo," Marta said, uncurling her arms to flap her apron at him. "Mallory, take Dr. O'Rourke to the cellar to help carry the wine. I predict this will be a two-bottle evening."

"Please, call me Connor," he said, smiling at Marta. "Do you need my help?" he asked, cocking an unsure eye at Mallory.

She said no at the same moment Marta declared, "Yes, she does." The housekeeper's insistence overpowered Mallory's denial.

Connor glanced uneasily up the stairs to see if Claire had surfaced yet. The only activity on the winding staircase was Bradford heading up. So, Connor followed Mallory as she snagged a ring of keys Marta tossed her.

Mallory wove through pots of greenery out in the courtyard. At the very back, she descended a narrow set of steps Connor hadn't realized were there. At the bottom of the dim stairwell stood a locked set of iron-banded doors that reminded Connor of pictures he'd seen of old European cask rooms.

"Sure you aren't taking me into the dungeon for beheading?"

Mallory shot him a long-suffering glare. "I didn't invite you to come with me."

As the door swung in on well-oiled hinges and a draft of cool air struck Connor, he snapped back, "No. The only place you'd invite me is a surgical ward where there'll be a team of doctors waiting to remove one of my kidneys."

Her shoulders bowed for an instant. Then Mallory stiffened her spine and reached inside to flip on a bank of soft incandescent lights.

As Connor came in behind her, she shut the door. "A successful wine cellar needs a consistent temperature at all times. You'll find Dad's white wine selection off to your right. Reds to your left. Specialty and after-dinner liqueurs just ahead. I'll get the brandy.''

"Are you hoping to show my ignorance by having me choose the wrong wine? Sorry to ruin your scheme, babe, but I've come up the social ladder since you knew me."

Connor made straight for the reds, quickly choosing a cabernet designed to complement beef. After tucking two bottles into the crook of his arm, he turned and watched Mallory lift two bottles of brandy.

"Is there an after-dinner port you and Claire could have?" he asked. "Or do you intend to let her flounder around the house by herself while your dad and I discuss my system?''

Mallory reached for a sherry, then put it back on the shelf. "I can't imagine that your fiancée would want to spend an evening making small talk with me. Apparently neither you nor Dad care that this is an awkward situation. I…I…just want it over. As I explained the night I came to see you in Miami, I'd make a pact with the devil to have Liddy Bea well again.''

"I think you made that clear enough."

"Don't shout. I'm not deaf." Gripping the bottles of brandy, Mallory jerked on the doorknob with a hand that shook badly. She cringed, feeling Connor's hot, angry breath on her neck. It hurt horribly to see and feel how furious he was with her.

"Unlike you, Mallory, I yell and slam things around when I'm pissed off," Connor said, giving a fair demonstration as he smacked the bank of light switches so hard his hand stung. "You and I never saw eye to eye on the way to handle problems."

"Because I prefer self-control over shouting?''

"Is that how you explain seven years of silence?"

"Me? I didn't...oh!" Mallory stumbled going up the steep steps. Conner shifted the cabernet and the sherry he'd grabbed to his left hand in order to keep Mallory from falling backward. His right hand slid beneath a waist-length crop top she'd teamed with walking shorts. As a result, his sweaty palm connected with her skin.

Connor's touch, which felt both familiar and foreign, zapped a bolt of remembered passion through Mallory that all but drove her to her knees.

"Don't touch me," she ordered, juggling the bottles while turning in an attempt to shrug off his fingers. All that did was bring them closer together.

Her breasts were flattened against Connor's chest when a low, angry voice from above froze them where they stood, leaning against each other.

"Well, isn't this cozy?"

Connor and Mallory turned raised glances aloft. Squinting into light from darkness, their eyes collided with Claire's accusing frown.

Connor's first inclination was to snatch back his hand. However, he hadn't done anything wrong, and he was getting damned tired of apologizing for nothing. "The stairs are steep," he said darkly. "Mallory tripped. Here, Claire, help us, please. Take a couple of these bottles,"

"Go to hell! What I'm inclined to do is phone for a cab to take me to the airport. I'm fed up with you making a fool of me." She tried her best to pull off her engagement ring. Clearly she wanted to heave it at Connor. But in the afternoon humidity, the ring refused to budge.

Marta stuck her head into the opening behind Claire and announced dinner. Bradford arrived a moment later.

"Good, good," he said, stretching to relieve Connor

of the cabernet. He passed Marta both bottles. In the next breath, he instructed Mallory to drop the brandy off in his study. "It'll be my pleasure to escort your lovely fiancée to the table, Connor. I already sneaked a peek in there," he confided. "Dinner looks and smells delicious." The senator clamped a hand around Claire's elbow, apparently unaware that he'd defused a potential fracas between his daughter and his guests.

Until Brad turned the corner with her, Claire gazed unhappily back at Connor, who'd emerged from the stairwell still steadying Mallory.

Edgy from the feel of Mallory's soft skin and the intoxicating scent of her perfume, Connor detoured past the downstairs bathroom to wash again before going in to dinner. Staring into the mirror, he muttered to his reflection, "Let it go, O'Rourke. History is all you have with Mallory Forrest."

CHAPTER FIVE

THE FORRESTS' DINING-ROOM furniture was fashioned out of teak, so old and highly polished it appeared nearly black. Because the room was banked by tall, west-facing windows, the decorator had liberally used potted greenery for a cooling effect. Asian silk tapestries, woven in muted blues and greens, hung on the wall opposite a floor-to-ceiling china cabinet. A sideboard that ran between the entry to the kitchen and the exit into the living area served as a showcase for intricate jade carvings and fine porcelain figurines.

One in particular, a colorful Ming elephant, was the topic under discussion when Connor slid into his seat. He probably should've seen where the conversation was headed before Claire lobbed her barb at Mallory, but he didn't. And even if he had, it was doubtful he could have deflected it.

"I read somewhere that artists from the Ming dynasty painted good-luck symbols on each piece of their porcelain." Claire spread her napkin across her lap, then reached behind her for the elephant. "Is this another one of your family's lucky charms?"

Since Claire's remarks were directed at Mallory, she spared the piece a glance before shrugging negligently. "Luck played an important part in ancient Chinese culture. Much more so than in ours."

Claire accepted a basket of rolls from Bradford. Her

attention remained on Mallory even as she replaced the elephant. "So you're not superstitious?" she asked, tonging a roll onto her snowy-white bread-and-butter plate.

"I place my faith in science." Mallory handed the basket on to Connor.

Claire smiled sweetly. "Oh, I guess that's why your daughter has such a strong aversion to angels. Except she's fairly vocal about her good luck coming from a cheap glass elephant." Claire put a bowl of fluffy mashed potatoes in front of a confused Mallory. "Oh, maybe Connor didn't mention how she refused to touch an angel bear he brought her."

Bradford lifted his eyes from the roast he'd been carving. "Kids get funny ideas, Claire. I wouldn't place a lot of significance on them."

"Oh, I think the elephant is quite significant. Connor thought so, too. Isn't that right?" Claire extended her plate for the meat Bradford held between the carving fork and knife. The minute she set her plate back down, she drew their attention to the lightning-bolt pin she'd transferred from her suit jacket to the blouse she had on. "I consider nothing less than diamonds my lucky charms." Laughing, she blew Connor a kiss. "Fortunately, Connor can afford them now. His taste has greatly improved since you knew him, wouldn't you say?" She smiled at Mallory over the flash of the square-cut stone of her engagement ring.

Connor squeezed her right hand as a gentle warning. He'd never known Claire to be so catty. Her friend Janine, yes. But not Claire. Strangely enough, he partially understood her need to hurt as she'd obviously been hurt. He just didn't know how to make what had happened more palatable for her. "Claire helped me choose the angel bear," he said in an attempt to extricate them all. "Her niece is Liddy Bea's age and is really into angels. I appreciated Claire's input because I know zilch about what kids like. But then, why would I?" he said, not really cognizant that this was a pointed jab at Mallory, too.

Her dark lashes swept up, revealing penitent eyes. "I'm sure Liddy Bea didn't mean to hurt your feelings, Connor."

Bradford cleared his throat gruffly. "Connor knows better. Men don't get worked up over such things, Mallory. Let's drop this nonsense. What I'd like to know is how Connor's visit with Fredric went. I assume he arranged for your tests."

"Oh, Connor's not scheduled yet," Claire rushed to say. "We have a lot to consider after listening to Dr. Dahl today."

The senator, who'd placed slices of roast on everyone's plate but his own, paused in the act of cutting his portion. "That right? What's to consider?" he asked, leveling a stare at Connor. "A child—one tied to you by blood—needs a healthy kidney to lead a normal life. You undergo a few harmless tests, and if everything checks out, you give her one. What could be more straightforward?"

Mallory had barely tasted anything on her plate before this conversation. Now she dropped her knife and fork. She hadn't once considered that Connor might not agree. That he might back out. Suddenly the possibility clutched at her heart, making it shrivel from fear. Fear for Liddy Bea.

Connor cleared his throat.

Claire again spoke for both of them. "Stop pressuring Connor. First, the brochure says there is some risk to a donor. Donors have died, you know. Others have developed long-term infections. All donors are advised to avoid heavy lifting for up to six weeks after surgery. Connor scales rocky cliffs on his job. He sometimes dangles off radar towers. He's battled sharks, for goodness' sake.''

"Hold on, Claire. You make it sound as if I risk life and limb daily. I don't scramble around rocky coasts nearly as much as I used to. And aren't you exaggerating the possible complications? We both listened to Dahl. I didn't come away with the impression that there was much danger at all to a donor.''

Claire pursed her lips. ''You're only thirty-three, Connor. More than half of your life is ahead of you. Can they guarantee this operation won't take a toll on your health in the years to come? What about when you're forty or fifty or sixty?''

"Of course there aren't any rock-solid guarantees. The doctor said there are no guarantees for either party,'' Connor admitted, slanting an apologetic glance at Mallory and Bradford.

Mallory leaned forward. A metal button on her top struck her china plate with a resounding ring. ''I've had no ill effects whatsoever.''

"You butt out,'' Claire ordered. ''You have a vested interest in making sure Connor goes through with this. I'm addressing him. It's *our* future this could affect.''

Mallory wadded her napkin into a ball. ''Well, excuse me.'' She rose half out of her chair, a stricken expression darkening her eyes.

Bradford's face turned brilliant red, and a pulsing vein stood out on his forehead.

"Claire, there's no need for rudeness. This isn't appropriate dinner conversation, anyway,'' Connor said firmly. "It's a discussion better left for later, when we have time alone."

"Well, I don't agree. I feel as if everyone we've met, including the doctor, has conspired to close a net around you. And you can't see what going through with this might do to us. To our marriage."

"You're right." Connor shook his head. "I *don't* see a problem. The way I understood it, a person can function normally with one kidney."

"Would anyone who's trying to get one of yours tell you horror stories? No." She glared at Mallory as she spoke.

Mallory shoved back her chair. "You two obviously have issues to work through. Dad, my presence here makes Claire uncomfortable. I'm going to phone Mark and ask to bunk at his apartment until Connor and Claire go back to Miami."

"Mallory, no!" Connor sprang from his chair. "We're the intruders. Claire and I will go to a hotel. I should never have agreed to stay here."

His words fell on empty air. Mallory had fled the room. Connor saw her pluck her purse and car keys from the hall table. Not everyone at the table had the view he did, but he saw how badly her hands shook. Everyone, though, heard the front door slam in her wake.

Connor turned to Bradford. "I'm sorry. Please, try to understand Claire's situation. The news of Liddy Bea's existence came as quite a shock to her—and to me."

Brad lowered his eyes, and motioned Connor back into his seat. "Mallory's been rattled ever since Liddy began to reject her transplant. I'll have Marta pack an overnight bag and send Davis to Mark's apartment with it. Mallory'll be fine. Claire, why don't you tell us what your other concerns are? If necessary, I'll phone Fredric, so he can put your mind at ease.''

Claire smoothed out her napkin. ''For one thing, Dr. Dahl never explained what causes polycystic kidneys, except to say that was the reason Lydia's malfunctioned.''

''Correct.'' Bradford shifted his bulk in the chair, then took a minute to instruct Marta to gather a few things for Mallory. ''Now then, the term polycystic simply means that cysts riddle Liddy Bea's kidneys and hamper them from filtering her body's impurities. Some people are more prone to cysts than others. It's just one of those things. No one else in our family's ever had the condition as far as we know.''

''Then it's not something her mother passed to her genetically? So, what if the condition came from Connor's gene pool?''

Connor roused. He'd pushed his plate aside, but continued to sip his wine. ''There's no kidney disease in my family, either, Claire.''

''What if it's a sleeper? A recessive gene or something? What if we have kids and one of them needs a kidney? What then, Connor? If you're left with only one kidney, you certainly can't donate another.''

''Aren't you reaching a bit, Claire?''

''Am I?'' Her eyes dulled. ''Can you blame me for wanting promises?''

Connor looked away. Eventually, he gave a short, negative shake of his head. ''I'm not blaming you for anything, Claire. You're the innocent who's been hit with a double whammy.''

''Finally you see. Then you'll go back to Miami with me, and take time to consider all ramifications before you agree to any tests?''

"No-o-o." A grievous sound, torn from Connor's throat, seemed to reverberate around the room. "I can't—I can't explain, Claire. But the minute I saw Liddy Bea's picture, I knew I'd cut off my right arm to help her."

"I don't understand, Connor. Yes, you're technically related. But you've never laid eyes on her until today. You're virtual strangers."

"It's a connectedness I can't account for myself. I'd have to say, it just…is, Claire. I'm sorry I'm not making more sense. I really am." He grasped both her hands.

Tears sprang unexpectedly to Claire's eyes.

Connor didn't like knowing he was the cause. Claire wasn't the type to dissolve into tears. He'd done his best to put himself in her shoes. Yes, he'd sprung a former alliance on her, one that had resulted in a child. No small potatoes. But…surely she could see there was nothing he could do to change the outcome. "Claire, don't cry. Please…don't."

"I've got to leave. Now." Jumping up, she again tried to wrench off the ring he'd placed on her finger during happier times.

Connor tried to still her frantic tugging. "Don't. I'll get my cell phone and arrange a flight home for you. I'll stay and have the tests. After Dr. Dahl has the results, you and I can revisit my options. We owe ourselves that much, don't we?"

"I'll make the reservation," Bradford offered. "Unless you want me to send a tray upstairs, since you didn't eat much, and give yourself a night to think this over," he said to Claire.

She shook her head.

"I'll have Davis drop you off at the airport on his way to bring Mallory her stuff. I know I'm probably the last person you want advice from, Claire, but life is full of ups and downs. If you can separate yourself from your emotions, you'll see Connor needs your support in this matter.''

"I ca-can't. At least not now. Not...here.'' Neither her chin nor her hands were steady. "I'll wait for the tests. But I feel so *wronged,* Connor. I'm not sure I can ever get beyond that.''

His stomach pitched as they all walked away from a beautiful meal left almost untouched. His mind churned with fears of his own. Some included Claire. Others had to do with Mallory. Uppermost hovered feelings for a child he'd met just hours before. *His daughter.* The phrase had attached itself to his brain. He'd begun to seriously doubt that this strange sense of love would ever falter. For that reason, Connor voiced none of what he might have said to convince Claire to reconsider her decision.

Fifteen minutes later, the house was silent except for the ticking of a grandfather clock standing regally in the entry of the Forrest home. Connor, framed in the open door, solemnly watched Davis pull away from the steps. Claire looked small, huddled in the limo's back seat. He'd offered to accompany her, but she'd insisted on going to thc airport alone.

"Did you ever wish you could turn back the clock and repeat a segment of your life?'' Connor said slowly to Bradford, who stood behind him.

The senator jammed his hands deep in his pants pockets. Rattling loose change, he slanted Connor a wary look. "A man does what he can, based on the best evidence he has at the time he's forced to make a choice. No sense torturing yourself with what might have been. That's a game without end, my boy.''

"I suppose." Connor didn't sound convinced.

"The best recourse a man has is to immerse himself in work. How about it? Shall we retire to my study where you can fill me in on that brilliant invention of yours?"

Connor lingered in the doorway until well after the taillights of the senator's limousine had disappeared through the wrought-iron gates. "I guess it couldn't make my day any worse," he said, still not wanting to step inside and close the door on his departing fiancée. He'd never felt so torn.

"Brandy does wonders to restore a burned-out soul. Drunk in moderation, of course," Bradford was quick to add.

"I'm not sure I can handle liquor on an almost empty stomach."

"I'll ask Marta to bring us a tray of fruit, cheese and crackers. Or a couple of thick roast-beef sandwiches," the old man said, with obvious hope that Connor would agree.

"Fruit and cheese, I might manage. If you want a sandwich, sir, go right ahead. As it is, I feel bad about destroying Marta's hard work. I feel worse because you and Mallory missed your meal. And Claire. On a flight this late, she'll be lucky to get peanuts."

"Leaving was her choice. I offered to have a snack sent up, if she'd agree to just sleep on her decision."

"I know you did, Senator. I think I'm feeling the weight of the world on my shoulders about now. Claire never bargained for anything like this."

"All you can do is ask yourself how else you could have played the hand you were dealt." Bradford led Connor into his study, a room furnished in dark leathers and manly plaids.

"That's the hell of it," Connor said sadly, "I don't see any other way to play it."

Bradford poured two glasses of brandy. He tasted his, made a smacking sound with his lips, then handed Connor the second glass. "Sit. Tell me how this early storm-detection system of yours works. How much time does it give a city to evacuate?" The phone rang and Brad excused himself to take the call.

Connor accepted the glass, but he wandered around the room. The call went on for a good thirty minutes. Amazingly, on hanging up, Brad returned immediately to his earlier question.

"Before we get into any of that, do you mind answering a question for me?" Connor asked.

"If I'm able to, I will. I'm too wily a politician to promise answers until I've heard the question."

Connor tried but couldn't restrain a laugh. "Spoken like a man who's had too many dealings with the press. I'm not planning to broadcast your answer. Still, you might not like my asking something so personal. Why are you bending over backward to be nice to me? I'd think you'd act the opposite toward a guy who skipped the country, leaving your daughter unmarried and pregnant."

Obviously Bradford hadn't expected quite that question. He inhaled his brandy, and Connor had to pound him on the back several times in order to get him to breathe normally again.

"Sorry." Connor again paced the room. "It's an honest question, I think."

Brad took a big swallow of brandy. He let Connor wander the perimeter of the study for fifteen or twenty minutes. The younger man took an inordinate amount of time inspecting Brad's extensive law library and framed records of his accomplishments as a state senator.

Finally, Brad roused himself. "I'll answer your question with a question, my boy. Did you know Mallory was pregnant when you took off for the South Pacific?"

"No. And I swear that's the God's honest truth."

"Mmm. That happened the same week Beatrice was diagnosed with an inoperable brain tumor. I hope you'll forgive me for saying this, but I had more to consider than you and Mallory. Not that it didn't occur to me once or twice to use fatherly muscle and force you to do right by her. But Beatrice became deathly ill so fast. Mallory, God love her, devoted endless hours a day to her mother's care. And Bea didn't want anyone but Mallory ministering to her. The one time I brought up the idea of tracking you down, they both jumped down my throat."

"Mallory didn't discover she was pregnant until after I'd flown to the Pacific?"

"That I can't say. Looking back, I'd have to admit I operated in a fog that year."

"It must've been a bad time for the whole family. I hope you know that, grant of a lifetime or not, I'd have chucked it all and flown home if I'd had any inkling what was happening here. Thing is, I wrote Mallory. Three, maybe four letters. She never answered. Not so much as a stinking line."

Bradford seemed to sag in his chair. "Mallory had her hands full with Beatrice being so ill. And didn't you two squabble right before you left?"

"Seven years is a long time, but I'd remember an argument like that. We had a discussion, but I left thinking we'd agreed to correspond."

"To be frank, my boy, sometimes it's wiser just to

forget. Stirring old ashes too often starts new fires.'' The old man poured each of them another brandy. ''Here. Drown your sorrows in this.''

Connor hadn't realized he'd drained his glass. He swirled the golden liquid, trying to remember back seven years. He and Mallory had both been moody in the weeks before he graduated from FSU's master's program. Her folks had thrown a number of lavish campaign parties. Mallory had wanted him to accompany her. Connor remembered he'd been tired and had a thesis due. In addition, he worked four nights a week and didn't have time to waste hanging around with Tallahassee's rich and famous.

Damn, why couldn't he recall more? Back then, he and Mallory argued a lot over their social differences. Especially over the wishes of Mallory's mom.

Only now Beatrice Forrest was dead. The senator was probably right on one score. Why rekindle old animosities?

''Stop frowning. You'll look old before your time, my boy.'' Bradford smiled at his own joke. ''It's getting late. Take a load off your feet. I'm going to buzz Marta and see what happened to our snacks. Then I want to talk turkey with you about your system. I'm sure you're aware of the preliminary data being leaked by various weather services in South America and the Caribbean. There's been a higher than normal number of predictions regarding increased hurricane activity for the upcoming season.''

''I've seen the reports.'' Connor turned one of the leather chairs to face Bradford's. He waited to continue until the senator had finished speaking with Marta.

Connor remembered something he needed to do before they launched into work mode. He wanted to be sure Claire had arrived home safe and sound. So as not to disturb the senator, Connor retreated to a quiet corner of the study and took out his cell phone. The number he punched in rang five times before Claire picked up. "Hi. It's me. Just checking to see you made it home okay."

Silence stretched over the line. "I barely walked in the door. Dammit, Connor. I worked up a really great mad at you on the flight. Why do you have to go and be so blasted considerate?"

He smiled. "It probably comes from growing up an only child of a single mom. She pounded stuff like that into me."

"Yes, well, ordinarily it's a commendable trait. Now, if only you'd get the rest of your priorities straight."

"I believe they are straight. Granted, it's bad timing, Claire. I mean, learning I fathered a child. But I did. Would you really like the type of man who'd turn his back on his obligations?"

She sighed. "You don't know what I feel, Connor. *I* don't know what I feel. I know I need a while to sort it all out. Don't contact me again until you're sure which path you're going to take."

Connor was about to reiterate that he *was* sure, but the line went dead. He slowly released the breath he'd been holding.

"Is everything all right?" Bradford called from across the room.

"What? Yes. No." With a wry shrug, Connor shoved his cell phone back in its case. "Claire made it home. She's no happier with me now than when she left."

Bradford ambled over and gave Connor a bracing slap on the back. "Give her time, my boy. Give her time. That's another big difference between women and men. Women hold grudges longer. Oh, hey, here's Marta," he said as the door opened and the housekeeper walked in, carrying a tray.

"I heard that disparaging remark, Senator," Marta said. "Women are like that because our moms were such terrific travel agents, sending us on all those guilt trips."

The men chuckled before diving into the platter Marta had prepared. They'd hunkered down to talk by the time she left, closing them in the room.

MALLORY SHUT OFF THE VIDEO Liddy Bea had fallen asleep watching. After several seconds of blessed silence, she set the control aside and pulled a light sheet over her daughter. Since the last regimen of steroids had kicked in, Liddy Bea didn't resemble Connor quite as much as she had during the phase when she'd been nearly well. Then her angular cheekbones almost matched his. Mallory smoothed a tangle of tight curls back over Lydia's ear.

Removing all but one stuffed toy from the bed, she rechecked the sturdiness of the side rails before she tiptoed out to tell the night nurse she was leaving. She did her best to turn off her memories of Connor O'Rourke.

Connor and his caustic bride-to-be.

Even if Mallory hadn't dreamed of Connor reappearing in her life, she'd never have pictured him with a woman like Claire Dupree. The blonde was attractive but clingy. Connor never used to like clinginess. He'd been the outdoorsy sort. A kid into swimming, boating and surfing. He'd seemed to admire the way Mallory kept pace with him in all things. He had worked harder than anyone on the hurricane disaster-relief drills.

But perhaps Connor had changed. Maybe his focus had switched more to indoor sports, Mallory considered darkly as she walked out of the hospital. She recalled he'd been plenty adept at those, too.

Meandering up the tree-lined street that led to Mark's apartment, Mallory reminisced about Connor's abilities in the indoor arena. They'd started out high school friends. In college they'd taken friendship to the next level. During many a rainy afternoon that should have been spent studying, they'd made slow, delicious love on her narrow dorm bed.

Immersed in memories, Mallory almost walked past Mark's place. Disgusted with herself, she stamped up the steps and punched in the security code. Her brother's apartment, generally a place she thought warm and cozy, seemed lonely tonight.

She quickly went through the rooms, turning on lights. It wasn't until she ended up in the totally masculine bedroom that she attached a label to her oddly melancholy feelings. She was jealous, green-eyed jealous, of Claire Dupree. So jealous, Mallory didn't want the woman anywhere near Liddy Bea.

There it was in spades. Hardly a month had gone by in the past almost seven years that Mallory hadn't envisioned Connor showing up unannounced, a heartfelt apology on his lips for his long years of silence. Then he'd admit how mistaken he'd been. How his life, without her, had been bleak. He'd beg her to take him back.

Which she'd do after pretending to think about it. She'd say straight out that they had a daughter. It'd be love at first sight, and Connor would cradle Liddy Bea in his strong arms—in her fantasy. Then they'd all hug and kiss. Unfortunately, at this point, the scene she'd created automatically faded out on those happy images of her imagined family reunion.

It hurt like hell, knowing the familiar dream would

never come true. Stumbling forward, she fell facedown on Mark's bed and sobbed out the tears she'd become so good at holding in.

Mallory cried until her eyes were dry—until her shoulders and lungs ached. Then she got up and dragged herself off to shower away the red, puffy evidence, vowing these would be the last tears she'd ever shed for Connor O'Rourke.

She'd wasted half her life on him. On loving him while she watched him grow from a gangly, awkward boy into a handsome, self-possessed man. Always there'd been pride in his thoughtful, gentle manner. Pride in his intellect. In his dogged accomplishments, some forged against all odds. Those were gifts she'd tuck away in the dim recesses of her mind, until one day she might take them out and unwrap them for his daughter. Not now, though. Not when the feelings inside her were so raw. Someday she'd be strong enough to share the very best memories of Connor with Liddy Bea.

Unless she had to destroy them fighting him in court...

Frowning up into the fine spray, Mallory wondered where that thought had come from. But she *would* fight if he and Claire attempted to gain even partial custody. That woman, Claire, had been spiteful about Liddy Bea's lucky charm. The pink elephant might be modest compared to Claire's diamonds, but the circumstances under which Connor had purchased the gift was what made the elephant so very special.

Like Claire, Connor had once thought his gift tawdry. Compared to the other presents Mallory had received for her sixteenth birthday, he'd considered the little elephant insufficient, its newspaper wrapping an embarrassment.

As she left the shower to towel herself dry, Mallory

wished he knew she couldn't name one other gift she'd received that day. What had gone through his mind, she wondered, when he saw she'd kept the elephant?

Oh, damn! What if Liddy Bea had said she knew her daddy had given Mallory the elephant? If their paths ever crossed again, she might have to ask Connor that very question.

Relaxed from her shower and the purging tears, Mallory returned to the bedroom, oddly more content than she'd been in some time. Davis had delivered a suitcase filled with her clothes, including nightwear. But with Connor occupying her mind, it seemed more fitting to slide between the cool sheets in the altogether, as had been their habit when they lived together. She thought about the fact that Connor had been extra careful when it came to protection. Always. Which told her their daughter was meant to be.

A languid stretch brought new visions of Connor O'Rourke.

The two years they'd been roommates in that tiny, hot, third-floor walk-up, nude was the preferred attire—so to speak—for both of them.

Mallory smiled, betting that information would wipe the snide smile off Claire's face. Flopping to her side, Mallory stifled a giggle with a yawn. It felt good. She hadn't giggled since Liddy Bea's transplant began to go bad.

For her daughter's sake, Mallory couldn't let herself get too worked up or angry at Connor. After all, he'd told his fiancée that he intended to have the tests. Her opinion of him rose from the basement, where Mallory had let it tumble.

Closing her eyes, she silenced her mind. Tomorrow was a brand-new day. A day that could well bring Liddy Bea a step closer to a bright future, thanks to Connor.

CHAPTER SIX

CONNOR HEARD FOOTSTEPS going either upstairs or down as he emerged from his morning shower. If the senator was up and about this early after keeping him up till midnight talking hurricane predictions, then the old man must be in better shape than Dr. Dahl had led Connor to believe. Too much brandy and smoke from Bradford's cigars had left Connor groggy.

Normally not an early riser, he'd managed to roll out of bed at seven this morning. Mostly because he was determined to catch Dahl before his morning rounds. Last night as Connor tossed about, unable to sleep for worrying about the two women whose lives he'd disrupted, he decided to press Dahl to begin the tests ASAP.

It wasn't fair to drive Mallory from her home, and it wasn't fair to leave Claire dangling. If he proved to be a good donor for Liddy Bea, and there was no reason given the state of his health why he wouldn't be, then he needed to do it. He and Claire had to face and dispense with her doubts, fears or other reasons for not wanting him to offer a kidney.

Dressed and feeling pretty much presentable, Connor left his room, buttoning his wallet into his left hip pocket. Not expecting to see anyone, he was startled when he bumped smack into Mallory, who'd apparently left her room across the hall.

When she'd flown out of the house last evening, she'd

worn casual clothes—a crop top and walking shorts. She now had on a gold-colored sleeveless dress that brought out red lights in her thick curls. Curls that had once spread like fiery flames across their shared pillow.

Floored by the memory and the need that slammed through him, Connor halted in his tracks. "I, uh, thought you spent the night at Mark's apartment."

"I did." She adjusted a flat gold necklace. "I left here in such a huff, I forgot to take the notes I needed for a meeting I can't reschedule. Also," she said wryly, "it'd probably cause a riot around the hospital if I showed up at a meeting of wealthy local matrons wearing shorts. Dad sent stuff, but Marta didn't include work clothes."

Connor ran a hesitant gaze up, down and up her slender length again. "I always thought you could wear a garbage bag and look good."

He appeared so serious, Mallory hastily sobered. It was probably the coward's way out, but she gripped the banister and all but ran down the stairs. At the landing, she realized how short of breath she was.

"Hey, slow down. If you're headed to breakfast, I'll join you."

"Shouldn't you wait and have breakfast with your fiancée?"

"Claire flew back to Miami last night. If Dr. Dahl can arrange to test me today, I'll be leaving, too. I'll continue my research until he notifies me of the next step. If you have pull setting up lab stuff fast, you could be rid of me sooner."

Her heart did a series of drumbeats. "So you convinced Claire to let you proceed? Thanks, Connor. I know giving Liddy Bea a kidney can't be as easy a decision for you as for me. She's little more than a stranger to you."

"Whose fault is that?"

They'd reached the kitchen door, where the smell of fresh coffee permeated the air. Mallory stopped and absorbed his smoldering glare. "Enough, already. Tell me, Connor, should I have trapped you into staying in Tallahassee with the news of my pregnancy? Was I supposed to demand you abandon your dream? How? The first thing you said to me that night was to suggest I stay behind, forget you and hook up with one of the yuppie lawyers Mother was forever parading past me. Well, I'm sorry, Connor. I needed to keep some portion of my pride intact."

"I probably said a lot of dumb things. I don't remember. Dammit, Mallory, at least give me credit for trying to do *something* right. Your mother made it clear enough that you could and should do better than marrying me. If it's retribution you want, the truth is I'd barely landed on Guam when I knew that letting you go was the biggest mistake of my life."

"Then why didn't you—" Marta suddenly blocked the doorway.

"Why are you two yelling at each other at this early hour? Come have breakfast, and try and act civilized."

Mallory gave her watch a quick check. "Yikes, I need to go. I'm meeting those prospective hospital benefactors at eight-thirty. I'll have coffee and a roll there."

Connor watched her execute a smooth exit. He remained rooted to the floor, staring after her as she dashed upstairs and came back a moment later carrying a bulging attaché and her purse. She seemed surprised he was still there. "I'll phone Fredric. The tests are fairly straightforward, Connor," she said, latching on to the first thing that might return them to a less volatile footing. "It's necessary to fast, and since you haven't eaten, they can probably work you in this morning. That way, you can catch an afternoon flight to Miami. I'll assume this works out, so I'll say goodbye now. *Thank you* seems inadequate, Connor, but I'll say it again—from the bottom of my heart and Liddy's.''

The finality of the door closing behind her took Connor aback. Damn, he wished Marta hadn't interrupted them earlier. What had Mallory been about to say? *Why didn't he...what? Phone?* The atoll where he'd been flown immediately after touching down on Guam had no phone reception.

But he'd written. Letters he'd sent out on a supply boat.

Marta's stern features again appeared in his line of vision. ''Davis is at the back door wondering when you want to leave for town. He said Mr. Brad left at six. Tell me why a body bothers cooking meals around here.''

Feeling a little guilty, Connor followed her into the kitchen. ''I have no idea what time Dr. Dahl's office opens. Nine, I'd guess. Mallory said they'll need me to fast for those tests. I'm sorry you went to the trouble of cooking. Everything smells great.''

Davis stepped into the room and removed his cap. ''Do you still want to go by the cemetery this morning, sir? The senator spoke with Dr. Dahl while we were on the way to his office. Apparently I should have you at the laboratory at ten. He estimates you'll be finished by one or two, but he's sorry he can't meet you for lunch. Said he figured you'd want to head back to Miami before he winds down, anyway.''

Connor nodded, glancing at the kitchen wall clock. ''I was hoping to catch an afternoon flight.''

''Oh, another thing Mr. Brad asked me to relay. Said he'll phone you the minute he gets authorization for funding. Didn't say funding for what. I guess you know.''

Connor's jaw dropped. Last night, the senator had joked about raising money to move Connor's research program from Miami to Tallahassee. Obviously it hadn't been a joke, after all. But why would he take the senator seriously? For one thing, he doubted it'd be simple to find the necessary bucks to make the switch. ''I, ah, guess I'll run up and pack. Marta, thank you, and be sure to thank the senator. He has no reason to go out of his way for me,'' Connor muttered.

Feeling suddenly as claustrophobic in this luxuriant home as he had at sixteen, Connor couldn't leave fast enough. ''Davis, it'll take me only a minute to toss my gear together and phone the airline. Will we still have time to go by the cemetery?''

''I think so, yes. Tell Marta what flowers you'd like for your mother's grave, and she can phone in your order.''

''My mom's favorite flowers were yellow carnations, and those little blue ones with yellow centers. I don't know what they're called.''

''Forget-me-nots,'' Marta supplied. ''Odd, those are Miss Mallory's favorites, too.''

For a second, Connor floundered. ''I, uh, must've given you the wrong flowers. My mom's favorites were, uh, yellow roses. And daisies.''

''A logical mistake,'' Marta murmured, gazing on Connor with narrowed eyes. The Forrests' housekeeper didn't think his mistake was logical at all.

Connor smoothed his tie. ''And please order a bouquet of Mallory's favorites sent to her at work. Have it signed from me and Claire. Maybe flowers will make partial amends for driving Mallory from her bed last night.''

''She'd rather have her own place. She and Miss Liddy gave up their house when Miss Mallory elected to donate a kidney. They were making plans to move back there when the transplant failed.''

''That explains why they live with the senator,'' Connor said, rubbing a thumb over his bottom lip. ''I'm afraid there's a lot I don't know about my daughter, Marta.''

''Humph!'' The housekeeper swung away and snatched up the kitchen wall phone. ''Appears to me that if a father wanted to know more about his child, he wouldn't be so anxious to hightail it out of town.''

That barb struck deep, as Marta had meant it to. But since Connor had nothing to say in his own defense and because she'd turned away, he simply excused himself with no further comment.

Less than fifteen minutes later, his bag packed and a flight secured, Connor found that his detour past the cemetery was far more gut-wrenching than he'd expected. Painful memories of the day he'd buried Lydia O'Rourke threatened to drown him as surely as if he'd been caught in a riptide. Adding to the sensation of being in over his head was the fact that someone else had left a bouquet on his mother's grave. Who? Claire? They'd talked about it yesterday. She could have phoned a florist.

As they drew closer, Connor realized the bouquet was wilted. While Connor tried to get his bearings, Davis efficiently whisked the old bouquet from the in-ground vase and hurried away to toss the faded flowers into a nearby trash receptacle.

About to ask Davis if there was a card with the bouquet, Connor saw that the senator's driver had withdrawn a discreet distance—presumably to allow Connor time to get control of his emotions. Which he eventually managed to do, long enough to whisper a remembered prayer. Something Mallory had taught him in the dark aftermath of a hurricane that had altered his life forever.

Mallory. She'd been such an integral part of his existence back then. Connor would never have guessed, seven or eight years ago, that they'd ever reach the point of trying to avoid being in the same room together.

"Sir," Davis said quietly. "Traffic is picking up. If I'm going to get you to the clinic on time, we'd better leave now."

Connor rose shakily from where he'd knelt in recently mowed grass. He slowly dusted grass clippings from the knees of his slacks as he moved toward Davis, who held the limo door open. "Those flowers, Davis. The ones you tossed. Any idea who might have put them there?"

Davis glanced over his shoulder. "I'd guess Miss Mallory and Miss Lydia came by before she went back into the hospital. The senator and I occasionally see them here. Miss Mallory sees to it that her daughter regularly visits her grandmothers."

"She does?" Connor's throat went too dry to say more. Did that mean Mallory spoke to Liddy Bea about him, as well? If so, wouldn't the child have recognized his name? Or had he not given his name when he'd introduced himself and Claire?

"We're at the clinic, sir. I have errands to run for Marta. Page me when you're finished. Here's the number."

"I appreciate the senator's placing you at my disposal, Davis. And thanks for the side trip to the cemetery. But I won't tie you up further. I couldn't get a flight out until nine-thirty tonight. After the tests, I'll catch a cab to the hospital and maybe spend a couple of hours getting to know my daughter.''

"Very good, sir." Davis beamed. "But I'd be most happy to chauffeur you. Otherwise Marta might suggest I clean the garage. That woman does love to boss me around when Senator Brad's at work.''

Connor grinned. "In that case, I'll leave my bags in the limo and page you when I'm done."

Davis slid back into the car and drove off.

Dr. Dahl's receptionist, Rhonda, glanced up when Connor opened the door. "Dr. O'Rourke." She rose gracefully and motioned him through a full waiting room. "Our lab techs will be overjoyed to see how prompt you are. Follow me, please. I think they're ready for you.''

"Like good little vampires?" Connor teased with more levity than he felt. The clinic had the antiseptic smell of a hospital. His stomach began to churn.

The woman led him down a hallway he hadn't noticed yesterday. She laughed at his lame joke. "That's good. I'll have to sew the techs black capes next Halloween. By the way, you haven't eaten, have you?''

"Not even coffee, so I hope you guys know you're taking your lives in your hands messing with me this morning. Which doesn't mean I don't appreciate such fast service.''

"We want to accommodate you, Dr. O'Rourke."

Connor shot her a veiled glance.

Rhonda smiled. "Don't look so worried. The whole staff is rooting for Liddy Bea. She's a great kid."

"My daughter's been through quite a struggle with this kidney problem, hasn't she," he said, following Rhonda into a gleaming white room.

The receptionist's dark eyes shifted, and then a shutter fell. "You'd have to discuss that with her mother. Mallory Forrest is your daughter's legal guardian."

"Only because she neglected to inform me of Lydia's existence," Connor muttered angrily.

Rhonda dropped a Request for Services form into an empty basket sitting just inside the lab. "Have a seat, Doctor. Lynn or Donna will be right with you."

"It's Connor, please. And look, I didn't mean to bite your head off. I just don't want you all to get the impression I'm a deadbeat dad."

Rhonda withdrew without another word. Not that Connor would have explained his situation in any greater detail. But he did stew a bit, wondering what Mallory's friends thought about his leaving her to raise Liddy Bea alone.

A perky blonde showed up to snatch the form. "I'm Lynn. I'll be relieving you of several vials of blood, Dr. O'Rourke. Then Donna will escort you across the hall, where she's set up for your tissue biopsy and pyelogram. Intravenous pyelogram," she elaborated. "An X ray, oh, and somewhere in between, you'll have to pee in this cup." She handed him a covered plastic cup emblazoned with his name.

"Dr. Dahl didn't mention anything about an X ray or tissue biopsy."

Lynn pointed him to a cubicle and asked him to sit. As Connor unbuttoned his shirtsleeve and rolled it up past his elbow, Lynn explained the X ray. "The doctor needs to cover all the bases with you. Not only are you a long-distance donor, but the recipient has had one failed transplant. A tissue sample is very helpful. An IVP tracks radiopaque dye through your urinary system and shows any glitches or abnormalities. Next week, a radiologist and Dr. Dahl will read your films. Then the team will decide whether you're a viable candidate.''

"Oh. Makes sense to check everything, I suppose. But can't you take my word for the fact that output from my kidneys is fine?''

She grinned a little at that, rubber-banded his arm and flicked a vein with her forefinger. The minute his vein puffed up, she jabbed Connor with the needle and loosened the band.''

"Hey, take it easy,'' he said. But this technician knew her job. Almost before he'd fully released his pent-up breath, Lynn had her four vials of blood.

As if by some silent signal, a dark-haired woman appeared. "I'm Donna. If you'll come with me, I'll point you toward the men's rest room. I've left a gown in there for you to change into.''

"A gown?'' Connor glanced up from where Lynn plastered a fat gauze patch over the spot she'd stabbed.

"Yes. An IVP necessitates inserting a catheter.''

Connor tried not to let either of the women see how the mere thought of a catheter made him grimace. Clearly, they knew. Despite their professionalism, these women, these friends of his daughter's, shared an unflattering view of him, and Connor got the message. Absent fathers didn't rank high with them. And he couldn't blame them for their attitude. He'd been a kid whose own dad took a hike. Connor knew how tough it'd made life for the parent left alone—and for a kid, who'd always wondered if he was to blame. But that was his story, not Liddy's. He wasn't anything like his old man. He'd never abandon his child.

After that, Connor didn't try to strike up a conversation with Donna. In spite of the long silence, the IVP went smoothly. The dye traveled its distance in due course, and eventually she announced that his X rays and tissue biopsy were complete.

"So, there's nothing more you need from me?" he asked once she'd helped him sit up and had handed him a sheet detailing the side effects to be aware of. "I mean, nothing except wait until Dr. Dahl phones me with the results?"

"That's right. If the tests are all satisfactory, I think Dr. Dahl mentioned scheduling surgery sometime in mid-August."

Connor paused at the doorway to the men's room, holding his gown together in the back. "Why the delay?"

"To allow Liddy Bea's most recent incision to heal. Hasn't anyone gone over the transplant procedure with you?"

"Dr. Dahl concentrated on discussing my role."

"Oh. Well, if possible, a recipient retains his or her failed kidneys. The donor organ is attached through a frontal opening. Liddy Bea's undergone two surgeries at the same site within one year. In addition to looking at all aspects of such an intrusive procedure, we have to consider repeat anesthesia, as well."

"I didn't realize..." His voice trailed off. "Dr. Dahl gave me and my fiancée some information to study. I'll read it thoroughly on the plane trip back to Miami this evening. I figured, since I was already in town, that I should get this part out of the way."

"I see. Okay, someone will be in touch, then. You're free to go. Oh, do you need a ride to the airport? Dr. Dahl said he'd have Rhonda take you."

"No, thanks. I've made other arrangements. But thank Dr. Dahl for the offer."

"Goodbye then, and good luck."

Connor munched gratefully on an energy bar Marta had given him. Donna's words kept ringing in his ears as he waited outside for Davis to pick him up. The term *good luck* seemed to imply that there was a degree of risk involved. Claire had expressed concern about that, even though he'd done his best to brush her worry aside. Should he get a second opinion?

Davis pulled in before Connor had worked that out in his mind. "You're still standing, sir," Davis joked. "The tests must have gone well," he said after closing the car door.

"Nothing to them so far."

"What time is your flight, sir?" Davis asked after a while. "Senator Brad has an evening meeting he only learned about an hour ago."

"Not to worry, Davis. I'll take my duffel bag with me and grab a cab to the airport. I didn't pack much. Unlike Claire."

"Mrs. B. used to do that, too. When the senator grumbled, she'd say he had no idea what it took her to do him proud."

"Mallory traveled light. At least when she was in high school and college. We went to a number of hurricane-volunteer training camps together," Connor said, noticing that Davis was studying him oddly in the mirror. All at once he saw it was because they were parked beneath the hospital portico.

"Jeez, how'd we get here so fast? This is my jumping-off spot. Thanks, Davis. To you and the senator," Connor said as he exited the limo.

"Nice meeting you, sir. Give my best to Miss Liddy." Davis moved briskly to the trunk and hauled out Connor's bag, which he sat on the ground. Connor, after emerging from the car, stared pensively at the hospital's upper-story windows.

"Nervous, sir?"

Connor gave a sheepish shrug. "It seems so. Tell me, Davis, why am I daunted by a six-year-old when I've gone on national TV and given speeches in front of the world's leading scientists?"

"Children have a way of looking clear to a man's soul. Maybe you're worried about what she'll see in there."

"I guess. I know I'm curious about how she'd react if she found out I'm her father. Okay, so I'm worried, too. And I can't really understand those feelings. I haven't done anything to be ashamed of. Had I known about her, I'd have been there for her. It's as simple as that."

Davis shifted uncomfortably, making Connor realize he shouldn't put a Forrest employee in the middle of a debate that could only be settled by him and Mallory. He abruptly grabbed and shook Davis's hand. "I'm wasting time we could both use more effectively. Thanks again." Slinging the duffel over one tense shoulder, Connor shoved through the first set of glass doors.

In the lobby, he passed the gift shop. Then he had second thoughts and retraced his steps. Inside, he took his time looking over the merchandise. He didn't want to be a man who had to buy his child's affections. But he felt bad for having disappointed her yesterday. He rejected the stuffed pink elephant, keenly aware of Claire's objections to it.

In a far corner, on a shelf of knickknacks, Connor saw four whimsical glass frogs whose broad grins appealed to him. Obviously a band, as each frog held a musical instrument. Lord, he didn't even know if Liddy Bea liked music. And normally, he supposed, glass wouldn't be appropriate for a six-year-old. Yet, he'd seen how she adored her mother's glass elephant. And these frogs made him smile. If Mallory deemed them inappropriate, she could take them away until Liddy Bea was older. Gathering the pieces, he carried them to the counter.

"Oh, I love these," the clerk exclaimed. "They'll bring joy to some lucky patient."

Appreciating her approval, Connor offered his most charming smile. The clerk, smiling back, arranged the frogs in a pretty gift box and tied it with a bright red bow.

Upstairs on the ward, Connor glanced nervously through the window of his daughter's private room. Though no longer attached to an IV, she appeared restless. Bored, he thought. Or maybe—lonely.

Yesterday, he'd had Claire behind him, urging him to go in. Today, he had no one, and admittedly no basis for the fear that gripped him by the throat. Finally, taking a deep breath, he thrust open the door and stepped inside.

The girl looked up from a doll she'd been listlessly flopping about. "Oh," she said, her eyes wide. "You did come back. I hoped you would. This morning when I asked Mommy if you might, she said no."

Connor set his duffel under one of the two vacant chairs. "I'm leaving for Miami later tonight. That's why I'm carrying my suitcase."

Liddy Bea craned her neck to peer behind Connor. "Where's the grumpy lady?"

Connor realized she meant Claire. "Uh…she had to go home early. Claire's not normally grumpy. I think maybe she was disappointed that you didn't like the angel bear."

The child fiddled with her doll's bonnet. Eventually she gazed up contritely. "Mommy said next time I'm sp'osed to just say thank you. What's in the box? Did you bring me another present? If you do, I know I'll like it." She edged up higher on the pillows.

Connor tipped back his head and laughed heartily. "How can you be so sure until you see what it is?"

"'Cause I love everything that comes in little boxes."

"In that case, here. Have a look." Connor put the package in her lap. "I've got to warn you, though. It's not a toy."

Liddy Bea already had the ribbon untied and the lid off. With care, she unrolled the first frog from its tissue, then cradled the piece ever so reverently in a pudgy hand. Tracing the frog's bulging eyes, she smiled softly. "How did you know I wanted my very own good-luck charm? 'Cause I'm afraid I'll break Mommy's elephant."

"Dig deeper in the box, honey. Your frog has three friends."

"Goody! So, if one breaks, I'll still have luck." She unwrapped the others and exclaimed over each frog in turn. When all four rested on her lap, she batted her long eyelashes at Connor and prettily lifted her arms for a hug.

Bending awkwardly, he accepted his due. Something about knowing that this child, with her soft, sweet-smelling skin, was a direct creation of his and Mallory's sent Connor's already jumpy nerves reeling. Perhaps the knot he felt in his gut made him squeeze her too tightly. At any rate, Liddy Bea ducked away before Connor was ready to let her go.

"Thanks. I, um, forgot your name," the child said, clearly not sure about having him so close now.

"It's Connor. Oh, wait—does your mom let you call adults by their first names?"

"Maybe." Liddy Bea nibbled on her lip, gazing solemnly at Connor's face. Apparently having solved whatever momentary concern she'd wrestled with, Liddy Bea carefully picked up her frogs. "I'll bet Mommy'll be surprised."

"Indeed, Mommy is," declared a troubled voice from the door.

Neither Connor nor Liddy Bea had heard Mallory open the door. Both aimed guilty glances her way.

Straightening, Connor tugged on his tie. "Mallory. I figured you probably had to work until at least five o'clock."

"The ward nurse phoned, asking if I'd authorized any male visitors for Liddy Bea today. Since I hadn't, naturally I rushed right upstairs. I work on the first floor."

"Mommy, we know Connor, don't we?" Liddy caught her mother's eye.

"I explained last night, baby. He's an old friend," Mallory said, her voice husky. "But you met him only yesterday."

Liddy Bea sighed aloud. "I feel like I've seen him lots of times."

Mallory and Connor shared a puzzled lift of the eyebrows. The truth dawned first on Mallory. Connor was slower to realize the girl probably only recognized a similarity to herself each time she looked in a mirror.

Mallory gasped weakly, clearly not wanting to be forced into explanations.

Fortunately, Liddy skipped easily on to the next item of importance in her life; namely, Connor's gift. "Mommy, come see what your friend gave me." Liddy pointed to the man she had no clue was her father.

"These are my very own good-luck frogs. So you can take Ellie home and put her back in her special place."

Mallory sidled past Connor, careful not to touch him. She took an inordinate amount of time examining the frogs, even though she felt Connor's eyes burning into her back. He was, she knew, dying to hear more about the special place where she kept his gift. But she'd be darned if she'd let him find out Ellie still watched over her while she slept, as the little figurine had done since the day she turned sixteen. Mallory had waged battles with her mother, who on many occasions tried to spirit Ellie into the trash.

Never had Mallory let Beatrice know how often her daughter's last act of the day was to kiss the elephant's trunk and make a wish that Connor would one day return to her. A silly ritual. And it had been patently clear for years that her faith in the good-luck charm had been sadly misplaced. Liddy Bea, chattering merrily about her windfall, seemed destined to travel a similar path.

"Mommy, please put my frogs where I can see them every morning when I wake up. You know what? I think maybe Connor knew my daddy. I'll bet my good-luck frogs will lead Daddy home. Do you think so? You said Connor's been gone a long time. And now he's back."

Mallory bristled at the very suggestion. "Connor's not really back. He lives in Miami, and he's leaving again. Aren't you?" she said, rounding on him in a way that could only be termed rude.

He leaned negligently against Liddy Bea's bed and found he actually enjoyed Mallory's discomfort. A discomfort she'd brought on herself, dammit, when she made the decision to cut him out of his child's life.

But as always, Mallory's intense blue eyes had the power to melt him into submission. The passage of time apparently hadn't altered that, in spite of their current adversarial relationship. Especially as those same blue eyes pleaded with him not to give away her secret.

Disgusted at letting himself be so easily manipulated, Connor uncrossed his arms and ankles, and angrily grabbed up his duffel. There remained, however, a tiny, defensive twinge, demanding he not let Mallory off scot-free. He glanced at his watch and noted that it was quarter after four. "If I'm going, how about a lift to the airport? You don't mind taking me, do you, Mallory? My flight's not till nine-thirty, so there's lots of time before then for us to grab a bite to eat. Otherwise, I guess I can phone the kitchen and ask to have a tray sent up with Liddy Bea's. If I recall from last night, you said that's an option."

"It's not your option," Mallory snapped. "I'd intended to work late...I'm preparing for my upcoming leave. But...oh, all right. Bring your bag. We'll stop at my office so I can shut down my computer, at least." Grinding her back teeth, Mallory kissed Liddy Bea. "Tell Connor goodbye, baby. I'll see you later."

"He could stay, and we could all have a pretend tea party."

"Maybe next time I'm in town," Connor told the child, totally ignoring Mallory's scowl.

"'Kay." Somewhat mollified, Liddy Bea smiled and waved them off, after turning on her side to better see the frog band her mom had set on the table near her bed.

Connor expected Mallory to let him have it once they were out of Liddy Bea's hearing. Instead, she clammed up, leaving him to match her furious strides down two flights of back stairs.

"Dammit, Mallory! Maybe you'd better define my role a little better—explain what you want from me."

Glowering, she slammed into her office, not inviting him to follow. He stepped in, anyway, taking grim satisfaction in the surreptitious glances the staff threw his way.

"Ah. I see you got the flowers." He fingered a pale carnation in a vase full of carnations and forget-me-nots.

"So you're the one who sent Mallory the bouquet?" her secretary gushed—a comment more or less forcing Mallory to complete terse introductions.

"Dr. O'Rourke's an old acquaintance. He's leaving town soon. This afternoon," she stressed to the still-giddy secretary. "Mandy, tell Alec I'm running out to the airport and back. I'll try to catch up with him at six or so in the cafeteria. If not, I'll see him in the morning."

Connor waited until Mallory marched past him and out the door. He turned to Mandy, who continued to eye him with interest. "Scrap the cafeteria message. Tell Alec whoever-he-is, I'm taking Mallory to an early dinner on our way to the airport. She can get together with him tomorrow." Connor shut the door solidly, then caught a sputtering Mallory by the elbow. Pulling her against his side, he forcibly walked her to the employee garage.

"You have some nerve," she exploded after he'd stopped beside her car and released her.

"You bet I do," he blazed. "Gumption was something your mother was sure I lacked, right? Well, as you can see, that's changed. So you might want to think twice about taking off without me, which is exactly what's on your mind. I've got no qualms about going back in there and telling your secretary exactly how it used to be with us."

"Bastard!" Her eyes sprouting angry tears, Mallory jabbed her key at the door lock.

Connor took the keys from her icy fingers and did the honors, handing them back with a flourish. "By any dictionary's definition, that term *does* fit me. But I'd be careful about flinging it around too freely, as it also applies to Liddy Bea. Your fault. Not mine. Now...if we're finished trading barbs, might I suggest stopping someplace relatively upscale to eat? If for no reason other than to ensure that we'll be civilized to each other for an hour or so."

With a last dirty look, Mallory slid into the driver's seat of her aging BMW.

CHAPTER SEVEN

MALLORY NAVIGATED THE BUSY downtown traffic without acknowledging Connor's presence.

While far from content with the way things were going between them, he gave her space. Until she turned onto one of the area's canopy roads—so named for the huge oaks whose spreading branches formed a long canopy over the corridors leading out of the city. "I wasn't kidding about us stopping to eat," he said bluntly. "Because of the tests, I missed breakfast *and* lunch, so I'm starved. All I've had is an energy bar Marta insisted I take. Anyway, isn't it high time we have a straightforward discussion about our daughter?"

Mallory tore her eyes from the road. "What do you mean, *our* daughter?"

He exhaled harshly. "I mean, how long are we going to dance around the truth? I'm Lydia's natural father. You can avoid the fact, but you can't change it."

Color drained from Mallory's face, and her body shuddered so noticeably, Connor reacted to her pain. "God, Mallory. If I could turn back the clock and relive our pasts, don't you think I would?"

"That's where we differ," she retorted sharply. "Even with all of life's ups and downs, I wouldn't skip having Liddy Bea for anything. Not for anything in the world."

"I didn't mean I'd erase the pregnancy. I only meant

I'd never have left you alone to deal with caring for her. Pull off here,'' he snapped. ''It's the Inn. I remember you always claimed they served great food.''

Mallory reacted automatically to his curt command. If she'd taken time to reconsider, she'd have driven past the cozy wayside restaurant, where the staff knew her on sight. This was Alec's favorite haunt. On nights when they both worked late, he often brought her here to compare notes. Before this moment, Mallory had studiously avoided attaching importance to the frequency with which her boss asked her to accompany him to cocktail parties and civic functions.

Suddenly, as she pulled into the parking lot, seated next to the only man to whom she'd ever given her body and her heart, Mallory was forced to face another truth. Her boss wanted to be more than a boss.

''What's the matter? Why are you staring at me? Aren't I dressed okay for this place? I have a sports jacket in my duffel. It's probably wrinkled, but—''

''You look fine.'' Mallory took the key from the ignition, averting her eyes from Connor O'Rourke. Still, she couldn't help noticing that one tanned, muscled arm was casually draped over the back of her seat. He looked slightly piratical with his dark, windblown hair swept back from a distinctive widow's peak. His sharply angular face, creased by a dimple on one side, lessened his rakish appearance. She'd seen the other day how his chest and shoulders had filled out in seven years. Not a detriment. He looked fabulous enough to send her heart into a tailspin.

From the corner of her eye, Mallory tried to study, instead, the strong, brown fingers Connor drummed nervously on the dash. She'd always loved his hands. Those long, clever, well-manicured fingers had never felt rough against her skin. Only now did she wonder why, when he often worked at labor-intensive jobs.

"Drive on," he growled. "Surely there's someplace not so fancy. I don't want to embarrass you. I never did. Although if your mom was still alive, she'd say I did that just by living."

"That's not true," Mallory blurted. "Well," she reneged unhappily, "it's true Mother made snide remarks a few times. It's not true you embarrassed me. I was always proud of you, Connor. I still am," she admitted in a ragged whisper.

That declaration caused Connor to straighten in his seat and stop the tattoo of his fingers on the padded dash. "Proud? Of me?"

"Of your work," she hastily corrected him. "Your professors thought an early-warning system to detect hurricanes was a pipe dream. You've shown them all."

"You've kept track since I left Tallahassee?" Both his confusion and underlying bitterness were achingly evident.

"No. No, I haven't," Mallory said, trying to combat his impression. "I read an article recently on your research in one of Dad's business magazines. And I happened to see an interview Miami TV did shortly after you joined their meteorological team there."

"Oh. Sorry I jumped to conclusions. You want to eat here, then?" He prepared to open his door.

"How long before you have to check in for your flight?" Mallory asked, turning businesslike again.

"Three hours or so."

"Well, it's only five now, so I, uh, suppose we have time to eat here. They're never in a rush to serve patrons. But if you have until eight, there shouldn't be a problem." Patting the space between them, Mallory found and retrieved her purse, which she'd put there as a barrier.

The small action reminded Connor of his gentlemanly duties. He'd been lost in assessing how pretty Mallory looked in the gold dress he'd admired earlier. Vaulting suddenly from his seat, he hurried around the car to assist her out. What he found most disconcerting was the fact that he had to mentally scold himself for letting memories creep in of the way Mallory used to look wearing nothing but a lazy, sexy smile.

He felt sick. Damn, he shouldn't have to remind himself that he had a fiancée awaiting him in Miami.

Connor knew he should be mature enough now to blot out lust-filled memories of a woman he'd once loved. But he wasn't succeeding. "What a mess," he mumbled, as he handed Mallory from the car.

"Are you referring to me?" Mallory stumbled a little.

"No," he said, startled. "I didn't realize I'd spoken aloud. I was referring to our situation. We're kind of caught between a rock and a hard place, aren't we, Mallory?"

"No. Not if we watch what we say around Liddy Bea, and if you and I limit our contact with each other. Once the transplant is over, we'll each go about our business as before."

Did she really believe that? Connor let her stride ahead while he dropped back to smooth his tie with a sweating hand. He'd have to make it very clear that he wasn't willing to disappear out of his daughter's life again.

Mallory reached the entry ahead of him. Connor, still a step behind, stretched one arm over her head to open the door. An elderly couple was just leaving, so he held the door to let them pass. He caught up to Mallory as the maître d' addressed her by name. "Ms. Forrest. If you're joining Dr. Robinson tonight, I believe you've beaten him here. Will you wait for him in the foyer or shall I prepare your favorite table?"

"I, ah, I'm dining with someone else this evening." Red seeped up her neck as she glanced self-consciously over her shoulder at Connor. Feeling trapped, she spun toward the host again. "We're in a bit of a rush to get to the airport. Any table will do, Dominic."

Connor gave in to a slow burn working its way past his lungs. "Come now, Mallory. We're not in that big a rush. By all means, you should enjoy Dr. Robinson's favorite table."

"Very good, sir." Dominic bowed stiffly and disappeared into the dim interior.

"That's unnecessary, Connor," Mallory hissed. "Any table would do."

"Do you recall me trying to save up enough money to bring you here on your twenty-first birthday? Two days before, I blew the spare tire on the old Ford, and that took all the cash I had. I know how hard you tried not to let your disappointment show. It was hell on me, since I was the reason your mom cut off all money except your tuition. I hated ending up in the college cafeteria when it should have been a special day for you."

"I'd forgotten that. What's your point, Connor?"

"Frankly, I'm curious about the guy who managed to make this place routine for you. Tell me more about your Dr. Robinson. Neither you nor your dad mentioned you were seeing someone."

Mallory put a hand to her temple where a troublesome pressure was building behind her eyes. "Alec, Dr. Robinson, is Forrest Memorial's chief administrator. Most of our visits here could be classed as working dinners."

"But not all?"

"What are you getting at, Connor? You're engaged, for heaven's sake! My position in PR reports directly to Alec. We work together a fair bit."

"Don't bite my head off. I'm interested in hearing about the people in your life now, Mallory. Because those same folks are in Liddy's life. If you want the unvarnished truth, I'm surprised you aren't married."

"Why? To whom? You and I dated exclusively for eight years."

"I've been gone almost seven since then. Even when we were living together, your mom kept trying to fix you up with a lineup of lawyers, regardless of how old some of them were. Say, how old *is* this Alec?"

"Fifty-six. Not that it's any of your business."

Connor would have shared his opinion of a twenty-four-year age difference had the maître d' not come back to collect them.

Mallory read Connor's views plainly enough. And she didn't care to hear what he thought. She all but tore the wine list out of Dominic's hand, plopped down hard in the chair he pulled out and hid behind the tooled leather binder.

"Is everything all right, Ms. Forrest?" Dominic inquired. "You'd like a different type of wine tonight, perhaps, rather than Dr. Robinson's preferred extra-dry pinot Grigio?"

Mallory's eyelids snapped open wide. "Wine? Oh, we're not having wine. It's not *that* kind of dinner, Dominic."

Staring at her oddly, the man discreetly plucked the wine folder from Mallory's grip, replacing it with the menu.

Connor lowered his head to hide a grin. "The lady is

the designated driver," he mumbled. "I'm merely along for the ride. I'll have a glass of cabernet." Connor rattled off several more exclusive brands. "Any one of those will be fine."

Dominic snapped his fingers. "Very good, sir. I'll leave you with Josef, our sommelier. Carlisle will be your waiter."

Like magic, Josef materialized. Following a brief discussion pertaining to what vintages the restaurant stocked, Connor settled on one.

Josef briskly closed the wine list, bowing as he backed away.

Connor watched the ritual, then glanced around, eyeing the gleam of silver against a backdrop of candles, snowy linen and lead crystal. The whole place had the smell of old money.

"Now that I can afford to patronize a restaurant of this caliber, I find it excessively formal. I can't imagine considering anyplace this stuffy my favorite."

"What's wrong with it?" Mallory unfolded her napkin.

"I still prefer that hole-in-the-wall crab shack you and I used to steal away to down in Apalachicola whenever I scraped together enough money to eat out."

Mallory laughed in spite of herself. "The air inside that place was so thick and humid, not even the overhead fans could get rid of the odor of fried seafood and hush puppies."

"I know. Yet, I've often thought about our trips there. We had a lot of laughs while we cracked that greasy crab." It dawned on him that he'd be afraid to laugh here at the Inn, afraid he'd be thrown out for disturbing the funereal atmosphere. That observation was interrupted by Josef coming to pour his wine. After he'd tested it and approved, Mallory buried her nose in her menu, adding no further comments, no other memories. Connor was aware of a vague disappointment as he turned to his own menu.

Their waiter appeared out of the darkness like a silent wraith. Mallory set her menu aside and, in a low voice, gave her order. Folding her hands together on the table, she and Carlisle gazed expectantly at Connor.

He continued to take his sweet time reading the hand-scripted gold pages, until Mallory's irritation became palpable. The air surrounding their secluded table sang like the taut bowstrings of the annoying, screeching violin playing in the background.

"For God's sake, Connor, choose something." Mallory leaned forward, slapping his menu aside.

Carlisle sucked in a breath.

Connor hiked one eyebrow. "You never used to be so uptight, Mallory. What's the matter—are you afraid old Alec will waltz in and find you at his special table, knee to knee with a strange man?"

"No." She drew back as if the idea was completely foreign.

Their knees *had* been comfortably touching—as Connor noted the minute she jerked hers to one side. Turning a smile toward the waiter, Connor asked questions about various items on the menu. At a point seconds before he sensed Mallory might explode, he named his selection and sat calmly back to enjoy his wine.

She twisted the gold necklace she wore around and around one finger. Her gaze darted right, then left and right again, never coming to rest on Connor.

"Get it off your chest, Mallory, before you strangle yourself with your necklace."

"All right." She leaned forward, the very picture of

fury. "You don't even like me, Connor. Why are you playing out this elaborate charade?"

He choked on his gulp of wine. He might have guessed any number of reasons for her annoyance. Her belief that he didn't like her was the last thing he'd expected to hear. "Seven years ago, who ran out on whom, Mallory? I seem to recall chasing you all the way to the parking lot, where you vanished into thin air. When you didn't come back to the apartment, I phoned your folks to see if you'd gone to their place. The housekeeper admitted you had. Next morning before I left for the airport, I phoned Forrest House twice, asking to speak with you. I was told you'd gone out." He shook his head. "You know…I'd forgotten that, but it's all coming back now."

"That's a lie! I was home all day."

"Your mother said you weren't. I want you to know I felt like crap leaving without even saying goodbye."

"Mother wouldn't be so mean. She knew I was cry—" Mallory shrugged and broke off, twisting the necklace even tighter until it left marks above her collarbones.

Connor set down his wineglass. He, too, leaned tensely across the small table. He opened his mouth to present his side but was forced to wait as Carlisle arrived with their salads. Angry sparks danced above the pepper mill as the waiter ground some on both salads. "Thanks," Connor snapped. "That's enough." And Carlisle scurried away.

Picking up her fork, Mallory stabbed her lettuce. "I sent a letter in care of the address you'd left for your headquarters in Guam. You never even tried to get in touch with me, Connor."

"The hell I didn't," he roared so loudly that diners

at several tables around broke off talking and eating to stare at the disruptive party.

Mallory touched a napkin to tightly pursed lips. "I don't have to listen to you trying to put the blame for our breakup on me. And I've lost my appetite." Tossing down her napkin, Mallory gathered her purse. "Phone a cab to take you to the airport after you finish your dinner." She rose, her dark eyes filled with pain.

Connor shackled her wrist. "Don't stop now, Mallory. Your fictional version of this is just getting good. Sit. It's damn well time we got to the bottom of something that's obviously been festering in both of us for years."

An evenly modulated voice spoke Mallory's name from above and to Connor's right.

"Alec," she exclaimed, her face going chalky in the candle glow. "I had no idea you planned to come here tonight. You never mentioned it at work."

"That's because you seemed preoccupied all day, Mallory."

Connor, forced by good manners to drop Mallory's hand and to stand and extend his to the newcomer, used the moment to measure the older man. Alec Robinson didn't look fifty-six. Slightly less than Connor's six feet in height, the hospital administrator wore his three-piece suit without bulge or wrinkle. There was no gray in his mustache, and only a trace in the otherwise ash-blond hair. The handshake he laid on Connor spoke of a man who worked to stay fit. Connor couldn't readily identify why the salad he'd hardly tasted seemed in danger of not staying down.

"Alec, this is Connor O'Rourke. Connor, Dr. Robinson...er...Alec. Technically, Connor's a doctor, too. He has a Ph.D. in meteorology." Mallory seemed reluctant to elaborate further on any personal details regarding either man.

"Poor Dominic almost had apoplexy, trying to tell me you'd already claimed our table, Mallory." Alec eyed Connor coldly, although he issued a dry chuckle. "Dom explained that you were on your way to the airport with a gentleman. If you'll excuse me for eavesdropping, I'm sure I heard you telling Dr. O'Rourke to call a cab. Does that mean you're heading back to the hospital? If so, I'll follow you."

The maître d', hovering behind Robinson, fluttered around like a demented butterfly. "Sirs and madam, we're creating a small scene here," he hissed. "Shall I add a third chair or will you be wanting your own table, Dr. Robinson?"

Mallory's color drained even more, if that was possible. While Connor would've liked to boot the good Dr. Robinson into outer space, he'd let Mallory deal with the situation.

"Dominic, please seat Alec elsewhere this evening. I've developed a splitting headache, I'm afraid," she said, speaking in a low, rapid voice. "I did ask Connor to call a cab. I'm going home to take care of myself. Alec, I'll see you at the hospital tomorrow. Connor, goodbye." She gripped her purse tightly and attempted to slip between the two men.

Alec gazed after her, his eyes confused. Connor took a giant sidestep and blocked her exit. "Are you feeling well enough to drive home?" he asked, his voice heavy with concern.

"I...yes. Thank you for asking."

They stood awkwardly for a moment, with Connor gazing down on her bent head, troubled by so many things that remained unspoken. But from her body language, he could tell she wasn't receptive and just wanted to leave. "We'll talk when I hear about my tests," he said, moving aside.

Mallory shook her head. "I can't handle the added stress, Connor. Please, for Liddy Bea's sake if not for mine, confine any further dealings to Fredric's office." She wove through the tables, practically at a run.

Connor pulled out a money clip, peeled off several bills and dropped them between their unfinished salads. Spinning from where he stood, he bumped into Carlisle, who was carrying their entrées. "You're leaving, sir?" the waiter gasped.

"Yes. Sorry, but I've got to run. I left my bags in the lady's car." Connor sprinted to the entry, only to see Mallory's taillights as she screeched out of the lot.

He stopped short and swore. He wondered when she'd discover she had his duffel and briefcase. Thank God he had a ticketless reservation.

"Does that outburst mean Mallory's left you stranded in Tallahassee?"

Connor turned around and met Alec Robinson's hard, black stare. "What business is that of yours?" Connor demanded testily.

"It isn't. But in the six years I've known Mallory, she's been unflappable, even though she's gone through plenty of things to flap about. Until tonight."

Connor ignored Forrest Memorial's top dog. Brushing by him, Connor felt in his pocket for loose change. He stalked inside the restaurant and found the pay phone in the Inn's foyer. He'd deposited the money and had the receiver to his ear to call a cab, when Robinson's hand flashed over Connor's shoulder.

Alec depressed the switch, and coins rattled as they fell into the coin box.

"Excuse me..." Connor dug out the change to redeposit it.

"I'll give you a lift to the airport," Alec said roughly. "There've been rumors floating around the hospital for the past couple of days, to the effect that Lydia's father blew into town on his white charger, intent on saving the day. As a rule I don't pay much attention to hospital scuttlebutt. It just occurred to me that perhaps this time I should've listened more carefully."

"Yeah, well, I understand a man's hearing is the first to go in the aging process." Hunching his shoulders, Connor opened the phone book again to the section listing cabs. He imagined he could hear Alec's teeth gnashing as he punched in the cab company's number a second time. He completed his call without interruption. But when he hung up and turned around, prepared to wait the few minutes they'd said it would take for his cab to get there, Alec still lurked at Connor's elbow.

"Look, smart-ass. You think you're pretty clever. Well, know this. I wield a lot of power at Forrest Memorial. Senator Forrest and I are like this." Robinson crossed his fingers and shook them in Connor's face. "I have more than a passing interest in Mallory—with Bradford's full blessing. It'd be wise for you to do as she said and confine all your dealings in this case to Fredric Dahl."

Connor noticed Dr. Robinson didn't look nearly so cool and collected now. "I think a man your age should watch his blood pressure," he said mildly.

Fortunately, before Robinson could manage any response, Connor's cab arrived. Dashing out, Connor jumped into the back seat. "Airport," he said, his voice still calm. But, dammit, his own blood pressure had risen. Who in hell did Robinson think he was, warning

Connor away from the woman who was the mother of his child?

He fumed all the way to the airport and during the entire hop-skip-and-a-jump flight to Miami. It didn't dawn on him until he opened the door to his apartment and walked into his bedroom—where the first thing he set eyes on was Claire's photo—that he hadn't thought of his fiancée once in the past several hours.

Falling onto his bed fully clothed, he pinched the bridge of his nose, blocking Claire's picture from sight. Being with Mallory tonight, before Alec Robinson showed up, had felt like old times. But if he still carried such strong feelings for Mallory, what did that say about his commitment to Claire?

Connor rolled over with a groan and snapped off the bedroom light. He'd better get his feelings sorted out before he went to work the next day and ran into Paul. His assistant dated Lauren, Claire's good friend. And Paul had a way of noticing things.

Needing sleep more than anything, Connor put both women out of his mind.

The phone, jangling loudly on the bedside next to his ear, awakened him from an unpleasant dream. His alarm clock said eleven-fifteen. A.m. or p.m.? More than half-groggy, he dragged the receiver to his ear. "Hello," he croaked. His sleepy greeting was met with silence. Assuming it was a crank call, Connor cursed and started to hang up.

"Connor?" His name, spoken softly, reached through the line, jolting him.

"Mallory?" Rolling onto an elbow, he did his best to make sense of the fact that she was phoning him at night.

"I'm sorry. It sounds as if I woke you. I hadn't expected you to even be home yet. I intended to leave a message.''

''That's okay. I got to the airport ahead of schedule. They had a cancellation on an earlier flight. What's up?'' he asked, hating to think she was phoning because old Alec had rushed right out and contacted her dad.

''After Davis brought my father home from a late meeting, he went to put my car in the garage and found you'd left your duffel and a briefcase in the back seat. I feel horrible having stormed from the restaurant with your things. I'll courier them to you in the morning. I hope there's nothing crucial in them that you need for work.''

''Nothing vital. I'd ask you hang on to the lot until I hear about tests and return to Tallahassee. Except the brochures Dr. Dahl gave me on transplants are in my briefcase.''

''Doesn't Claire have a set?''

''Yes, but we...uh...decided to take a breather from each other until after I hear if I'm an acceptable donor.''

''That's my fault, isn't it? I feel awful, Connor.''

''No need. You have enough to contend with. If we're going to apportion blame, Mallory, I probably deserve the lion's share. At the time we parted, I thought I was doing the right thing. Just after I got the grant, I overheard someone in the presentation party say how glad your mom would be to get rid of me. The more they talked, the more I began to realize I'd been holding you back.''

''That's absurd!''

''Wait, don't interrupt, let me finish,'' he said over Mallory's protest. ''This needs to be out in the open. That lady, who was from the civil weather patrol, spoke the truth. She knew your family well. Your mom headed the volunteer program. Anyhow, on the way home, I started thinking that I could be broke for another five to ten years, depending on how my research went. You deserved a better life than I had any hope of providing. I suddenly saw everything you'd sacrificed for me, and I didn't like being a taker. A user.''

Her breath caught in a little sob. ''Why didn't you explain all this back then?

''Probably because I've matured and have developed some finesse,'' he said with a self-deprecating laugh. ''But that's all history. It's too late to change our destinies. We can only go forward from here.''

''You're right. There's nothing to gain by rehashing the past. I wish I didn't feel that we've somehow cheated Liddy Bea.''

''*You* haven't, Mallory. You've been there from the minute she gave her first cry. Any way you cut it, I come off looking like the villain.'' He paused, rubbing his face. ''Didn't you ever once consider that I had a right to know about her?'' His voice grew thin. Bleak. ''You of all people knew how I felt about my own father's irresponsible behavior.''

''I would have notified you if you'd shown a glimmer of interest in how I fared after you left. It would only have taken a postcard. A word. Anything, Connor.''

''Yeah,'' he drawled. ''That's why didn't you answer a damn one of my letters.''

''Letters? You wrote?'' The question hung between them.

''Look, I'll buy into the probability that your folks' housekeeper didn't tell you I called. And I'll accept that your mom lied about you being home. But no way in hell will I believe the U.S. Postal Services lost all four of my letters.''

Static came and went on the line, but there was no sound from either Mallory or Connor except for their erratic breathing.

"You're saying you actually mailed letters to me? No way! I received *nothing*."

"You don't have to keep up the charade, Mallory," he said tiredly. "What's done is done."

"Connor, I'm not lying." Mallory's voice rose. "I swear on your mother's Bible—which, by the way, you left in the apartment and I've saved for you—that I never got so much as a postcard from you. I swear."

Connor jackknifed upright. He didn't know why he needed light to take in what Mallory was saying. He just did. He groped for the switch and flooded the room. In the process, he knocked down a tray that held his car keys and change.

"Are you still there? What happened? Connor, did you fall out of bed?"

"No. I knocked some stuff off my nightstand. About the Bible. I forgot you rummaged around the ruins of our house and unearthed Mom's Bible, and dried it out. Do you think someday Liddy Bea might, uh, like it?" He seemed at once hopeful and anxious. "If so, just hang on to it."

"Okay. One day it'll mean a lot to her to have something of her paternal grandmother's. Dad put a piece or two of Mom's jewelry in a safety-deposit box with Lydia in mind. Can we forget the Bible for a minute and get back to those letters you allegedly wrote?"

"No alleged about it. *I wrote to you.*" He enunciated each word.

"When? Where did you send them? The apartment?" Mallory demanded.

"I don't have exact dates off the top of my head. I'd

been on the island a couple of days when I wrote the first one, addressed to the apartment. I missed you, and I was homesick as hell. They only shipped supplies in twice a month. I think, when I didn't hear back from you, I sent subsequent letters to your folks' address.''

"Liddy Bea was three months old when I moved to a place of my own."

"Yeah. Marta told me you had. I suppose the letters could have ended up in a dead-letter bin somewhere."

"The apartment rent was paid up through the end of the summer. But I moved home right away, because Mom felt so lousy. She died the day Liddy was born. Dad begged me to stay at home and take over Mom's role as his political hostess. It was a really difficult time for all of us, Connor. Alec had already offered me a job at the clinic. He helped me locate a condo and a nanny. Alec went out of his way to be kind."

"I'll just bet old Alec did."

"What does that mean? Did you start something with him after I left the Inn?"

"Why would you automatically assume I picked the fight, and not the other way around?"

"Because Alec is a born gentleman."

"As opposed to me sprouting from a trailer-trash housemaid, you mean?"

"Stop putting words in my mouth. I meant no such thing. If you must know, Connor, you're making my point for me. You've always had a temper. I've never heard Alec raise his voice in anger."

Connor laughed. "Then you should have been a mouse in the corner outside the restaurant tonight, sugar. Old Alec sounded downright hostile when he warned me to stay away from you. In case I didn't get the message, he invoked your father's name. Was the senator figuring he'd be getting a two-for-one deal when he hired Robinson at the hospital? If so, you'd better ask your old man if he got rid of my letters.''

"Two-for-one? What are you talking about?''

"Hospital administrator cum son-in-law. Or are you going to try and tell me Alec doesn't see himself as more than your employer?''

"Even if he does, Connor O'Rourke, that's none of your business. You gave up the right to have any say in who I do or do not keep company with.'' Mallory knew her voice was shaking, but she had one last thing to say to Connor. "Shouldn't you tend to your own backyard? I wonder if Claire would appreciate your sounding like a jealous lover.''

The noise of the receiver cracking into the cradle on Mallory's end left Connor's ear ringing. Still, it was quite a few minutes before he unclenched his hand from his own phone. It annoyed him to discover that Mallory's assessment was dead-on. He was mad-dog jealous of Alec Robinson. And what was worse, he knew it was wrong.

CHAPTER EIGHT

MALLORY HAD DIFFICULTY believing that Connor had written her after he left Tallahassee. Yet he'd sounded so adamant. So definite.

Although it was closing in on midnight, she hadn't heard her father come upstairs. Throwing on a robe, she rushed downstairs. Sure enough, light spilled from under his study door. Upset as she was, Mallory burst in on him without knocking.

Glancing up from the papers spread across his desk, the senator first frowned, then smiled and removed his half glasses. "Mallory. Marta thought you'd gone to bed with a headache. Once again I arrived home too late for supper. Poor Marta, her meals have gone begging lately. But I guess you're feeling better."

Mallory laced her fingers together tightly. "Dad, do you know if Connor tried to correspond with me here at Forrest House after he went to the island?"

Bradford's smile faltered, and he fell back in his chair. "That was so long ago, darlin'. What possible relevance could a simple note or two have now?"

Zeroing in on his guilty expression and his specific mention of a note or two, Mallory stepped up to his desk and planted both palms on his papers. "If you destroyed mail addressed to me from Connor, then you knowingly interfered with Liddy Bea's right to a relationship with her father."

"Me? I didn't destroy anything."

"Then who? Our house staff? If so, you ordered it. They'd never take that responsibility on their own."

"Not staff." He sighed loudly. "Sit, Mallory. I'll tell you what happened. But, I swear to God, I learned all of this too late to make any difference."

Not liking the ravaged look that entered her father's eyes, Mallory slid bonelessly into the leather chair across from him. She was glad for the width of the old oak desk.

Bradford dropped the pen he'd been holding and stared past her at the floor-to-ceiling bookcases that lined the room. "Early the morning before your mother died, she put in an urgent call for me and Dr. Padgett, our Episcopal priest. It was time to unburden her soul, she said."

"Mother? *She* was responsible? I—I'd have thought she was too ill."

Shaking his head, the senator opened his humidor and took out a cigar. He didn't light it, but worried it nervously between thumb and forefinger. "Let me tell this my way. The call terrified me. I couldn't imagine anything as grave as Beatrice made it sound. At first, I tried to leave her alone with the priest. You see, she seemed frantic, and she wouldn't look at me. I was afraid she was going to admit to having an affair with one of my colleagues or something."

"Oh, Dad," Mallory whispered. "Mother loved you from the bottom of her heart. You should've known she'd never do anything to hurt you."

"Yes. Well, she loved you, too, Mallory. I have to believe that's why she acted as she did. Out of overwhelming motherly love."

"Tell me, please. What mischief did she do?"

"To start with, she underwrote Connor's original grant. Funded it from her private trust with a stipulation that he be sent to the most remote hurricane center available."

Mallory bolted from her chair. "*Why? She had to know how much I loved him,*" she murmured.

"Bea never believed the boy would amount to anything. Sit, Mallory. I've only begun—there's much more. Your mother confessed that when the first note arrived from Connor, she opened it. He was begging you to move to Hawaii to be closer to him. Beatrice said she already suspected you were pregnant. By then, of course, she'd been diagnosed with an inoperable brain tumor. Beside herself, she said she couldn't bear to think of you taking our only grandchild halfway across the world to live like who-knew-what kind of nomad."

Brad rocked forward and back, caught up in his story. Mallory knew he'd forgotten she was even there. He was reliving being in that hospital room with his wife.

Finally, he roused. "Right then, I believe she crossed the line of no return. Beatrice had decided to intercept all of your incoming and outgoing mail, in case you got it in your head to contact him. She claimed you tried only once that she knew of. But she swore his letters stopped coming before her illness intensified to the point of requiring full-time hospitalization." He paused to take a breath, and Mallory leaned toward him.

"I can't believe remorse wouldn't have driven Mother to disclose this to me. I sat by her bedside every day, even on days when I had morning sickness so badly I could barely hold up my head. I can't forgive her," Mallory cried. "Mother knew how horribly I missed him."

"Darlin', Beatrice said she might have told you, except that when her conscience finally nagged her to confess, Alec Robinson had taken to dropping by regularly to chat you up. He'd asked you to step into the fundraiser position at the hospital after you had the baby. Bea said you seemed to want that, too. On lucid days, she figured it was a sign from God. After all, your degree is in public relations, Mallory."

So, had her mother played matchmaker in dealing with Alec, too? Was that how he might have mistakenly assumed their relationship could be more than a working one? Mallory felt the throbbing headache return.

"But, Dad," Mallory said brokenly, "when Mom confessed this to you, why didn't you come to me and set the record straight?"

Brad tossed the unlit cigar back in its box. "A number of reasons. That very day, while Beatrice clung to life, I made discreet inquiries about O'Rourke. I discovered that some of the biggest names in meteorology thought he was brilliant. His research had begun to be noticed by important scientists in the field. Could I in good conscience, I asked myself, take all that away from him? I shouldn't have to tell you what his research could mean in terms of lives saved in our state and many others."

Mallory nodded. How could she fault her dad's thinking when it so closely mirrored her own reasons for letting Connor go?

"Honey, while I weighed whether or not to involve myself, and if so, to what extent…we lost Bea. I fell into a black pit of depression for weeks. Possibly months."

"I know you did," Mallory acknowledged sadly. "So did I. If I hadn't had the job Alec arranged, after Liddy Bea arrived the very day Mom died, Lord only knows how I would've survived that year. Oh, Dad, how can I blame Mother, considering the magnitude of her illness and suffering?''

"I hope you don't, Mallory. Like I said at the start of our conversation, what's to be gained by raking over old coals?''

"Connor's aware that I didn't ever receive his letters. I telephoned to tell him I accidentally took off with his bags tonight. I don't know how the subject came up, but he said he'd written to me. I was first shocked, and then furious—and I all but called him a liar. *Did* call him a liar. Oh, Dad, I owe him a huge apology. But how can I say I'm sorry, without making Mother appear petty and manipulative?''

"Forget it ever came up. By getting it out in the open, you probably cleared the air. If I know scientists, and I think I do, nothing short of being told the planet's on the verge of extinction can distract them from their work for long. Let Connor's research provide his balm. His work and Claire. You're not forgetting he's engaged to be married, are you, Mallory?''

"No-o-o. It's just…well, he sounded so angry before we signed off. And more…hurt, I guess. That part shook me, Dad. I've always blamed *him*.''

"I suspect his reaction is partly latent guilt attached to having met Liddy Bea. Hmm. You've got to feel for the spot Connor's in. Perhaps you should phone him again and tell him the truth. Stress two things. Make him understand how sick Beatrice was at the time. And re-assure him that you aren't out to screw up his life or make any monetary demands on him. Claire certainly has reservations along those lines, even if Connor doesn't. Going back to the conversation at dinner the other night, it could well be what had that woman so bugged. She probably thinks you'll hit Connor up for retroactive child support. You could do a lot by reassuring them both that Connor's involvement with Lydia Beatrice begins and ends with his forking over a kidney.''

''Dad! You make what I'm asking of Connor sound completely mercenary.''

''Practical, not mercenary. I'm a practical man. I'd like our dealings with Connor to remain amicable. I want the Panhandle to have the fruits of his research. Since your mother funded his grant, dammit, why should Miami reap the rewards of his early-hurricane-detection system? I want his first trials to protect *our* coastline this fall.''

''You do?''

''Darn tootin'. I don't want you to breathe a word, but I'm pulling strings left and right to transfer his project from Florida International University's Hurricane Center to our own FSU Department of Meteorology.''

''That doesn't sound ethical. Is it?''

''You think I'm trying to steal his invention? On the contrary, I'll see he's paid handsomely, plus secure him a full professorship at the U. I did some snooping. Miami's only provided him with a token associate post. Believe me, Mallory, if Connor's operation works the way he claims, he'll be well compensated worldwide. If his system fails right off the starting block, my deal allows him to teach while he goes back to the drawing board. If he fails in Miami, it's all over for him.''

Mallory gazed blankly at her father for several moments, never uttering a word.

''I can see you're too beat to appreciate what I'm trying to do for him, darlin'. Run on up to bed. I've probably been insensitive, forgetting how tough it's been on you having to deal with Connor. Let me explain your mother's machinations to him. I'll phone tomorrow or the next day and smooth his ruffled feathers. There's no reason for you two to cross swords again. Just go on about your business. Devote your time and energy to taking care of our girl.''

Did her father have no idea how much she *wanted* to set things right between her and Connor? Obviously not. Anyway, it was all so pointless. He had Claire now. ''All right, Dad. I'll leave it in your hands, and I'll…carry on.'' Mallory climbed shakily to her feet. ''Which reminds me. Fredric phoned to say Liddy Bea can come home the day after tomorrow. Apparently the incision for her peritoneal catheter is healing nicely. Also the site where they removed my…my kidney.''

''Why, that's the best news I've heard in days, Mallory. By Jove, I'll leave Marta a note on the kitchen bulletin board. She can fix Liddy Bea's favorite meal. I guaran-damn-tee that meal won't go begging. We'll make it a celebration, why don't we? I'll phone Mark to see if he can drive up from Pensacola. You invite Fredric and Alec.''

Mallory had reached the door when that bomb fell. She whirled to face him. ''Alec? Why would I include him in a family dinner?''

Bradford arched a silvery eyebrow. ''Because Alec's in the habit of expecting you to work after hours. Inviting him ensures he'll let you leave the office on time. Why else? Mallory, I declare, you're acting very odd tonight.''

''I'm sorry. It's been a stressful couple of days.''

''I agree. Maybe you should start your leave before Liddy Bea comes home.''

''No. I want to work ahead as much as possible. I'll

be fine. I haven't been sleeping well. I wake up listening for her, and then I can't seem to fall back asleep.''

"It'll be nice to have her home, won't it? Save us so many extra trips to Forrest Memorial, too. Though, Lord knows, we ought to be used to it.''

"Dad.'' Mallory hesitated midway out the door. "I...don't want you to take this wrong. But after Liddy Bea's released, I'm going to look for a place of my own again.''

"You are still mad because I promised Liddy Bea I'd arrange a circus for her end-of-the-year class party.''

"Not that specifically. In general we rely on you too much. I'm thirty-two, Dad. I have a job. A daughter. Dammit, I shouldn't still live at home. I need to get a life.''

Bradford leaned forward on his elbows. "No reason you can't do that and live here. This house has everything any kid could ever want or need. I talked to a man the other day about buying a pony. Liddy Bea would love that. Why struggle out on your own when life would be so much easier if you lived here? I know Beatrice talked with you about that very thing before she passed away.''

"Oh, you bet. Did it never occur to you or Mother that I was born with a mind?'' Mallory pounded her chest. "Successes or mistakes were mine to make—and solve!'' She stomped out, slamming his door behind her. Upstairs, in her room, she realized she'd taken a long-overdue stand.

It felt good, except that she didn't sleep a wink all night.

CONNOR'S CELL PHONE RANG as he sat reading the morning headlines over a cup of coffee in a back booth of his favorite greasy spoon. "O'Rourke," he said, after thumbing open the phone. "Senator?" Connor dropped his paper and swore under his breath when an errant corner landed in his cup. "Uh, is everything okay in Tallahassee? Liddy Bea's all right? Mallory?" Tension gripped his stomach.

A garbled explanation had Connor straining to hear above the noisy breakfast crowd. Finally making sense of Bradford's words, Connor felt his temper begin to climb. "Hold on. Let me get this straight. You're saying I didn't win that first grant on merit, as I was led to believe? Dammit! Why tell me now?"

Again the caller replied. This time Connor thought he'd blow his top as, little by little, he began to understand the full extent of Mallory's mother's interference. "You're asking me to forgive your wife's selfish actions for the sole reason that she had cancer? She played God with my life! I'm sorry, but that's a lot to ask, Senator," Connor said, wanting to throw the phone across the room. "Explain to me why you feel the need to spill your guts now?"

The senator's voice became clearer. "I never should have let this much time pass. Last night, Mallory mentioned that you two had words because of a few letters Beatrice trashed. It's useless to rail at Mallory, nor does it make sense to blame the dead. I'm sure you'll reach the same conclusion after you've calmed down."

"Why didn't Mallory phone and do her own dirty work?"

"I volunteered. You've both carved out separate lives, my boy. You're standing on the precipice of an opportunity that can solidify your career. All Mallory wants is for Lydia Beatrice to live normally. Otherwise, I think you'll have to admit she's managed these past seven years rather well. So has the girl. Liddy Bea's content as she is.''

"So, what are you saying? I should go on about my life as if I'd never learned my daughter existed?''

"In offering her a kidney, Connor, you're giving her the ultimate gift—a second chance at life. For that reason, you'll always be her savior. Is it imperative she know *who* you are? Wouldn't that only confuse her? Do Liddy Bea a favor, son. Ask yourself if popping in and out of her life as a part-time dad, simply because you have a guilty conscience over getting her mother pregnant, isn't as selfish as the act committed by my wife?'' He paused significantly. ''You need time to think about what I've said, Connor. We'll talk again soon.''

Had the waitress not come by to warm his cooling coffee, Connor didn't know how long he'd have sat there listening to a buzzing line. With the matter-of-fact way Bradford explained things, he'd be damned if on some level it didn't make sense.

Or it might have, if he were a saint. On every other level, Connor wanted to shout and punch things. He wanted to kick a brick wall until his toes hurt more than the ache he felt deep in his heart.

Some thread of sanity refused to believe his stepping down, out of the picture, was the best thing for his daughter. His and Mallory's child. A child they'd discussed long ago, in vague ''someday'' terms—often in the aftermath of loving. There'd always been the assumption that someday they'd marry and have kids. Promises made when Mallory's heart beat hard and fast against his. He'd almost forgotten those old hopes and dreams.

Dammit, he didn't *want* to believe that all Mallory wanted was the cold detachment from him the senator had outlined. But maybe Brad was speaking for her. Theirs had been the hopes, dreams and promises of youth. They'd both changed. During Mallory's brief visit to inform him of Liddy Bea's existence, hadn't she made it plain that the only thing she wanted from him was a kidney? She wouldn't have even offered to let him visit Liddy Bea if he hadn't pressed the issue.

"Son of a bitch!" Connor's reverie was interrupted by a slap on the shoulder. He glanced up, into the faces of Greg Dugan and Paul Caldwell, colleagues and his two best friends since he'd moved to Miami.

"You look like hell, buddy," Greg announced, shoving Connor over in the booth so he could sit beside him. Paul folded Connor's paper and took the opposite seat.

"Doesn't surprise me." Paul motioned to the waitress, who carried a coffeepot. He didn't elaborate until he and Greg both had mugs filled with thick chicory brew. "Lauren and the other bridesmaids spent yesterday consoling Claire. What the hell went on in Tallahassee?"

"I told you I was taking a few days to consult the doctor in charge of my daughter's case. I figured Lauren would let you know Claire decided to go along."

"Yeah? So, have you and Claire called off the wedding for good? Is that why she came home early?"

"What did Claire say?" Connor hated to reveal more than Claire might want spread around. That was the least he owed her until they talked again.

Paul shrugged. "I only ever listen to Lauren with half an ear." He grinned. "Stimulating conversation isn't the reason I date her, you know."

"Knowing you'll blab to anyone about your sex life doesn't make me anxious to tell you what's going on between me and Claire." Connor eyed his associate over the rim of his mug.

Paul snickered. "Glad you didn't try to insinuate that you and Claire *had* a sex life. Since you postponed the wedding, she's complained about that to anyone who'll listen."

"She has?" That bit of information didn't sit well with Connor.

Greg lowered his mug. "Janine's the blabbermouth. She's slept her way through most of the men who work at the South Atlantic hurricane center. Even though she claims to be Claire's friend, it galls her that you're one of the few who didn't end up in her bed, Connor. Now she's trying to convince Claire there's something…uh… wrong with you."

"Is there?" Paul asked point-blank. "At your age it's practically unheard of not to sample the wares." Paul eventually flushed under Connor's flinty gaze.

Greg kicked Paul's shin. "Connor has a kid, dumbass," he informed Paul. "So his johnson obviously works. Anyway, we didn't come here to talk about women. Last night, I was at a barbecue at Jay Durham's beach house. He said he got an odd call from the head honcho at Florida State University's Meteorology and Oceanography program. The dean of science asked Jay to fax him a copy of your doctoral certificate and an overview of your current project. Jay thinks you lied to him about why you went to Tallahassee. He's sure you had a job interview. What went on over there, man?"

"Come on. Quit pulling my leg. Like I'm gonna believe our deputy director invited plebeians like you to his beach barbecue. A guy who hobnobs with naval commanders—because he believes they'll recommend him to the National Oceanographic and Atmospheric Administration for the European post he wants so bad he can taste it."

"It was a last-minute invite. Looking back, I told Paul I think Jay just wanted to pump somebody who knew you."

"What did you tell him?"

"I didn't tell him you found out you had a kid. Although bigmouthed Janine probably already did. I stuck to the story you wanted them to have at work. I said you lived in Tallahassee before you went to the Pacific to do research, and some family business surfaced that you needed to handle."

"That's no lie," Connor said in his own defense. "Besides, technically I'd have been gone this week, anyway—on my honeymoon. I wanted you to give him that story partly because I know Jay would learn the wedding had been postponed."

"Are you avoiding the question? Why FSU *is* interested in you?"

"I'm not avoiding it. I'm not sure. My daughter's grandfather is a state senator. We discussed my research. Senator Forrest promised to find the funds to transfer me from Miami, but I didn't think he was serious. Or even if he was, that he wielded the kind of power to make that happen overnight."

"Senator Bradford Forrest? Good Lord, Connor, you messed around with that guy's daughter? I've heard him talk on TV about different of environmental issues. He strikes me as one tough nut. I'd say he wields a whole lot of power."

Connor nodded. He wasn't thinking about the possibility of moving his research program, though. He was thinking about his latest conversation with Mallory's dad. Clearly he shouldn't underestimate the senator. Connor always had his nose stuck in his graphs and weather charts—what did he really know about the power of politicians?

"We'd better head for the center, guys. If all three of us waltz in late, heads will roll."

"Greg." Connor pulled him aside after they'd paid their bills and were walking toward their cars. "Thanks for warning me. But at this point I'm gonna play dumb. Frankly, I'm not sure that Senator Forrest is behind the inquiry from FSU. They have a fairly advanced research setup. Unless it's improved in seven years, though, they're not equipped to provide everything I need to round out my research."

"That's probably true," Paul readily agreed. "Speaking of which, you need to drop by my office as soon as we all get to the center. One of the seismic units you have me monitoring showed some interesting activity while you were gone. If your control data is accurate, we may be looking at early hurricane activity this year."

"No kidding? Is something building in the West Indies?"

"Nope, these reports are coming in from your monitors out in the straits between Cuba and Cozumel."

"Hmm. I'll go straight to your office and check the patterns myself. If need be, are you available to fly out there with me today to pull up the monitor so we can see if it's malfunctioned?"

"Sure, but don't you trust your own engineering?"

"The control tests I did last year in the Pacific all came in accurately with early warnings on stage-three and four hurricanes. If the reports are equally accurate this year in the Gulf and the Atlantic, by next year I'll be ready to discuss using the technique universally. Until then, I'm not crying wolf. Understood?"

"Yes, boss," Paul drawled, bowing and scraping as he backed toward his SUV.

"Beat it, clown. Get outta here." He scowled. "I guess I'd better stop and talk to Jay before I swing by your office. It doesn't pay to let the man holding the reins on your project stew too long."

Connor was correct in that assumption. Jay Durham lay in wait, ready to grab him the minute he walked into the building. "O'Rourke, step into my office, please."

Connor walked off from Paul and Greg, who'd arrived right on his heels, but he didn't miss the histrionics of his friends rolling their eyes. "I intended to come by and see you, Jay. Paul reported some suspicious deep-water activity on an electronic monitor I planted off Cozumel. I'll need a floatplane so we can run out there today to check on things. It's a beautiful day for flying. Can I interest you in tagging along?"

Durham cocked his head to one side. Whatever he'd been prepared to berate Connor for now hung at bay, forgotten for the moment. "Suspicious deep-water activity? Nothing's come in from our satellites." He shook his head. "It's far too early for hurricanes. I told you either the sharks would eat your damned monitors or the salt water would corrode them. No, I won't waste a workday. What I *will* do if those idiots from FSU phone back and want you is transfer your ass to them so fast your head will swim. Let *them* look like fools when they rely on your false data."

"Well, Jay, why don't you tell me what you really think about my research?" Connor said mildly as he started to duck back out the door.

"Wait! I hear you knocked up some woman in Tallahassee. Keep a lock on your zipper while you're still in my fleet, O'Rourke. Maybe the crew you worked for in the Pacific tolerated that nonsense. I run a tight ship.''

Connor clenched his hands at his sides, but leaned closer to Jay. ''I'd advise you to watch what you say when you talk about my daughter and her mother. Her dad's the ranking state senator.'' Fuming silently, Connor stormed from Durham's office.

His temper had cooled a bit by the time he reached Paul Caldwell's cubbyhole office. Once he went inside and began reading over the printouts Paul had mentioned, he forgot totally about Jay's outburst.

Only hours later, as he flew high over a glass-smooth ocean, did Jay's diatribe surface again. And that was because Paul brought it up.

''One of the part-time clerks told my secretary she heard you raise your voice to Jay this morning. What happened? Granted he's a jerk, but he's *jerk, sir,* to us. He's in charge of this data facility, Connor.''

''Yeah? Well, he pissed me off.''

''Must have. Did he say any more about FSU?''

Connor circled, then began his descent. ''He bad-mouthed Mallory, and he has no idea what he's talking about. He doesn't even know her.''

''Mallory?'' Paul's eyebrows puckered.

''The woman who showed up at my bachelor party. God, that seems so long ago.''

''Hey, I thought you acted plenty steamed at her, too. Shouldn't you still be? If you ask me, she pretty much screwed up your life, springing a kid on you like that.''

Connor's features softened. ''Mallory's mother sabotaged us both, it turns out. It's a long story, Paul. I'm glad I was wrong, though. She's doing a great job of raising our daughter. Now, there's a cutie pie,'' he said, sounding like a proud father, as he set the floatplane down neatly on the ocean surface.

Paul nudged Connor out of his momentary reverie, indicating they should tie up to a naval buoy. "Listen to you. I understand now why Claire's all shook up. You've still got the hots for your old lover."

Connor sucked in a huge mouthful of salt air as he climbed out on the pontoon, prepared to deny Paul's statement. Then, his denial slowly fading away, Connor privately admitted there was a hint of truth to Paul's observation.

"Man, oh, man!" Paul reached out and grasped the float frame. "Know what I think? You're in trouble, pal."

Connor lashed the plane tight. He thought he probably looked a little green around the gills. And not from choppy seas. The water barely rippled.

Paul, taking no notice of Connor's torment, continued blithely giving advice. "If we were talking about me or Greg, I'd say juggle both women for a while. Hell, for quite a while. Me, I'm not one to commit, even though Lauren's badgering me for a ring. But you don't strike me as a good juggler, Connor. And Claire, she doesn't strike me as the type to share her man. Not even with a kid."

Connor stiffened. "I don't have even partial custody of my daughter, Paul. But if I did, I'm sure Claire would welcome her in our home. That's assuming she and I go ahead and get married."

"I've known Claire longer than you have. Read my lips, old son. Claire is not the nanny type."

"She wouldn't be a nanny. She'd be Lydia's step-mother."

"Same difference. You're *engaged* to the woman, for

God's sake. Haven't you noticed she's—what's the word—narcissistic. Yeah, I think that's what Lauren calls her. It means self-centered," he added, staring into Connor's blank gray eyes.

"I know what it means. I can't believe Lauren would say such a thing. I thought she and Claire were friends."

"They are. Lauren sees these traits in Claire because they're a lot alike. Which is why I haven't jumped right out to buy the rock Lauren's picked out."

"If that's how you feel, why don't you find someone else?"

Paul grinned wickedly. "Together, we set fire to the sack, if you get my drift."

"Don't you ever feel like settling down with one woman? You know, come home to the same person every night?"

"Nope. My brother says it'll happen. The marriage bug bit him at twenty-eight. Me, I'm thirty-four and I still want more women. A lot more."

"Paul, you're hopeless. Hey, there's my marker. The orange bob with the green markings. Shift your pontoon so I can reel in the tracking unit."

It took another hour to complete the task. They'd landed in the shallowest point in the channel, but the water was still plenty deep. Once he'd dredged up the waterproof case that housed his intricate electronic system, Connor connected his test gear and began checking computer chips. Personal concerns were shoved aside.

"So, how's it look?" Paul lit a cigarette and blew smoke into the wind.

"I'm not detecting any malfunction. Maybe it was a rare tornadic pulse offshore near Venezuela. I saw satellite reports on that before I left Tallahassee. Curaçao's remote reported really choppy seas last week. They have no explanation. The activity apparently didn't result in a storm.''

"You think it's a freak incident?"

"At this point, that's all I can think. Let's increase our readings of all my Caribbean monitors for the next two weeks. Instead of once a day, we'll set up a new schedule and check them twice. We'll split up the readings.'' Connor dumped the housing overboard and watched it settle out of sight in the depths of the murky green water.

"Okay," Paul grumbled, "but it's a waste of time. It's not even officially summer."

Connor glanced up and blinked. "It will be next week." He sighed. "Claire had her heart set on a spring wedding."

Paul clapped him on the back and climbed back into the plane. "Time flies when you're having fun. Why not wait till next year to tie the knot?"

Connor grimaced, donned his earphones and reported their takeoff to the nearest tower. Considering how confused his personal life was, he'd hardly call what he was going through *fun*. Especially since he had to face the fact that when he got home from Tallahassee, he hadn't been in any rush to phone the woman who wore his engagement ring. He should put Mallory out of his mind. But she continued to invade his dreams. As if that wasn't trouble enough, he had a daughter to think about now. One question in particular was plaguing him: Would she, as her grandfather suggested, be better off if Connor just donated a kidney and dropped out of her life?

That question weighed heavily on him. So much so, the flight over Gulf waters under a midday sun, which should have been relaxing, sent him back to the office twice as tense as when he'd left it.

Paul noticed and obviously couldn't resist poking at him. "Your conscience won't let you sleep with both women, Connor. Florida law sure doesn't allow you to marry two. You might want to consider that old black magic. I know a guy who consults some voodoo woman down in the swamps before he goes to the racetrack. What?" Paul said as Connor spun on him, a scowl darkening his face.

"Caldwell, honest to God—butt out of my life, okay?"

"Sure, sure." Paul spread his palms and backed away. "But if ever I saw a guy who'd benefit from a little love potion, you're it."

Connor watched Paul saunter off. "Love potion," Connor snorted. "Yeah, right," he grumbled at his reflection in the window. "All I need is a dozen more women stomping on my heart."

Work, that was the key. He'd lose himself in his work. It was the one thing that had gotten him through past losses.

CHAPTER NINE

LIDDY BEA accepted her due as the center of attention at the dinner table the evening she came home from the hospital. Her mother, grandfather, Uncle Mark and Dr. Dahl were there. Also Alec. To Mallory's dismay, Fredric Dahl had showed up with Dr. Robinson in tow. Alec was never at ease around her daughter, and tonight was no exception.

"Mallory, you're letting the child get overstimulated." Alec pulled back a snowy-white shirt cuff and glanced at the flat gold watch strapped to his wrist. "Shouldn't she be heading off to bed?"

Bradford frowned at the speaker. "Marta hasn't even served dessert yet, Alec. She fixed—what, Lydia Beatrice? It's your favorite," he said in a singsong voice, tapping Liddy's button nose.

"Strawberry shortcake?" Her gray eyes lit up. "I'm full, though, Grandpapa. 'Cept I don't wanna go to sleep yet," she inserted quickly, sending a disgruntled look at the man who'd dared say she should be in bed.

"She can sleep in tomorrow, can't she?" Mark interjected.

Mallory nodded. "Since you missed your class party, Grandpapa and I decided to stretch your bedtime tonight."

"Goody! Mommy, when's Connor coming to see me again?" Liddy Bea rearranged her frog band around her plate for the hundredth time. The glass figurines had never been out of her sight since she'd left the hospital.

Caught off guard, Mallory swept a glance around those seated at the table. She immediately noticed Alec's disapproval. Hurriedly, she transferred her attention to Liddy Bea. "Did Mr. O'Rourke say he'd see you again, baby?"

"I can't 'member. I wish he'd come to dinner tonight. I want him to see how much I love the frogs he gave me. They can't really play music," she announced to the table at large. "But I pretend they're playing *bring back, bring back, bring back my daddy to me...ee...ee!*" Her voice warbled.

Alec Robinson snorted inelegantly. "Where on earth did you hear that old Scottish ballad? The correct words are bring back my *bonnie* to me. Not to be pedantic, but it refers to Bonnie Prince Charlie, of course."

Mark Forrest touched his napkin to his lips and flashed a dark look at his sister and then her boss.

"Nurse MacDougal taught me the right words. She said it's okay if I make up my own verses." Liddy Bea pouted prettily.

Mallory squeezed the child's hand as Bradford and Dr. Dahl exchanged interested smiles. "Liddy, hon," Mallory said softly, "you can sing with your frogs in your bedroom. It's not polite to sing at the dinner table." She might have said more, but Marta's arrival with a four-layered strawberry shortcake diverted everyone.

Even Liddy Bea said she couldn't pass up eating a few bites of her favorite dessert. She promptly gobbled it up, then asked to be excused. Her mother nodded absently. The little girl kissed her mother, her grandfather and Uncle Mark. She collected her frogs and went to play in her own room.

The adults settled down to enjoy their dessert, coffee and conversation. "When do you expect the results of Connor's blood work?" Mark asked. "I'm sorry I missed seeing him. He and I have a lot of old times to talk over. I wonder if we weren't in Hawaii around the same time one year. If I'd known for sure, I'd have looked him up."

Fredric Dahl polished off his last bite. "Well, it's time for me to get home to the family. Before I forget to tell you, David Hinze, our best radiologist, is on vacation this week and next. But reading O'Rourke's IVP is at the top of his list as soon as he's back. I expect the cross match and tissue tests will be in by then, too. So by the Monday after, we should know how clean a match O'Rourke is. I'll shoot for that target date to reschedule his next visit."

"So soon?" Mallory set her fork aside. "I don't know why I'm so nervous," she said to no one in particular. "You said Liddy won't be ready to have the surgery for several weeks."

"Are you worried Connor will change his mind?" Mark asked.

Mallory shook her head.

"I know I said we'd need to wait." This from Dahl. "However, Liddy's healing very nicely. Depending on how her antibodies build or subside, we may not have to wait."

"Really?" Tears swarmed in Mallory's eyes, forcing her to blot them away with her napkin. "Sorry, but that's the best news I've had in months. Now, if Connor can take off work to come here for the transplant on such short notice, I'll be the happiest woman alive."

"Does he need to come here?" Alec asked sharply. "Why can't he donate at the transplant center in Miami and have them fly the organ to us? It's handled that way through the national donor program."

Fredric shook his head. "In the case of live donors, it's preferable to have the patients in adjacent surgical rooms. And Miami's so close."

Bradford pulled a cigar out of his breast pocket, placed it between his lips, then lit it. After he puffed a few times, he smiled like the Cheshire cat, wreathed in smoke. "Proximity may not be an issue. The powers that be in FSU's meteorology graduate program are salivating over the possibility of adding Dr. O'Rourke to their staff. All that's needed to make him a firm offer is deciding on an amount. And what do you think of this? I'm funding a special section of baroclinic instability studies myself. Out of the Beatrice Forrest Foundation."

Mark choked on his last swig of coffee. Mallory gasped. "Is there a foundation set up in Mother's name?"

"Took the words out of my mouth," Mark murmured.

"Not yet." Bradford puffed some more. "I'm talking to Joel Ferris about establishing one. It's fitting, don't y'all think? To honor the work your mother did with hurricane-relief volunteers? It came to me after we talked last night, Mallory."

"If the foundation's providing Connor with funds to work here in Tallahassee, Mom would turn over in her grave," Mark blurted.

Mallory shot him a dirty look.

"Come on," he said. "She sent him to the middle of nowhere. Or rather she got the volunteer board to front Connor's grant. They might've thought she did it to further the cause of hurricane detection, but I knew it was to make him disappear from your life, Mallory."

She reached across the corner of the table and

slammed her fist into Mark's arm. "That's for not telling me. Did you imagine I *wanted* to be a single mom?"

Mark rubbed his arm. "Jeez. I didn't know you were p.g. when I left for the naval academy. At Mom's funeral, you never mentioned Connor. I think when I said how much Liddy Bea looked like him, you told me to shut my mouth."

Liddy Bea came skipping back into the dining room. "Who do I look like, Uncle Mark?"

"Yourself, baby," Mallory said, glaring murderously at Mark. "Goodness, it's time for your nightly exchange, Liddy Bea." Pushing back from the table, Mallory grabbed her daughter's hand. The others rose with a scrape of their chairs.

"I should be going, unless you need my help," Dr. Dahl said.

"I, uh, me, too," Alec mumbled. "Unless…well, you aren't planning to do her exchange right here, are you, Mallory? If not, I'll stay and chat with your dad."

"We can do them anywhere, but Liddy likes her privacy. You could come up and talk to me for the half hour or so it takes," Mallory said peevishly, finally understanding why she kept Alec at arm's length. Ever since Liddy Bea was diagnosed with renal failure, Alec—who had a private practice before he became Forrest Memorial's chief administrator—had held himself aloof from Liddy's illness.

"No, thanks. I shouldn't stay, anyway. I've got a busy schedule in the morning. Will you be in tomorrow, Mallory? I know you said you had some things to square away."

"Mark's only in town for a few days. I'd like him to help me find a place to live. Mostly, though, I prefer not to leave Liddy Bea alone with Marta quite yet. Not until I know how she's going to react to home dialysis.''

Mark watched his dad prepare to walk Fredric and Alec to the door. ''You want to sublet my apartment, Mallory? The navy thinks it's time for me to pull another two-year tour overseas. I'd planned to list the place with a leasing agency tomorrow.''

''You're a big help, son,'' Bradford complained from the hall. ''I've got this huge house. I don't know why either one of you needs a separate apartment.''

Mallory opened her mouth, but Mark answered first. ''We're not kids anymore, Dad. It's damned awkward sneaking someone in here to spend the night, you know.'' He sent his sister a surreptitious wink.

Bradford puffed furiously on his cigar. ''At your age you both ought to find permanent partners. Quit having flings.''

Alec sought Mallory's eyes from across the room.

''Mark isn't speaking for me.'' She lowered her lashes, as she quickly led Liddy Bea up the winding stairs.

''I wish you'd reconsider facilitating O'Rourke's move to Tallahassee,'' Alec said quietly to Bradford.

''Why?'' Brad leveled a frown at the speaker.

''Do you honestly think O'Rourke won't start making demands on Mallory if he's living in town?''

''What I think is now that he's had a look at Liddy Bea, his conscience will nag him to spend more time with her. Mallory won't want Lydia flying off to Miami for regular visits. Nor do I. To be blunt, Alec, what business is it of yours?''

Alec paled under his tan. ''Apparently you've forgotten how badly he treated Mallory. Why give him a second opportunity?''

"He's engaged to be married, Alec. Connor postponed his wedding to be tested as a kidney donor. You're worrying for nothing."

"Am I? We'll see. Mark my words, you'll live to regret aiding and abetting that man, Bradford." Alec hurried after Fredric Dahl.

CONNOR DID AS HE'D ALWAYS done during times of personal crisis—he threw himself into his sensors and graphs. He also vowed to get his relationship back on track. But he and Claire played phone tag for the remainder of the week. Late the next Wednesday, he finally connected with her. "Hi, stranger. I heard Jay has you teaching a class in operational computer support out at Key Biscayne."

"Do you have the results of your tests yet?"

"Nope. I phoned the clinic this morning. Rhonda said their radiologist is on vacation. He'll be back next week, I guess."

"There's really no point in our talking until then, Connor."

"We're engaged, Claire. I thought you might like to have dinner and catch a movie this weekend."

"Are you ready to consider my objections to your donating a kidney?"

The wire crackled. "If I'm a match, Claire, I'm giving Liddy Bea a kidney. Period."

"Then call me when you know."

"What difference does it make? It's my body."

"Because, Connor, I'm really not sure I'm prepared to marry half a man."

"Half a—" The connection broke off in Connor's ear. He stared at the receiver for several minutes before slamming it down. He paced his apartment for an hour. An-

gry, hurt and lonely, he grabbed the phone again. He
wanted...*needed* to speak with Mallory. Until now, he'd
resisted phoning to see how Liddy Bea was getting on.
The main reason for that was his fear that he'd be taking
something away from Claire. Now he was too furious
with her to give a damn. Liddy Bea was his daughter!

Bradford, not Mallory answered. "Hi. It's Connor.
Sorry to bother you so late in the evening, but I've been
putting in some grueling hours at the center. I'm curious
as to how Liddy Bea's doing after her release."

"Fine. She's feeling so well, we held a celebration
dinner Monday. Mark even flew up from Pensacola."

"Good. That's great."

"Maybe yes. Maybe no. The fool boy put his furniture
in storage and sublet his apartment to Mallory. She and
Liddy Bea have moved. I'm rattling around this damned
mausoleum by myself."

"No. You have Marta and Davis."

"It's not the same. Now I'll have to phone ahead to
see my grandchild. Damn, I miss her already."

"Funny, I don't know her anywhere nearly as well as
you do, but I miss her, too."

"Say, I may have a partial solution for the fix you're
in."

"Oh?"

"Yes. Beatrice came to our marriage with consider-
able family money. She used to dip into it now and again
to surprise me or the kids with special gifts. When she
died, I was shocked to discover her trust had grown considerably. She'd set some aside for charities, plus small
trusts for Mark and Mallory. The bulk sits there gaining
interest."

"Forgive me, Senator, if I can't see how your wife's
money pertains to me."

"That's just it. She…did you wrong, in a way. You'll never get back the years you lost with…uh…Lydia. At any rate, I've set up a foundation up with Bea's money. I'm prepared to fund your research project. As well, FSU will offer you a full professorship in their meteorology program. You can live closer to Liddy Bea, and keep tabs on her without disrupting her life, or yours."

"I'm stunned, Senator." Connor let a few seconds tick by. "And this proviso meets with Mallory's approval?"

"Haven't exactly run the whole deal by her. She knows about the foundation funding your research. And she's aware the university wants you on staff. Claire will like living in the capital city, won't she? She struck me as a woman who'd enjoy the culture here."

"Claire loves it in Miami. She has a lot of friends and a good job."

"Tell her I'm not without contacts in high places, Connor. I'm positive we can improve her salary."

"I will." Connor wasn't sure whether or not more money figured into Claire's future plans. Truthfully, he felt pressured from both sides and needed to pull back.

"I'll courier the transfer forms to you tomorrow, Connor. If everything meets with your approval, we can firm this up when you fly over for your test results. Leave your flight number on my voice mail and I'll have Davis meet you. Oh, and Fredric's pretty sure all your test results will be in by next week. This way, you can sit down with him and go over them in person. See them, rather than have to digest stuff over the phone."

"I guess. Sure. Send me the forms. This is all so sudden, I'd like some time to study everything. I'll make a decision as soon as possible, though."

The men had little more to say to each other. After

he'd hung up, Connor's heart raced in anticipation of spending more time around Mal—no, Liddy Bea.

Whoa! Connor stared off into space, attempting to corral thoughts run amok. This job transfer was definitely a matter he had to talk over with Claire. Preferably today.

Unfortunately, his attempts to reach her again failed. He left messages on her home voice mail and at work, saying they needed to get together. He'd been purposely vague about why. By Friday night, he'd grown really irritated. "Claire, I have a great job offer from the university in Tallahassee. I'm flying over there on Monday to get the results of my tests. Help me out here. We need to discuss this before I go. I can't very well accept or reject a possible transfer without your input."

There was a message when he came in from his midmorning run on Saturday. Dang, he'd put off going until late, thinking Claire would sleep in. He'd decided she must have spent the night with Lauren or Janine.

It was Claire, but she was no help. "Relocate to Tallahassee? Are you crazy? I'm in the Keys with friends, scuba diving. I won't be back until Monday morning. Phone me at work after your lab results have been deciphered."

Connor yanked the sweaty towel from around his neck, knocking the phone off the hall credenza. It didn't give him the satisfaction he sought. And he'd broken it, which meant he had to go shopping for another one.

A job he tackled immediately after showering. A good move as it turned out. Minutes after he returned and plugged in his new phone, Dr. Dahl called. "Brad tells me your flight gets in at nine, and that Davis is picking you up. He'll take you straight to a breakfast with department heads from FSU. I've spoken with Dr. Hinze, the radiologist who'll read your X rays. He's promised to read them here, so he and I can go over them together before you arrive. I've arranged my schedule to fit you in at eleven. Let's hope that by lunch, we all can go out and celebrate.''

Connor agreed to all the arrangements, feeling somewhat dazed as he hung up. Perhaps he could string the group at FSU along. He'd just tell them Claire was out of town. It was the truth.

MONDAY, HE DRESSED IN his best suit. And he considered it a good omen that his flight landed early and Davis was waiting. His luggage this trip consisted only of the briefcase Mallory had shipped back. The leather still carried the faint scent of her perfume—or so he fancied.

"Good morning, sir." Smiling, Davis fell into step beside him. "You may want to remove your suit jacket before we go out to the car. It's muggy. You'd think it was August instead of June."

They both laughed, but Connor shrugged out of his coat and loosened his tie. They passed old familiar sights as they left the airport. Connor was struck by a sense of coming home. Dumb. Most likely he wouldn't accept the offer. Claire had certainly made her feelings clear.

Not wanting to think about that right now, he opened his case and removed the proposal. A sweet deal if there ever was one. Possibly a once-in-a-lifetime offer containing everything he could possibly need in the way of testing his detection system.

Gazing out the window, he thought he should have tracked Claire down in the Keys and made her listen. He knew better than to get her out of bed this morning before his flight left. She was not a morning person under the best of circumstances.

"Davis," Connor said on the spur of the moment. "Do I have time to see Liddy Bea before I need to be at that breakfast with the college staff?"

"She and Miss Mallory moved into Mr. Mark's apartment." He shook his head. "Mr. Bradford's been a mopey dog all week."

"So is that a *no?* I suppose Mallory's back at work. Whoever she has watching Liddy Bea would probably call the cops, right?" he said glumly. "I just thought—there's so much at stake today…it'd be nice to… Well, never mind."

Davis squinted in the side mirror and changed lanes. "Miss Mallory's taken a temporary leave, except for cleaning up a few things at work. She and Miss Lydia will certainly be up. Their apartment's on our route to the university."

"Really? Thanks, Davis. I'll only take a minute to say hi."

Luck seemed to accompany Connor today. Two cars pulled away from the curb in front of Mallory's complex, leaving a space big enough to park the limo. "We've got fifteen minutes to spare," Davis informed Connor. "Twenty max."

Wearing a huge grin, Connor leaped from the car. He'd gone barely two steps when he was back, rapping on the window. "Which apartment?" he asked sheepishly.

"Two eleven. I can see that number in my sleep, sir. The senator, Mr. Mark and I helped Miss Mallory carry a hundred boxes up those two flights."

"No elevator?"

"Of sorts. We're in the historic district, sir."

"Why didn't she have movers?"

"Apparently because she didn't think she had much

stuff to move from Forrest House. Movers did transfer
the furniture she had in storage, though.''

''Huh. So, did Alec Robinson pitch in and help?''

''No. It was a family affair, sir. Why?''

''No reason.'' Nevertheless, Connor whistled as he
bypassed the ancient-looking elevator and lunged up two
flights. He thought the jog would give him a few moments to organize his thoughts. Too soon he found himself staring at Mallory's door—and he couldn't explain
a sudden urge to turn tail and run. His hand was less
than steady when he knocked.

Light footsteps approached the door. Double locks
turned slowly, and the door opened the width of a chain.
One of Mallory's eyes and a portion of her rumpled hair
came into view. ''Connor? Wh-what are you d-doing
here?'' Her hand came up to clutch a silky robe under
her chin.

''Sorry to barge in without calling.'' He braced a hand
on the molding. ''I'm in town on a whirlwind visit. But
you probably know that. I just…just felt like seeing
Liddy Bea.'' He was careful not to say he also felt like
seeing her.

''Who's at the door, Mommy?'' Liddy Bea peered
from behind her mom, trying to see their caller.

''It's Mr. O'Rourke, baby.''

''Yippee! I knew he'd come see where I keep my
lucky frogs. Let him in, Mommy. I wanna show them
to him now. Uh…oh…do we hafta make my bed?''

Mallory laughed at her child's adult-sounding concerns. ''I'm sure Connor's seen an unmade bed before,
Liddy.'' She unfastened the chain and opened the door.
''I look like a mess, but at least I can offer you a cup
of coffee.''

''I can only stay a minute.'' He stepped over the

threshold while checking his watch. "Ten, tops. I barely have time to do more than take a gander at those f-frogs." Connor happened to glance up and his tongue stumbled over the last word. Backlit by sun streaming through the living-room window, Mallory, dressed in a red satin robe, seemed to have caught fire. "You're no mess," he blurted. "God, Mallory, you're more beautiful than ever."

She blushed furiously while Liddy Bea giggled. "I think she is, too. Grandpapa says I'm going to look 'xactly like her some day."

Tearing his gaze away from Mallory, Connor muttered, "That you are, Miss Lydia. That you are." Feeling a decided tilt in the floor beneath his feet, he rested a hand on his daughter's baby-fine hair. "Uh…your mom and grandfather are going to be beating boys off with a big stick about the time you turn sixteen." Dammit, he wanted to check out the boys who came calling on his daughter, wanted a say in what she did and whom she saw. He couldn't very well do that if he lived in Miami and she resided in Tallahassee.

"Connor, you look as if you might keel over. Are you feeling okay?" Mallory plucked at his shirtsleeve.

"No, I'm not okay." He jerked from her loose grasp, suddenly angry with Mallory again. "If you must know, my life's been a roller coaster since the night you showed up at my apartment."

Her pale hands fluttered to her waist, where she nervously tightened the sash of her robe. "Not a day goes by that I don't wish things had been different, Connor."

Liddy Bea wedged between the couple, her big eyes taking in first one, then the other. She slipped her small hand in Connor's larger, sweaty one. "I'm taking Connor to see my room. Oh!" Her eyes grew even larger.

"Is it okay if I call you that, or do I gotta say Mr. O'Rourke?"

A nerve in Connor's jaw jumped erratically as he ground his teeth to keep from telling Liddy Bea to call him Daddy.

Mallory read his uncertainty and a few other emotions he probably didn't know he was revealing. Fortunately, Liddy Bea was unaware of his tension. "Connor's fine for now, baby. Another day, when there's more time, he and Mommy will have to settle on what you should call him." She turned to Connor. "If you're going to see what Lydia's done with the frog band you gave her, you two had better scoot. I think Davis just tooted the horn. It's his five-minute warning." She pulled aside the curtain and waved to Davis.

Her matter-of-fact approach to their serious dilemma knocked the stuffing out of Connor as few other things would have. He simply nodded and fell into step with his daughter. Just being here with this fantastic kid he'd helped bring into the world jumbled his thoughts. Especially since his daughter didn't even know him for who he was...

Liddy Bea's bedroom was any little girl's dream. White antique furniture. A canopy bed with lacy covers. Shelves spilling over with toys. A closet stuffed with frilly dresses, and also clothes for play. Connor noted with a lump in his throat that his gift of funny glass frogs claimed a prominent place on a stand beside her bed.

"Grandpapa said I should name them Accordion, Clarinet, Saxophone and Conductor, 'cause that's what they're doing." She giggled. "They're special, so I gave them special names." She touched each one. "Brad, Fredric, Mark and Connor," she whispered. "That's a secret. 'Cause I'm not s'posed to use grown-ups' first names.''

"They're your frogs, kitten. You call them whatever you like." He was decidedly pleased that she hadn't named one Alec. "I've got to run, Liddy Bea. I have an important appointment, and I can't be late."

"'Kay. But I wanted to show you Mommy's bedroom. Come see where she keeps Ellie, the pink elephant my daddy gave her."

The mere thought of setting foot inside Mallory's bedroom sent hot and cold chills racing up Connor's backbone. Based on experience, he knew that the scent of her perfume would linger there, subtly pervading the entire room.

"Davis is probably getting impatient," Mallory called from the hallway. "Dad told me about your possible transfer, Connor. Do you think you'll accept it?"

"Do you want me to?"

The direct question caught her off guard. Again her fingers flew to her throat, this time to twist the top button of a sleeveless blouse. She'd used the time Connor spent with Liddy Bea to throw on a blouse, a pair of shorts and to run a comb through her hair. Recovering belatedly, she murmured, "That's for you and Claire to decide, isn't it?"

"I think it involves you, too. Or did you imagine once you brought me kicking and screaming into Lydia's life, I'd just slink away without a whimper?"

"Connor, please." Mallory's hands shook as she clamped them on Liddy's shoulders. The girl had her head tipped back. Her puzzled gaze moved from Connor to her mother.

"You did think that." He made the assessment, looking deep into Mallory's shocked eyes. And he was, in turn, furious. "Having lived most of your life with a lawyer, I can't believe you'd be that naive."

She marched to the door and flung it wide as Liddy ran into the adjacent room to peer out the window. "Are you warning me to hire one?"

"If you figured I'd pop in, leave a kidney and silently disappear again, then yes. I hadn't decided until this minute, Mallory, but I want to be more to Liddy Bea than a kidney. I *will* be more."

Mallory shook all over now. In a stab at control, she wrapped both arms around her waist and asked in a quavering voice, "Are you planning to wage a custody war?"

"If I have to." He felt exhilarated at having reached a conclusion, and he also felt like a heel. The last time he'd seen Mallory in such a state was the night he'd gotten his master's degree and announced he'd be leaving town.

Now that scene flooded back. He'd refused to hear of her following him to the South Seas. Grasping at anything to make her stay, while at the same time assuaging his guilt for following his own dream, he'd said she should forget him and take up with one of the lawyers Beatrice was forever parading past her. Mallory had worn this same shell-shocked expression then. She hadn't stood her ground. She'd run. It'd been the last time he'd seen her for seven interminable years.

Davis gave the horn a quick blast. Connor had no choice but to leave things hanging.

Mallory gladly escorted him out. In fact, she slammed the door so hard, his entire body jerked at the sound.

Panting from his mad dash downstairs, Connor jumped into the limo. "Sorry I took so long." Glancing up as he shut his door, he saw that Mallory and Liddy

Bea had parted the curtains. Tears streaked Mallory's face. That was the picture Connor took with him into the breakfast meeting with the meteorology department heads.

In spite of that, the meeting went well. The men were sincere about everything in their offer. Connor stared at the dotted line for several minutes. If he returned to Miami without this position, he was convinced that Mallory would fight him over his parental rights. But if he lived here, they might not need a court to work out an amicable agreement. Almost certain that Claire would misunderstand, he uncapped the pen and scrawled his name on all three copies of the contract.

Two professors walked him to the reception area, where Davis waited to take him to his appointment with Dr. Dahl. "We've already cleared office and laboratory space for you, Dr. O'Rourke. We've freed up James Kirkpatrick, our most promising field studies senior student. He's available to help set up your equipment anytime."

Connor clasped the men's hands, one at a time. Breathing deeply, he marveled at the freedom he already felt. Under Jay Durham in Miami, he felt stifled. "Gentlemen, I plan to give notice in Miami tomorrow. By afternoon, I'll start shipping equipment. I don't want my transmitters to be off-line for more than a day or two at most. Tell Kirkpatrick to prepare for the first shipment in a couple of days."

"Very good. We're anxious to see how this system of yours works. We've allowed you the entire summer to work at your own pace. Your first classes are scheduled in the fall. But be aware, O'Rourke—there are some in the scientific community here who are skeptical about your results."

The warning, one he'd often heard before, gave Connor pause for thought as he headed toward his next meeting. Should he have been so hasty? Maybe he was trading one jerk of a deputy director for a whole host of naysayers.

AT ELEVEN-FIFTEEN, Fredric Dahl received Connor into his office without a smile. "If my being late has pressed you for time, I can switch my return flight to a later one," Connor offered genially.

Fredric shook his head. "Be seated, please, Dr. O'Rourke. I'm afraid I don't bear the good news we've all been hoping for."

"What?" Connor found himself falling into the chair across from Dahl. "I'm Liddy Bea's natural father. Surely my blood matches hers."

"Blood isn't the problem." Sighing, Fredric handed Connor a cross-cut, colorful picture of a bean-shaped organ. A kidney. Turning aside, he snapped on a magnifying light set up to display X rays. Presumably Connor's.

"My films?" Connor asked, squinting into the light.

"Yes. Normally a kidney has one renal artery and a renal vein passing blood through the organ. You have double veins attached to both kidneys. It's not a totally uncommon anomaly and poses no threat to you. But the veins don't match Liddy's."

Dr. Dahl fell silent as both he and Connor stared at the aberration someone had circled on Connor's X rays with a red Hi-Liter.

Dahl stirred first. "In adults, I've seen cases where a transplant team piggybacked one vein on top of other. Or they've used a T connection of sorts. Not all of these procedures fail, but there's a higher risk and any possibility of failure concerns me. Especially as Liddy Bea has already endured one rejection. We can't afford another. I've already broken the bad news to Mallory. She knows we have to wait for a match on the national donor list.''

"But…but…but…" Connor sputtered. "So this is it? We're not even going to try?" His stomach knotted so painfully he couldn't think what questions to ask. He felt a crushing weight pressing in on him.

"Don't you think I'd attempt it if I thought her chances were better than half?" the doctor snapped. "Sometime you need to sit down with Mallory and have her explain everything Liddy's already gone through. Right now she's stable. Until that changes, or until an appropriate donor kidney becomes available, we'll leave things as they are." Clearly signaling the end of their meeting, Dahl rose and headed for the door, leaving Connor slumped in his chair, dabbing moisture from his eyes with a handkerchief he'd fumbled from his breast pocket.

It took Connor a while to gather his wits—until he knew his legs would support him. He still felt disoriented as Rhonda appeared at the door, a sad expression marring her ordinarily smooth skin. "Would you like a cup of strong coffee before you leave, Dr. O'Rourke? Or I can give you one to go. The senator's driver is waiting to take you to the airport. For what it's worth, I'm really, really sorry about this. We all had our fingers crossed."

"Yes," Connor mumbled. "So am I. Damned sorry. Does Senator Forrest know?"

"Yes, I believe Dr. Dahl contacted him."

Connor expelled a tight breath. "So, now we just wait for a miracle? Tell me, Rhonda, how long do miracles take?"

"The most dire cases go to the head of the donor list. Liddy Bea's right up there. If a match shows up anywhere in the U.S. it'll have her name on it. There's just no guarantee it'll be today, tomorrow, next week or even next year."

"I see. You're not very encouraging," he said, finally forcing himself to leave. He didn't blame Dr. Dahl for disappearing. Mallory and Liddy Bea were counting on him, and he'd let them down. On top of that, he'd arranged to move to Tallahassee. Would Mallory or Bradford ever be able to stomach seeing him again?

Walking out, Connor doubled his fist and smashed it into a pillar. The pain radiating up his arm didn't compare to the agony that gripped his heart.

CHAPTER TEN

DAVIS SAW CONNOR and emerged quickly to open the limo door. "Goodness, sir! Your hand is bloody."

Belatedly feeling the pain, Connor realized he must have skinned his knuckles. Patting his pocket, he found the tear-damp handkerchief to wrap around his hand.

"You didn't…ah…strike Dr. Dahl, did you?" Davis asked in hushed tones.

"No. None of this is his fault. I guess you heard…I have a…defect."

The old driver's face fell sadly. "It's disappointing for everyone. After Miss Mallory gave her a kidney, Miss Liddy was like a new girl. We all prayed you could make it happen again. But don't blame yourself. You did everything you could. Shall we get you to your flight, sir?"

"Yes. No." Connor shook his head. "I can't go without seeing Mallory. What kind of man slinks off to lick his wounds and leaves his family hurting?" he muttered.

Davis perked up considerably. "Very good, sir."

Connor's brain, briefly numbed by Dr. Dahl's blunt words, had begun to function again. In the eyes of the law, Mallory and Liddy Bea technically *weren't* his family. But over these last weeks, he'd laid claim to his child—in his mind and in his heart. And by association…Mallory.

Only—there was someone who took priority. *Claire.*

Finding his cell phone, Connor listlessly punched in her work number. If he actually got her and not her voice mail, he wasn't sure what he was going to say.

Claire did answer her own extension. Her groggy voice suggested she'd gotten too much scuba diving and not enough rest.

"Claire, it's Connor. I've seen Dahl." His throat worked spasmodically as he waited for her to ask what he couldn't bear to admit—the result of his tests. She said nothing. Unable to keep his voice from cracking, Connor explained in brief terms that he wasn't a match.

"That's fantastic!" Claire seemed to rally. "Now you can get your body back to Miami where you belong, and forget those people. We'll reschedule the wedding. Soon as we hang up, I'll call Janine, Lauren, Greg and Paul. We'll cobble together a celebration of sorts for tonight— invite our friends and colleagues. What time do you get in?"

"Celebrate? I said I *can't* give my daughter the kidney she so desperately needs, and you see that as a reason to celebrate?"

"Yes," she said warily. "Don't you understand, Connor? That frees you from any real or imagined sense of obligation. You can quit feeling guilty."

"Claire, I can't believe you said that. Lydia Beatrice is my child. Part of me. She's named for my mother. I may not be the donor she needs, but that doesn't mean I'm just going to turn my back on her."

"So, what are you saying, Connor?"

He shut his eyes and shifted the phone to his other ear. "I, uh, want to be in her life. It'll mean some sort of partial custody."

Claire sucked in a lungful of air. Then the line cracked for a moment with static. "We never discussed having children, Connor. I'm not ready to take on that chore yet. If and when it's time, I want kids of my own. I don't see myself in the role of stepmother.''

"I'm sorry you feel that way. If you loved me, you'd try to make room in your life for Liddy Bea.''

"Wrong, Connor. If you loved *me,* you wouldn't ask me to welcome your illegitimate child with open arms.''

"Don't do this, Claire. Don't force me to choose.''

"That's exactly how I see it. Me or a kid you don't know from Adam.''

"I'd hoped we could sit down and talk about this and a few other things when I got home, but…'' He hesitated ever so briefly. "This morning, I signed on with the university here in Tallahassee. I'm relocating my project. Part of the reason for making this change, is to give me a chance to know Liddy Bea. If you have a problem with that…''

"I do. A big problem. I guess…it's over between us. But if you think I'm handing back my engagement ring, think again. You owe me, Connor. You've humiliated me in front of our friends, co-workers and my family. I hope you rot in hell!'' She slammed the phone down in his ear.

He stared vacantly into space a moment, then quietly closed his cellular. As he did, he felt a weight fly off his shoulders. He didn't care about the ring. Originally, he'd intended to give his grandmother's ring to his fiancée. The ring his mom had stored in a safety-deposit box. It was one of very few family items that remained after the hurricane destroyed their mobile home. Now he thought it was probably significant that he'd never shown Claire that ring. Instead, he'd purchased the one she and her friends had picked out. A setting far flashier than his grandmother's. Her small diamond lay buried in hammered gold rose petals. Mallory had loved the antique setting from the first moment she'd seen it.

One day, perhaps, he'd give it to Liddy Bea.

"Are you all right, sir? I couldn't help overhearing," Davis said, turning slightly to glance at Connor.

"I'm okay." Connor took a deep breath. "Frankly, I should feel worse." A cell phone rang, cutting off his reply. He flipped his phone open, only to discover it wasn't his.

"Good timing," the driver said as he clicked off his car phone. "That was Senator Brad. His meeting's going long. He was checking to see if I'd got you to the airport."

"Did you tell him I was swinging by to see Mallory?"

"Yes. He said she may throw you out."

"Can't say I'd blame her, Davis. I still need to tell her I'm sorry. I'll miss my flight, but maybe I'll stay over an extra day. I should contact a leasing agent and find a place to rent. Now that I've essentially cut all ties to Miami, I'm ready to move on."

"Mr. Mark's apartment has four bedrooms. I heard Miss Mallory tell Senator Brad that the rent was higher than she expected. She's considering advertising for a roommate."

"I doubt she'd sublet to me," Connor said wryly.

"You never know. You did tell Ms. Claire that one reason for moving here is to get to know Miss Liddy better. That hectic job of Miss Mallory's, along with constant worry over Miss Liddy, is wearing her down," Davis remarked casually as he double-parked. Bounding from the car, he whisked open Connor's door. "Good luck, sir," he muttered as Connor stepped to the curb. "Lord willing, Miss Mallory will see she needs you for more than just a kidney."

Connor puzzled over Davis's statement on his trek upstairs. Davis and Claire both twisted things—making it sound as if his involvement here was about him and Mallory. It wasn't. It was about Liddy Bea. And about the fact that he wanted an active role in her life.

Connor's light knock resulted in Mallory abruptly yanking the door open. "Oh," she exclaimed, her eyes dark-ringed and smudged from recent tears. "What are you doing here? I thought you were Dad. He phoned after Fredric called him, wanting to rush right over, even though I said there wasn't anything he could do."

Connor thought someone needed to be here for her. Granted, he'd missed her other hours of need. But he was here now.

Liddy Bea pushed a doll buggy into the room and stopped. "Connor, hi! I heard Mommy tell Grandpapa you can't give me a kidney." She ran up and tackled his thighs. "Don't be sad like Uncle Mark and Grandpapa were when they tried to give me one. I love you, anyway." Her chubby arms tightened, threatening to tip Connor off balance.

Mallory gasped. "Liddy Bea. You can't love someone you hardly know."

Letting go, the child shrugged. "It feels like I do…know him, Mommy."

Mallory appeared so flustered by that, her hand slid off the knob. Connor took advantage of her lapse in attention. He wedged through the opening and shut the door.

Mallory rubbed her bare arms. "I thought you'd be on your way to Miami. Why aren't you?" she asked in a dull voice.

"For a variety of reasons. Not all of them are clear in my mind. The biggest, I suppose, is that I couldn't leave without trying to explain to you the impotent rage I feel over not being a donor. Dr. Dahl mentioned that there are cases where surgeons have made the double vein-artery anomaly work. Maybe we should get a second opinion.''

''I trust Fredric. He's the top in his field. If you only knew how many doctors we saw before he diagnosed Liddy Bea's condition. Explore more avenues if you'd like, Connor. I can't deal with added discouragement right now.'' She grasped the knob again, as if expecting him to take his leave. ''It…uh…means a lot that you stopped by. I'm sorry we argued earlier. Sorrier, of course, that you aren't a match. But this way, you and Claire won't have to leave Miami.''

''Claire and I…ended our engagement. I took the job at FSU.''

Mallory's hand flew to her lips. ''Why? Oh, God, I'm so sorry. I should never have tracked you down. I've totally screwed up your life, haven't I?''

''No, you didn't.'' Connor's eyes rotated toward Liddy Bea, who'd gone to the dining-room window, presumably to look for Davis. ''We have quite a lot to discuss, Mallory. Would you like to sit down over a cup of coffee?''

''I…was…getting ready to do Liddy's midday exchange. Maybe another time.''

''I won't be put off, Mallory. Some of what we need to clear up has been hanging over our heads for seven years.''

Mallory swallowed air, which resulted in a massive coughing fit. Connor pounded her on the back. ''Good try, Mal. But I'm still not leaving. And fainting won't discourage me, either,'' he said when she closed her eyes and pressed a hand to her forehead.

That observation produced a narrow-eyed glare. "I've never fainted in my life. Not even when I was pregnant. Oh, all right, Connor. Except we can't talk here. Little pitchers. Big ears." She rolled her eyes toward Liddy Bea.

"If this isn't a stall tactic, Mallory, then name when and where we can meet. Today," he stressed.

"Dinner? At Barnacle Bill's? It's casual and medium priced. This isn't a date, Connor. We'll split the check."

Connor felt his temper surge. "No. Things have changed, Mallory. I'll let you pick the place, but I'm not the dead-broke student you once had to sneak money to the maître d' for."

She blanched.

"I only let you get away with it because I hated having you miss out on going to places you frequented before you and I met."

"I never needed fancy restaurants. If I occasionally arranged to pay in advance, it was because you worked so hard, Connor. I thought you deserved a night out once in a while—without worrying about which budget item we'd have to juggle or skip."

"See, this only proves what I said. Talking is seriously overdue."

"I agree. Especially if those are some of the mistaken impressions you've carried around. Is eight satisfactory? I'll arrange a sitter for after Liddy Bea's evening exchange. Shall we meet outside Bill's?"

"Eight's fine. But we'll both leave from here. First, I want to see how you do an exchange. Moreover, I have nowhere else to go. I didn't plan on staying in Tallahassee tonight—my decision to lay over came out of the blue. In fact, I was hoping you'd help me find a rental nearby."

"Can't Connor stay with us, Mommy?" Liddy Bea, who'd just returned, tugged Mallory's hand.

"Absolutely not." Mallory sounded as if the suggestion was unthinkable.

Connor gazed at her steadily. "A little bird told me you're considering taking on a roommate."

"I was—am. These last few years have all but depleted the trust Mother left me. I could ask Dad for help, but I won't, as a matter of principle. Oh, this discussion is ridiculous. We can't be roommates, Connor."

"No? We shared quarters once. Am I the only one who thought we got along fine?"

Mallory vividly recalled some of the *fine* nights spent in Connor's arms. Heat rolled over her, making her knees go weak.

Liddy Bea danced around excitedly. "Please, Mommy! Please, let him stay. Grandpapa said you needed to find a man to paint where Uncle Mark's pictures used to be. And after you broke my mirror, you said you needed a man to hang stuff."

Mallory's jaw tightened. "Baby, your grandfather and I were talking about paying a handyman to do some of the heavy chores."

"Isn't Connor handy?" Liddy Bea leaned back and gazed adoringly up at him.

He grinned and ruffled the girl's bobbing curls. "Exactly, kitten. In the workplace they call it job-sharing. Two people split a single workload. Each person is assigned the work he or she does best. Now, me, I make a mess of laundry. But I'm a terrific painter and picture-hanger. I'm a so-so cook. Better at cleaning the kitchen. Oh, and I vacuum up a storm. I can already see definite possibilities for your mom and me in such an arrangement."

Mallory clenched her hands at her sides. "You two, *stop*. Liddy Bea, you know I want a grandmotherly kind of lady to sit with you while I work. Someone who'll cook, clean and otherwise fill my shoes after school starts in the fall."

"Can't the lady clean Connor's room, too?" Liddy Bea met her mother's frown. "Uh-oh. I forgot you said I gotta call him something dif'rent."

"Coincidentally, I have the summer free, Mallory." Connor produced his trump card. "The university isn't scheduling me to teach until fall. They've allowed time for me to set up my system and make sure it's operational. Once the equipment's in place, it's a matter of training student aides to read the printouts. Until fall, I can name my hours. For instance...nights. Leaving me free to stay with Liddy Bea during your workday. That way, you won't have to extend your leave."

"What?" Mallory yelped over Liddy's shouts of "Goody, goody!"

Employing a hopeful smile, Connor pressed harder. "I really wasn't looking forward to having so much spare time on my hands. I feel better about it now. This is a workable plan, don't you agree, Mallory?"

"But, but, but..."

"Liddy Bea's the real winner. She gets round-the-clock supervision by the two people who care most about her welfare."

"It's a crazy notion. Insane!"

"Practical. We split the rent down the middle. The house is mine by day. Yours by night. If you work late, I'll adjust my schedule. I'm offering to share the whole domestic load, Mallory."

She felt herself toppling—almost ready to try his crazy idea. It was his willingness to adjust his schedule that tipped the scales. Fund-raising work demanded erratic hours. "I can't decide something this important at a snap of the fingers. I'll think about it, Connor. Not everyone's cut out to deal with a chronically ill child. I'll definitely need to see how well you handle Liddy's exchanges."

"Absolutely." He tossed his briefcase on the couch and loosened his tie. Turning expectantly, he was surprised to discover that Mallory had moved in so close he nearly landed on her foot. Connor grabbed for her in an effort to keep them from crashing into each other.

His aftershave tickled her nose, and Mallory sneezed.

"I'd offer you my handkerchief, but it's wrapped around my hand."

Mallory saw where blood still seeped through the white linen. "What on earth did you do?"

Stuffing his battered hand in his pocket, Connor shrugged negligently. "Nothing."

"It looks like something," Liddy Bea said, nosing her way in.

Mallory tugged his hand out so she could examine it. "You need to wash off that blood, put on antibiotic ointment and apply ice to the joints. Connor, your knuckles are swelling. I'd say you struck something hard." As she talked, Mallory dragged him down the hall toward a bathroom.

"Thanks," he managed to mutter. "I did it to myself. I was so mad after hearing Dahl's verdict, I smacked one of the clinic pillars on the way out. Not the brightest move I've ever made."

Mallory's lashes swept up. "I understand the feeling," she said quietly. "When Fredric phoned, I wanted to scream and kick. But, Connor, if you really want to spend time with Liddy Bea, you'll have to manage your anger better," she murmured, as Liddy careered into the room, her arms loaded with stuffed toys.

"These are to make Connor feel better," she said, thrusting them at him.

Connor sorted out a soft bear with his left hand and tucked it under his chin. That sent Liddy Bea into peals of delighted laughter.

Mallory stopped tending Connor's cuts. "I haven't heard her laugh like that in weeks." She was plainly shaken by the fact that credit for this belonged to Connor. "Maybe having you around would be, uh, good for her," she reluctantly admitted.

Turning serious, Connor ducked his head and forced her to look him in the eye. "Good for all of us, I hope."

"Yes. It's worth a try." She concentrated on applying the cream. Once she'd covered Connor's scrapes with soft gauze, she scrubbed her hands and arms with anti-bacterial soap. "Liddy Bea, baby, it's past time for your exchange. Today I'm showing Connor the process, okay?"

Liddy gazed solemnly at the man who was essentially still a stranger. Without saying a word, she sneaked a trusting hand into Connor's uninjured one.

"What exactly is an exchange?" he asked as she led him to her bedroom.

"You'll see." Mallory went to a storage closet stacked high with boxes. From one she pulled a plastic bag filled with clear liquid. "This is dialysate, used to replace fluid after we remove waste from her system." Two polyethylene tubes were attached to the bag; one dead-ended at a second, empty container. "Liddy has a permanent catheter imbedded in her abdomen."

Connor nodded, though he couldn't imagine what she meant.

"Attach the bag of dialysate to that hook we screwed into the wall. Clip off hose A and plug the other end into her catheter. Then unclip hose B, which leads to the empty bag you set on the floor."

Connor leaned over Mallory, who knelt beside Liddy. His warm breath ruffled the hair on the back of Mallory's neck. She shifted, hardly able to believe the tiny licks of tension squeezing low in her stomach. It'd been so long since she'd experienced anything remotely sexual. More annoyed than anything, Mallory dashed any such possibilities from her mind. Besides...she darted a fast glance at Connor, and he seemed intent and unmoved. Which, she suddenly remembered, was the way it often used to be between her and Connor. She'd fallen head over heels for him the day they met. For several years, he'd considered her nothing more than a pal.

This roommate thing could probably work—if she taught herself to be as emotionless as he was. Digging deep, she ignored the mounting tension.

"Okay, see, Connor? It's connected. Unclip hose B and the waste goes into the bag. When it's full, clip it off and open the bag of solution. Gravitational pull empties the dialysate into Liddy's system via hose A. It's pretty simple, really, once you get the hang of it. All in all, it takes forty minutes or so to complete the cycle."

Connor nodded, not trusting himself to speak. A plastic stump protruded from his precious baby's flesh, and there was a puckered, red scar angling across her abdomen. He thought he might be sick, but was determined not to be.

Mallory's voice droned on above the buzz in his ears. "Always make sure your hands are clean. The cannula must be covered after we're done. I worry about infection. She's had so many," Mallory murmured, getting up to sit in the rocker. She pulled Liddy Bea into her lap. "This is better than hemodialysis, which takes four to five hours each time.

"She goes through this how often?" Light-headed, and trying desperately not to show it, Connor sank down on the end of Liddy's pink-and-white bed.

"Three." Liddy Bea held up three pudgy fingers. "Sometimes more."

"It's three now," Mallory explained. "Fredric checked her creatinine and BUN levels yesterday. Three's not getting the job done. He'll probably up her to four."

Swallowing hard, Connor nodded again. If Mallory could do this and remain unaffected, by God, so could he. Maybe if he looked at the process clinically—sort of like working with his own sensitive equipment—he wouldn't trip and fall on his face. "Uh, if you two are set here for a while, I'll go somewhere quiet and make a few phone calls. I need to start the ball rolling on my move."

"Sure. I'll read Liddy Bea a story. This gives us one-on-one time for reading, doesn't it, baby?"

"Uh-huh. Next time, can Connor read to me?"

"You bet, kitten." Moved by her earnest little face, Connor lifted her chin and kissed the tip of her nose before he left the room. *Fled* might be a more apt term for his hasty exit. What if he couldn't do what Mallory managed with apparent ease?

Of course he could. But he'd never again take Mallory's role for granted. She'd humbled him with her efficiency and her capacity to adapt.

"LIDDY BEA FELL ASLEEP during her exchange," Mallory said, when she found Connor some forty-five minutes later, seated at her kitchen table. "Is that fresh coffee I smell?" She let her nose lead her to the pot.

"I hope you don't mind that I rummaged around and helped myself to coffee. After listening to the chief of Miami's center call me a traitor for ten minutes, I really needed a jolt of caffeine."

Mallory filled her cup and carried it to the counter to stir in sugar. "Maybe you should listen to him. What if you *are* making the mistake of your life?"

"In what way?" Connor tilted back in his chair. He sawed a finger thoughtfully across one hollow cheek.

"When it was time to bring your project back home, was Tallahassee a place you considered applying?"

He ran his gaze up and down her tense body and realized his answer was important. He'd be damned if he knew where this was leading, though. Something was bothering Mallory. Connor wished he could read her better. "The station in Miami approached me first," he finally admitted. "I didn't contact them."

"Really? Wow. Your work did get noticed in high places."

"Have you forgotten how closed the meteorological community is?"

She blew ripples on her coffee before sipping. "I haven't thought about it at all," she lied. Of course she had. She'd logged on to the Internet from time to time, looking for any information linked to hurricane detection—and Connor specifically. It irked her that she hadn't been better prepared for his homecoming. Her focus was on donating a kidney for Liddy Bea, so she hadn't ever been aware that Connor was in Miami. He'd obviously been there for a number of months by the time she saw the article in her dad's business magazine.

He studied her carefully. "Then this grilling has little or nothing to do with my job."

"Not true," she snapped. Hanging her head so that her hair obscured her face, she admitted warily, "I don't know what to have Liddy Bea call you. How'd I explain who you are, where you've been and why you suddenly showed up?"

"Try the truth." Connor stood and rammed both hands deep in his pants pockets. "Or I suppose you could wait until she puts two and two together. Thanks to your saving that elephant, she's already connected me with her dad. How do you think I felt that day at the hospital when she asked if I knew her father?"

Shoulders hunched, Mallory pulled out a chair and threw herself down. "She must have developed a curiosity about fathers at school," Mallory said morosely. "Probably from seeing her friends' dads. But she's never asked me any direct questions about you."

Connor felt a surge of the anger he thought he'd gotten rid of. "So how did you explain her grandmother Lydia? Davis said you two visit her grave."

Mallory's hands tightened around her coffee cup. "I never made a secret of the fact that you existed. I mean, I didn't say I found her in a cabbage patch, Connor. When I thought she was old enough to understand, I explained that her grandma Lydia, her daddy's mother, had died during a hurricane."

"Well, that's something at least."

Mallory sat up straight. "Don't take that tone with me, Connor. You weren't around. I never heard a word. I faced each day the best way I knew how."

"You never heard from me because your mother played God."

"She did. And I can't begin to tell you how sorry I

am. But you know what? Once I learned Mother was so ill, I'm not sure I could have gone against her wishes. Having a child, loving that child with every part of you, can lead to irrational decisions at times. I won't judge my mother for loving me, Connor.''

''Not even if her selfishness altered the course of your life, Liddy Bea's and mine?''

''The past is gone, never to be resurrected,'' she said sharply. ''I'm not the same person I was seven years ago. Nor do I want to be someone who can be that badly hurt again—if, for instance, another man I care about walks out on me. I rely on myself now.''

''Is this your way of saying you've had second thoughts about my offer to split parenting over the summer?''

''Second, third and fourth thoughts, Connor. I keep changing my mind. One minute I think, okay, this'll be fine, the next minute I don't see how we can make it work. A big question for me is, what course will you take if I decide to restrict your access to Liddy Bea?''

''You should've considered that *before* you landed on my doorstep in Miami, flashing baby pictures around. I don't want to take you to court to establish my rights as a father, Mallory. But I will if you try to cut me out of Lydia's life.''

''Haven't we all been hurt enough?''

''I hate to think that establishing a connection with my child would hurt any of us.''

''You're a harder man than I remember, Connor.''

He inclined his head, continuing to stare her down.

She sighed hugely. ''I don't want to throw Liddy Bea into the middle of a nasty custody fight. We both know you're her father and I'm her mother. I guess the arrangement you proposed is the best thing to do, for now, anyway.'' Liddy Bea, unaware of the portent of what she was interrupting, rushed into the kitchen, her face flushed from recent sleep.

"I want juice, Mommy.''

"I'll pour it.'' Connor offered. "Do you have a special glass?''

Liddy nodded. "I have a Hello Kitty glass. A cup and plate and a bowl, too.''

He followed her pointing finger, opened the cupboard door and saw the line of kitty faces grinning out at him. "Dr. Dahl warned me I should bone up on a blue dog and certain kitty paraphernalia.''

"Para...who?'' Liddy batted big, beguiling eyes.

"It's a big word that means *junk*. What kind of juice?'' Connor's voice echoed from the depths of the fridge.

"My favorite's grape. Mommy, did you buy grape juice at the store?''

"Oh, baby, I forgot. Can you drink cherry this time? I'll write down grape so I'll remember to buy it when I go out again.''

Connor, already pouring the cherry, set the glass on the table next to Mallory's cup. "Your mom and I are going out to eat tonight. We'll stop on the way home and get grape juice. Is there anything else you need?''

"Can I go out with you?''

Connor gnawed on the inside of his lip. "I...uh...well, kitten, your mom and I were planning on doing some grown-up talk.''

"Darn. I never get to go out and eat unless Grandpapa takes me. Mommy goes with Dr. Robinson all the time, and I have to stay home.'' Liddy crossed her pudgy arms and stuck out her lower lip. "It's not fair.''

"Liddy Bea, drink your juice." Mallory tugged out an adjacent chair for her daughter.

Alec Robinson's name hit Connor between the eyes. Perversely, he wanted to show Liddy Bea that he wasn't anything like the other man. "I guess your mother and I can talk another time. I think it'd be nice if the three of us went out and celebrated my job change, kitten."

"We could have, like, a party," Liddy said, suddenly enthusiastic.

"Connor, I—" Mallory's objection was interrupted when her daughter jumped in and said, "And we can cel'brate you moving in with us. Huh, Mommy?"

Two pairs of eyes suddenly pinned Mallory. She stuttered and stammered and in the end, she capitulated. "Okay, fine. After your evening exchange, Liddy Bea, we'll go out and toast Connor's move to Tallahassee. Uh…and his being our new roommate."

Connor smiled crookedly as he hoisted his cup of cold coffee and clinked it against Mallory's, then Liddy Bea's glass. A smooth-as-silk toast fell from his lips. "To my new job and to the two prettiest roommates a guy could ever hope to have."

Tension vibrated between the adults. If looks could kill, Mallory's scowl would have him being measured for a pine box.

CHAPTER ELEVEN

CONNOR SPENT THE REST of the afternoon making arrangements to have his equipment and belongings packed and shipped.

"You're nuts," Paul Caldwell told him. "Cutting all your ties in Miami doesn't seem smart to me. To say nothing of saddling yourself with a sick kid. That reeks of financial meltdown." Paul didn't specifically mention Connor's broken engagement to Claire, but Greg Dugan had no such hesitancy when he got on the line.

"What kind of jerk breaks his engagement over the phone?"

"Is that what Claire said I did?"

"Well, yeah. Maybe not in those exact words. But at lunch, she announced you two had split. And Janine said you phoned Claire right before noon."

"Claire called it quits, Greg. Not that it matters who broke up with whom. In the long run, it probably saved us both. We were doomed as a couple. It turns out we have different goals."

"I picked up some of your conversation with Paul. So you're jumping from the pan into the fire, is that it? You're reconciling with the mother of your kid?"

Connor glanced into the laundry room where Mallory stood folding a load of white clothes she'd taken from the dryer. For the last two hours she'd ignored him. He gave a short laugh. "I'm moving my project to Tallahassee because I have a daughter I'd like to get to know better. If her mother and I remain civil to each other, it'll be a miracle. Anyway, the move is permanent from my perspective. I wish you and Paul could join me. You've been a big help with my project."

"My family's here, plus I have a teaching fellowship for September. And Paul's really into the Miami babe scene. But thanks for thinking of us. Jay won't miss you." He laughed.

"That's a fact. When do you think you can begin shipping my equipment?"

Greg named a date about four days out.

"That'll work for me." After detailing instructions for packing the more delicate instruments—the ones he'd bought with earlier grant funds—Connor signed off.

Next, he notified his landlord of his plans and prevailed on him to ride herd over the movers he intended to hire for his personal belongings. Once the man agreed, Connor dialed the moving company. He felt as though his cell phone was attached to his ear by the time he'd finished shelling out his credit card information.

"It's six o'clock," Mallory announced, stepping to the door of the dining room as he hung up from his last call.

Connor snapped the cuff of his shirt back to look at his watch. "So it is." Rolling his head from side to side, he linked his fingers overhead and stretched. "Is six significant? Oh, does Liddy Bea have to eat at set times?"

"Within reason. Her exchanges need to be more regimented. It's time for another, and you did say you wanted to do this one. If you're backing out, that's okay, but she's counting on you to read to her."

"I'm not backing out. I had no idea it'd gotten so late."

"That's why our splitting up Liddy's care isn't practical, Connor. I can't go off to work, trusting you'll remember her exchanges. What if you forget?"

"Once I'm responsible for doing them, I'll keep better track of the time. My watch has an alarm, and if need be, I'll set it for each exchange, at least until remembering becomes automatic. Shared parenting will work if we want it to, Mallory." He hooked his thumbs loosely in his belt loops. "Are you hoping I'll screw up?"

"Let's say I have grave reservations."

"Why are you so angry with me, Mallory? If anyone's been wronged, it's probably me. Don't I deserve a chance to prove myself?"

"I'm sorry, Connor. Everything's been out of whack since I decided to find you. Fredric warned me you might want to take a more active role in Liddy Bea's life. I naturally thought there wasn't much chance of that. I figured if you'd wanted to look back at what you left behind in Tallahassee, you'd have done so way before now. So I went to see you—and found you were engaged to Claire. Considering all of that, how could I predict you'd turn your life, and mine, upside down by quitting your job and moving here?"

"You couldn't predict that I'd want to be a father to my daughter? Really? When you probably know the real me better than anyone alive, Mallory?" He gazed on her with great sadness as he spoke.

Unable to deal with the truth in his statement, she turned and walked to the dining-room window. Leaning her forehead against the cool glass, Mallory blinked away threatening tears. Tears for all the lost years.

Connor hesitated only briefly, then closed the distance between them. War waged inside him—should he touch her or not? He seemed to have little control over his hands as they curved lightly around her upper arms. Turning her, he pulled her face against his chest.

Memories of all the good—the *right*—moments they'd shared washed over him in successive waves. The perfect way she felt in his arms. The times he came home late after working two jobs and did nothing but hold her. Even her perfume acted as a balm.

"It's pointless trying to fight a past we can't change," he said gruffly. "For Liddy Bea's sake, can't we take the parts that did work and build on them?"

His rough voice was little more than a low rumble against Mallory's ear. She'd forgotten how secure and safe she used to feel being held by Connor. A hodgepodge of nostalgic moments flooded back, paralyzing her. The faint scent of his aftershave and the slight abrasive scrape of the starched cotton shirts he preferred added to the images already floating in her mind. She didn't trust herself to speak. Instead, she knotted her fingers in his shirt.

For an instant, his arms tightened. Then he wedged a space between them. "Listen. Liddy Bea's calling us. She's going to be really confused if she comes in here and finds us in a clinch. My aim is not to make life more difficult for either of us, Mallory. All I want is a chance to get to know my child."

Mallory shivered as the words sank in. Connor wasn't asking to resume their relationship. That wasn't what he wanted at all. Her mistake. And one she wouldn't repeat. Stepping away from him, she discreetly blotted her eyes on her sleeve. "Forgive me. I'm not usually the weepy sort. I guess I'm still shaken from the shock of finding out that you can't be the donor we were hoping for."

"Don't apologize, Mallory. Living in the same space, we're bound to stumble once in a while."

"No. For our situation to work, Connor, we need to set ground rules. I'll tackle that tomorrow. Do you mind booking into a hotel tonight? You can drop us off after dinner and take my car. I shouldn't need it tomorrow."

"What if you have an emergency? Never mind. I'll come in after dinner and watch you get Liddy Bea off to bed, then I'll phone a cab. I agree we can probably use a breather while we sort this out. But can we tell her tonight who I am?"

"Please, Connor. I need time to get used to sharing her. Coming, baby," she called, hearing Liddy Bea yell for them again.

"How long?" Connor pressed as he dogged Mallory's steps down the hall.

"Two weeks," she said off the top of her head. "By then, I'm sure we'll have established a routine. Kids need routine."

"I wouldn't know what kids need, Mallory. But I damn sure intend to learn."

"Another thing, Connor. Please don't swear. I've noticed you have a tendency to swear more than you used to."

"Not a lot," he said, growing defensive at her sudden attempt to push him aside and take charge. "Your dad swears quite a bit."

She nervously raked her hair back over one ear. "He has other bad habits, too, like smoking cigars. He tries to curb them for Liddy's sake. I'm only asking you to consider what effect little things like that might have on an impressionable child."

"That's reasonable. Now, what if we want to date?"

"D-date?" The word sounded strangled.

"Yes. Liddy Bea said you often go out to eat with Dr. Robinson."

"Oh, that. She's too young to realize those are working dinners."

"But Alec's old enough to know they're not dates, right?"

Mallory felt her cheeks grow warm. "The hospital board of directors expect Alec and me to host the hospital fund-raisers. We have a number of those each year."

Studying the red splotches that suddenly appeared on Mallory's cheeks, Connor decided he'd said enough on the subject of Alec Robinson. Changing tack, he stepped aside and motioned for Mallory to continue on to Liddy's room.

"Before you repeat the steps of Liddy Bea's exchange, let me see if I can remember them. First, we wash," he said, stopping at the hall bath.

She nodded. "Infection of any kind is a major threat to Liddy. We can't avoid every germ, of course, especially given her age. Just take my word for it—infections around shunts are nothing we ever want to deal with."

"No, I shouldn't think so." He dried his hands on a paper towel as they walked down the hall.

Both mustered grins for Liddy Bea as they entered her room. She'd gathered a host of stuffed animals and books near the rocking chair where Mallory had sat with her earlier. "Ready to muddle through this with me, are you, kitten? I hope I don't end up all fumble fingers."

"It's a cinch," she bragged. Then indecision spread over her face. "Well, I probably can't do it all alone. 'Cause I'm not tall enough to reach the hook Mommy put in Uncle Mark's wall. At Grandpapa's, we used

Grandma Beatrice's hat rack. I had a step stool, and I could hook my bag on it all by myself.''

"I could have brought the hat rack," Mallory said. "Maybe I'll have Dad drop it off. It moves easily, so we can do an exchange in any room."

Faced with connecting the tubing to Liddy Bea's shunt, Connor dug deep for the wherewithal and hooked her up. He managed by telling himself this unpleasant procedure did the work of her kidneys, and thus kept her free of poisons that would otherwise ravage her tiny body. He pulled it off without a hitch.

"Very good." Smiling, Mallory praised him. "Since you two look as if you're set for a month with all that reading material, I'll go shower and change clothes so when you're done we can head out to dinner."

Liddy Bea climbed up onto Connor's lap with minimal assistance from him. She handed him a book called *Chicka Chicka Boom Boom.* It was filled with silly alphabet rhymes, and in minutes he joined in her infectious laughter.

Mallory poked her head back into the room, a puzzled look on her face. "Ah, it's the book bringing the house down around my ears. I couldn't imagine what you two found so hilarious." She lounged against the door frame, lazily rubbing one bare foot on the opposite leg.

Connor's eyes cut to her legs. Long and tan and smooth. He swallowed his laughter. "I thought you were going to shower," he said, finally forcing the words past dry lips."

"I am. I was getting a towel when I heard you and decided you two were having way too much fun." She shrugged. But a crimson-polished, manicured toenail continued to slide up and down her calf.

Connor gripped the book so tightly, Liddy Bea

couldn't turn the pages. "Mommy," she sighed. "You're 'rupting our story." Her observation refocused Connor's attention on the child.

"Yeah, Mom," he scolded Mallory. "Stop 'rupting us." He thought to himself that could be *cor*rupting rather than *inter*rupting. He'd been near to salivating, and he hadn't experienced those edgy feelings over a woman in too long—including the year or so he'd spent with Claire. He realized that with more than a little shock. He should've known sooner, he supposed, feeling profound regret for having wasted her time.

Missing social outlets in his life, he'd met Claire through co-workers. And he'd more or less let her direct their relationship from then on. He should've recognized earlier that, while he was contented enough with Claire, he didn't love her.

"Okay, I'm going," Mallory said. Connor hastily turned the page and just as hastily finished the story. Liddy, totally oblivious to his inner turmoil, grabbed another book, which she declared her "second most favorite." Connor read on as if he hadn't been rendered numb by that stab of physical desire for his child's mother.

Boy, howdy! If Mallory had any idea what he was feeling, she'd toss him out on his ear so fast he wouldn't know what hit him. He sure hadn't been prepared for the sneak attack on his senses. Oh, he'd reminisced about the good times he and Mallory had shared but as often as not, he'd immediately switched to being furious with her for keeping her pregnancy a secret.

For the first time, Connor saw validity to drawing up rules for living in the same quarters. When he'd first proposed the arrangement, he'd had in mind something like the setup he'd read Prince Andrew and Fergie had created. Living in the same house, sharing parental duties, but outside of that, leading independent lives.

"Connor." Liddy Bea nudged him. "It's time to switch bags."

Rousing, Connor hurried to clip the tube to the waste fluid and unfasten the one that would carry the dialysate into her system. "I'll have to pay closer attention, kitten. I think your mommy's worried I'll screw up."

The child studied him from serious gray eyes, so like his own. "What's screw up?"

"It means make a mistake."

"Oh? Mommy's not grumpy 'bout mistakes. She says everybody makes 'em. We just gotta try and not make the same one twice."

"You're a lucky girl to have such a nice mother."

"Yep. Do you got a nice mommy?"

"I did have. She died a long time ago. In a hurricane," he added, anticipating Liddy Bea's next question.

"My grandma Lydia died in a hurricane, too." She snuggled into the hollow of Connor's shoulder and arm. "I don't like hurricanes."

"Me, neither, kitten." Connor hugged her, attempting to ward off the shiver that coursed through her body.

"At school, we saw a movie with a hurricane. My teacher showed us how we hafta make a straight line and follow her to a bus if we hear the siren. It was loud. Me and the other kids covered our ears. Didn't your mommy or my grandma Lydia know they should get on a bus to take them away from the hurricane?"

Connor wondered how on earth he'd manage if she asked more questions about his mother and her grandmother. He was going to have to watch more than his tendency to swear, it seemed. "I heard your mom's shower shut off. We need to finish reading this story before she comes and drags us off to eat.''

''Okay. I'm not very hungry, though.''

''Maybe you will be by the time we get to the restaurant. Your mama picked a fish place. Do you like fish?''

''It's okay. I like French fries better. But Mommy only lets me have a few. 'Cause Dr. Fred says.''

''If I'm going to stay with you during the day, your mother and Dr. Fred will have to write out a list of no-no foods. I'll probably be fixing your breakfast and lunch.''

''Uh-huh. And dinner when Mommy goes out to eat with Dr. Robinson.''

''She does that a lot, does she?''

''Yep. The days Grandpapa didn't get home early, me and Marta had a tea party in my room. She cut the center out of sandwiches with cookie cutters. It was fun. Maybe you and me can do that sometime, huh, Connor?''

''You and I, not you and me, kitten. I've never cut the center out of sandwiches with cookie cutters. I guess I have a lot to learn when it comes to cooking for little girls.''

''I don't think Marta cooked the sandwiches.''

''What's this about cooked sandwiches?'' Mallory asked as she whisked into the room.

''Connor and me—uh—I are gonna have a tea party with my dolls next time you hafta go eat with Dr. Robinson.''

Mallory blushed and sent a questioning glance at Connor.

He noticed the dialysate bag was empty and busied himself unhooking the apparatus. ''We were discussing me fixing breakfast and lunch. Liddy Bea said sometimes Marta fixed special dinners if you weren't home.

I'd appreciate you drawing up a list of foods Liddy Bea likes, and ones to avoid. Clip it to the rules when you get those set up. What's our next step here? What happens to the used bags, Mallory?''

"Right now there's a box inside my room. Each time it's full, I seal it and put it in one of the outside trash bins. That's a chore I won't mind sharing. The boxes are heavy. I'll try to find a more neutral place to put it. I think our bedrooms should be off-limits to the other person, don't you?''

Watching her, fresh from her shower, Connor thought bedrooms were the last place he'd want to be off-limits. However, those were fantasies that should be kept to himself. Or better yet, fantasies that should be extinguished completely. "I'm easy," he said, lifting Liddy Bea off his lap. "Maybe you can put this one in the box while I go wash again. Did Mark leave any clean shirts here? Otherwise, I'm stuck going to dinner in what I'm wearing.''

"Mark cleaned out everything. There's a mall near the restaurant if you'd like to stop afterward and pick up a few things to tide you over until your stuff arrives.''

"I'll have to." He rubbed a prickly jaw. "Unless you don't mind me looking like a bum for a few days, I'll need a razor. And at least a couple of shirts, jeans, socks and underwear.''

"Catching the last flight back to Miami might turn out to be less expensive for you, Connor. I've already arranged for this month off work. We don't have to start splitting day care tomorrow, you know.''

"What I know is that I've already lost too many days, months, weeks and years, Mallory. Even one more is too many.''

She looked guilty, and at the same time, bristled.

"I was stating facts, Mallory, not blaming you."

"I'm sorry, but that's what it sounded like, Connor. I think we should go eat and bring this conversation to an end."

Connor nodded, hoping they could keep things pleasant for their daughter's sake.

Mallory handed Liddy a light sweater. "I'll go stash the used bags, wash and then grab my own sweater. Liddy, honey, can you show Connor the way to the tenant parking lot?"

"Sure. Give me the keys, Mommy. I'll open the doors."

"They're in my purse. It's on the kitchen counter."

Liddy Bea grabbed Connor's hand. She ushered him into the kitchen, where she sorted the keys from other items in Mallory's purse, while he washed.

"We always lock the 'partment door when we go out to the car. But I guess Mommy'll do that when she comes out."

Liddy Bea led the way along the hall and down back steps into a courtyard Connor didn't know existed. There was a fenced swimming pool and a grassy area with barbecues and picnic tables shaded by gently swaying palms. Beyond, two women were playing tennis. Two other courts were vacant. Smaller fenced yards flanked the courts on either side. One yard held swings, a slide and a climbing fort. In the other, a man was letting his puppy chase a ball through the short grass.

"That's Mr. Peterson and his puppy, Big Foot. Hi, Mr. Peterson." Liddy dropped Connor's hand. She ran to the fence, sank down on one knee and stuck her hand through the mesh, all so fast, Connor barely had time to move from the spot where his feet seemed to have taken root.

His heart still did a double flip until he heard Liddy Bea's girlish giggle and he realized the setter pup was snuffling her arm and licking her fingers.

Turning her hand over, Liddy Bea scratched the dog's soft, coppery-colored ears. "Big Foot likes me, doesn't he, Mr. Peterson?"

"Sure does, little lady." The elderly man glanced at Connor and smiled. "Well, there, I guess Dad's been away on a trip." Still smiling at Connor, he added, "I've only ever seen the girl with her mama. I've told my wife it's a crying shame the little one doesn't have a dog. There's no kids living in our complex, but your daughter wouldn't get lonely if she had herself a pet."

Liddy Bea stopped stroking Big Foot's ears and squinted up at the adults. "Connor's a friend of my mommy's, Mr. Peterson. I don't have a daddy."

The old man straightened away from the fence. But not before he pushed his glasses up on his nose and gave Connor and Liddy Bea each a good long once-over.

Mallory hurried up just then, somewhat out of breath. "Oh, hello, Mr. Peterson. I went directly to the car and wondered what had held up Connor and Liddy Bea. I should've known. If Big Foot's anywhere outside, Liddy Bea can't pass by without petting him. Now you'll have to wash again at the restaurant, honey."

"I was telling the mister the little one needs a tail-wagger. A friend of my wife's works for the humane society. They're always looking for good homes."

As she gently lifted Liddy Bea away from the fence, Mallory's smile turned into a frown. "Oh, I don't think—"

"*Please,* Mommy," Liddy Bea implored. "Only two kids in my class don't have a puppy or a kitty or a goldfish. 'Cept I don't want a goldfish. Can I have a puppy, Mommy? Grandpapa said I could if we stayed at his house.''

''He did?'' Mallory sounded indignant. ''When?''

''The day Uncle Mark helped us move. We met Mr. Peterson and Big Foot. I said I wanted a dog just like Big Foot. Uncle Mark said he didn't think dogs belonged in 'partments. Grandpapa said if we came back to Forrest House, he'd buy me one.''

Mallory pressed her lips together tightly. Saying goodbye to Mr. Peterson, she hustled Liddy Bea off in the direction of the covered parking stalls.

''Nice meeting you, sir.'' Connor dipped his chin.

''Guess if you're the girl's uncle, that explains the strong resemblance.''

''Mark's her uncle. I'm Connor O'Rourke, Mr. Peterson. I'll be sharing the apartment with Liddy Bea and her mother, and I'll be assuming Liddy Bea's daytime care. Maybe I'll talk Mallory around to thinking about a dog. If I do, I'll get the address of the humane society from you or your wife.'' Connor jogged off after the others, feeling unsettled about the half-truths he was expected to give regarding his relationship to Liddy Bea. If even nearsighted strangers saw the likeness, one of these days someone was bound to say so in terms Liddy understood.

The ride to the restaurant would have been quiet if not for Liddy Bea's run-on chatter concerning Big Foot.

''Hush,'' Mallory finally said as she pulled into a parking lot next to the establishment. ''Liddy Bea, you can pet Big Foot whenever you're both outside. Think how often you've been in and out of the hospital, baby. The last thing Mommy needs is a dog to worry about on top of everything else.''

Liddy Bea's lower lip trembled, and her bubbly chatter died a sudden death.

Connor decided it wasn't a good time to talk to Mallory about getting a dog—or about explaining to Liddy Bea his real role in her life. He gave the hostess their names while Mallory took Liddy Bea to the women's washroom to wash her hands.

In spite of the rocky start, dinner went well. Liddy Bea was well behaved, and the waiter remarked on her good manners.

Mallory accepted the praise as her due. Connor was happy to let her. "You've done an excellent job raising her," he said after the waiter withdrew. "I wish I could see where you missed having a man around, but I can't say there's any evidence."

As Mallory contemplated how to respond to a remark of that nature, Liddy Bea, who'd chosen to sit by Connor, slid close and wrapped both hands around his arm. "In the hospital, the day you saw Mommy's elephant, it sounded like you knew my daddy. If you do, will you tell me and Mommy where he is?"

Neither Connor nor Mallory was prepared for that bombshell. Both shifted in their seats and scrabbled for something to say.

Mallory recovered first. "Baby, I want you to sit back and finish your dinner. Or if you're full, we'll ask the waiter to bring us a box so you can take the rest of your fish sticks home. We'll warm them up and you can have them with a salad for lunch tomorrow."

Liddy Bea lifted pleading eyes to Connor, as if expecting him to contradict her mother.

"Nice try, kitten. Eat. Your mom and I have to be on the same wavelength if we're going to work together successfully."

"Will we be a family?" Liddy Bea asked, scooting fully back on her chair.

"You and I *are* a family," Mallory said, gazing in confusion at her daughter.

Liddy Bea shook her head, making her curls dance. "Families have a mama, a daddy, kids and a dog."

"A dog?" Mallory and Connor said in unison.

Liddy Bea nodded. "Remember, Mommy? I brought a liberry book home and it had pictures of a house, a mommy, a daddy, a boy and girl. And a baby and a dog. You said the book was about families."

"I know I did, but—" Mallory pressed a hand to her head and dropped her elbow on the table.

Connor took pity on her. He wished she'd taken the opportunity to explain who he was, but he supposed he understood Mallory's hesitation. He needed to earn the right to be included in their family. "Liddy Bea, families come in different sizes, shapes and colors. They don't all live in houses and they don't all have pets. And I'll bet some of your schoolfriends have two grandmas and two grandpas, while you only have one grandpa. That's sometimes the way it is, kitten."

"Oh." Liddy Bea mulled over what he'd said, pinning him with eyes so like his own, Connor glanced away.

Rising, Mallory signaled the waiter. "We're ready for the check, and could we have a couple of boxes, please?"

Connor noticed then that Mallory had barely touched her food. If this was her habit, it was no wonder she'd lost weight from when he'd known her. Back then, she'd enjoyed eating. Not that she was even the slightest bit overweight. But she used to be solid. She skated, swam, jogged and biked several times a week, which kept her trim.

"I didn't see any of your sports equipment at the apartment. Of course I didn't poke through closets, but stuff like your bike and surfboard used to sit out."

Mallory turned in surprise. "My bike is gathering dust at Dad's. Mark had a friend who bought my surfboard five or so years ago. I pretty much stopped everything at the time Mom's illness got bad. Then, what with working irregular hours and taking care of a house and a baby, the stuff I did when I was single sort of fell by the wayside. What about you?" she asked, filling the containers the waiter dropped off on his way past their table.

"I still try to jog every day or so. I thought I'd surf on the island, but working on my hurricane-detection system filled a lot of hours. I did learn to fly. One of the guys who ferried supplies in gave me the books and a few lessons. As he had an instructor's license, he let me log the required hours on his plane."

"Nice. You always talked about learning to fly. Do you have your own plane?"

"Nope. That's out there in my dream column. But most municipal airports have rentals. I'll take you and Liddy Bea up one of these days before winter hits."

"Goody!" Liddy said excitedly.

"Liddy, honey, Mommy hasn't got much free time. Besides, it's probably better if we don't plan too many outings together."

"Why?" Connor was busy forking Liddy Bea's fish sticks into the box, but he paused to stare perplexedly at Mallory.

"Just because. We're sharing an apartment, Connor. As we're sharing responsibility for Liddy Bea. That's it. Otherwise, I thought we'd agreed to operate as separate entities."

His stomach did a funny sinking dive as he took out money for the tip.

"Oh, if you're getting the whole tip, let me pay for your dinner." Mallory plucked the check from the table. "We pay on the way out."

Standing, Connor gathered the boxes without a word. Up to now, he'd enjoyed their evening out. He had to agree with Liddy Bea—it felt like they *were* a family, dammit. Apparently Mallory was determined to keep them separate.

He juggled the boxes and his billfold. At the cash register, he shoved the boxes into Mallory's hands and snatched the check. "I said I was paying and I am, so don't give me any static." Once he'd paid, he grabbed Liddy Bea's hand. Stony-faced, he walked out, leaving Mallory to sputter and fend for herself.

There happened to be a couple of dogs in a car they drew abreast of at the first stoplight. Liddy Bea chattered the rest of the way home about everything she'd do if her mom let her have a puppy.

Connor was seconds from putting in his two cents' worth, making his plea to Mallory on Liddy Bea's behalf, when Mallory swung into her parking spot. Leaning negligently against the trunk of a Jaguar parked in the adjacent space was Alec Robinson, still dressed immaculately in shirt, tie and three-piece suit. Even his shoes gleamed in the fluorescent lights that ran the length of the garage.

Since the Jag was parked on Mallory's side, it was conceivable that Alec didn't see Connor until he stepped out of the car to open Liddy Bea's door.

Alec scowled. "What's he doing here?"

"What are you?" Mallory queried in return.

"Fredric told me what a disappointing day you had.

I thought I'd drop by to see how you were doing. I also brought the names of some new patrons to add to the ticket list for our winter fund-raiser.''

"Oh, I won't need that here at home. I'm coming back to work as early as Monday.''

"Really? That's great news.'' Alec continued to eye Connor. "Bradford said you were going to advertise for a live-in baby-sitter. I didn't realize you'd already done that.''

Mallory threw an uncomfortable glance toward Connor. But it was Liddy Bea who spilled the beans. "I don't gotta have a baby-sitter, Dr. Robinson. Connor's moving in with me and Mommy. He's gonna take care of me while she's at work.''

"What?'' Alec's harsh query bounced off the ceiling and reverberated faintly from the back wall of the garage.

Unable to stifle the grin that spread from ear to ear of its own accord, Connor swung Liddy Bea into his arms. He slammed her car door breezily. "Come on, kitten. If Mommy will toss me the keys, I'll take you upstairs and start getting you ready for bed. We'll let your mom explain our living arrangement to her boss.''

Mallory didn't seem able to comply with Connor's simple request.

"Connor, Mommy left the keys in the car,'' Liddy Bea said in a loud whisper.

"So she did.'' Connor opened the passenger door, bent inside and pulled the keys from the ignition. Next, he scooped up the boxes of food and handed them to the child. "We'll put these in the fridge,'' he announced. "Like your mommy suggested, I'll warm up the fish for your lunch tomorrow.''

He heard the angry rumble of Alec Robinson's deep

voice and quickened his pace to get Liddy Bea out of earshot. This was probably going to be an unpleasant scene and the child didn't need to hear it.

Connor also pocketed the keys, since Mallory had offered him the use of her car. He'd intended to call a cab, but they'd forgotten to stop at the mall and he needed to get there before it closed. A car would give him a faster getaway, too. Connor had no doubt that Mallory would be itching to take a chunk out of his hide once she sent Alec away and stormed back inside.

Still, it was worth facing her fury to have dealt that pompous windbag Robinson the shock of his life.

CHAPTER TWELVE

CONNOR HEARD THE FRONT DOOR of the apartment slam as he was tucking Liddy Bea into bed. "Here comes your mom. I thought we'd have time to read a book, but I'd better scoot out of here and go shopping and then find myself a place to stay for the night. Save this story for tomorrow."

"Okay." Liddy Bea sighed, but she snuggled down with her stuffed dog. She'd already fussed with her glass frog band, making sure each figure faced her bed. "Mommy leaves my door open so I can see the hall light."

"Don't like the dark, huh? I'm not fond of it, either, kitten." Connor stroked her hair as he stored that information. He realized it was just one of the many things he didn't know about his daughter—her fear of the dark.

She stretched out her arms to him for another hug.

Connor had helped her wash her face and hands after they came in. Her sweet soapy smell engulfed him as he bent over her again.

A shadow blocked the hall light as he disentangled Liddy's arms from around his neck.

"Connor, you can't toss a child in bed straight from dinner. This splitting care thing really isn't going to work. I don't know what made me ever think it would." Mallory sounded more weary than upset.

"We washed my hands and face and got me clean

jammies, Mommy." Liddy Bea sat up in bed, still clutching her stuffed toy and Connor's hand. "I 'splained how I can't have a real bath until my tummy heals."

"You washed her and found clean pj's?" Mallory turned surprised eyes on Connor.

"Yes. And I was just leaving," he said. "I changed my mind about borrowing your car. I could use it, if you're sure that's okay. We forgot to stop at the mall, and I need a few things until my movers arrive."

Mallory worried her top lip with her teeth. She glanced from Liddy's anxious face to Connor and back again, then led him into the hall and lowered her voice. "It's probably not a good idea. As Alec pointed out, nothing about this deal we made will seem sensible to anyone on the outside looking in."

"Funny, I recall we once had this conversation in reverse. Back when we lived together, I used to worry about what people might think. But you never cared about anyone else's opinion."

Mallory stiffened. "Time and motherhood have a way of changing one's perspective. You've remained a carefree bachelor, Connor."

"So marry me and correct all that. Then everything will look aboveboard to these people whose opinions you're suddenly so worried about."

"*Marry* you?" she gasped. "Connor, where did that come from? Oh, I see. You eavesdropped. You heard Alec ask me first."

"*What?* I did no such thing. People…uh…marry who have a lot less in common than we do." Turning red, Connor mumbled that he'd never thought she was serious about Robinson. "Sorry. Today's been…eventful. I'll go now. We both need a good night's rest. Tomorrow, we'll set some rules. Don't be hasty about any plans until then. We can make this work, I promise."

She seemed unable to move, and felt icy fingers of doubt tiptoe up her spine as Connor's body brushed hers in passing. At one time she would have snapped up his offer of marriage so fast it would've made his head swim. Now the knowledge that he'd just become unengaged to Claire Dupree left her too confused to believe she could ever feel the same love for Connor again.

Even though she heard the outer door close and lock, she couldn't seem to grasp everything that had transpired in the last half hour.

"If you married Connor, would he be my daddy?" Liddy's eager voice floated into the hall and broke into Mallory's thoughts. "Then he could stay here forever, right?" Liddy's overexcitement brought Mallory rushing back into the bedroom.

"Baby, Connor wasn't serious. He was being a smart aleck, asking me to marry him. It's not going to happen."

"Why not?" The little girl pouted. "He'd make the best daddy."

"You've seen him, what? Two or three times at most? Liddy Bea, there's more to being a good husband and daddy than Connor's shown us so far."

"I don't like Dr. Robinson. He said I'm spoiled 'cause I want a night-light. Connor doesn't like the dark. And he don't smell like lemons." Liddy's lower lip quivered.

Mallory almost laughed. Alec Robinson did go overboard on the lemony aftershave. It was also true that he'd been fairly vocal about her spoiling Lydia. Alec's views on child-rearing were one reason she'd never seriously entertained the idea of marrying him. There were others. A bitter divorce he refused to let go of. Followed closely by the fact that he had more in common with her dad than with her. Dinner in formal restaurants and attending the opera were Alec's only ideas of entertainment. He repeatedly said he didn't like anything that involved getting sweaty.

She supposed that also included sex. Although it'd been so long since she'd enjoyed the experience, she wondered if her memories might've been enhanced by deprivation.

Mallory crossed the room and sat on Liddy's bed. "Liddy Bea." She smoothed the child's still-damp curls. "I'm not going to marry Alec. I wouldn't marry anyone you didn't like. Furthermore, he'd have to love both of us a lot."

Liddy Bea nodded. "Connor loves us, Mommy."

Mallory's hand faltered, growing suddenly clammy. "What makes you think that?"

The child shrugged. "I just know. I'm sure glad he's not gonna marry the lady he brought to see me in the hospital. Aren't *you* glad, Mommy?"

"Honestly?" It was on the tip of Mallory's tongue to say she hadn't given Claire a thought. But if she was going to be honest... "Yes, baby, I'm glad Connor's not marrying Claire. But that's got to be our secret, okay? You lie down and go to sleep now. I need to type up some rules so that tomorrow when Connor comes, we have a routine."

"'Night, Mommy." Smiling, Liddy Bea flopped on her side and slung an arm over her stuffed dog.

CONNOR ARRIVED BEFORE breakfast the next morning. He juggled house and car keys, two cups of coffee, a carton of milk and a dozen assorted doughnuts.

Liddy Bea's eyes lit up. Mallory wore a scowl. "I

have a nutritious breakfast on the table. You should have called to check before you bought doughnuts. Fredric is trying to restrict Liddy's fat intake.''

"Oh. I thought you said we needed to go light on protein."

"That, too. Low sodium, low protein and low fat."

"What's left in the food chain?" Connor asked, plainly perplexed.

"It's balance we're striving for. Fredric isn't sure if certain foods increase her buildup of negative antibodies. If her antibody count gets too high, she's not a good candidate for transplant."

"Can I have one doughnut, please, Mommy?" Liddy asked in a beseeching tone.

Mallory sighed, and seeing her indecision, Connor stepped in. He put down the box of doughnuts and picked up the child. "Why don't we check out what your mother fixed for breakfast? Then maybe you and I will get out of her hair for a while. You know, give her some time to herself? We'll take the doughnuts to the university, where Da—um, where I'll soon be setting up my project. The staff will love us for bringing a treat. And I'll make a good first impression."

Mallory caught his almost-slip. She told Liddy Bea to go wash and watched the girl skip away after Connor set her down. Mallory pulled Connor aside. "Is that a good idea, Connor? What if people notice your similarities and think she's your child?"

"She *is* my child," he said clearly and concisely. "Your neighbor, Mr. Peterson, made the connection yesterday. As could anyone at a park, in the grocery store or the hospital—anywhere. I'm willing to allow you a reasonable amount of time to figure out what to tell her, but I'd like it settled before she starts school. I want their records set straight.''

He looked so big. So imposing. So serious. Mallory shut her eyes.

"I'm here to stay, Mal. I'm back in Tallahassee, and I'm not going away. Unless you move, and if you do, I'll pull up stakes and follow you.''

Connor was the only person who'd ever shortened her name. The only person who said *Mal* in a way that still conjured visions of being together in bed. He'd usually called her Mal in the throes of passion and at other highly emotional times. Which proved he was dead earnest about this.

"Two weeks, Connor. Give me two weeks starting Monday, when I go back to work. I have to be sure this isn't a passing fancy with you.'' Realizing he was about to protest vehemently, she held up a hand. "After nearly seven years, two weeks isn't much to ask. I know I probably don't deserve the added time. I should've let you know when she was born. But… I have to be sure! Parenting isn't anything you've ever done. Look at the number of dads who regularly opt out. Those numbers triple when a child is chronically ill. I've seen the statistics, Connor.''

"And I keep telling you I'm not one of those statistics. If I'd had any reason to suspect you were pregnant, the last six-plus years would've been different.''

"Yes, they would. You'd be able to blame me for ruining your career.''

"This sniping at each other is getting us nowhere.'' Connor paced the kitchen in short, quick steps. "Two weeks. Fine, I agree to two weeks.''

"Thank you.'' Mallory's voice cracked. "H-how will

you handle it if anyone else remarks on…the, uh, no-
ticeable similarity?''

"I'll wear sunglasses everywhere I go.''

Mallory dredged up a smile. ''I can't fault you for not
trying to accommodate my insecurities. Come on. Let's
eat. Let's discuss the rules we're going to establish. I
have a whole list.''

"Wait a sec. *Insecure* isn't a word I'd ever connect
with you, Mallory. The very opposite, in fact. It's something I always admired about you—that ability to move
easily in and among people from any walk of life. The
other volunteers in our hurricane-relief group looked to
you for leadership. So did I. When did you start feeling
insecure?''

"I never felt that kind of vulnerability before I had a
child. You know, Fredric warned me when I mentioned
finding you, Connor. He said courts look more favorably
on fathers now. And when you consider the facts alone,
it might appear that I've done you wrong.''

Approaching her, Connor lifted the hands she had un-
consciously clenched at her sides. He pried open her
fingers and curled them over his, lightly stroking her
knuckles with his thumbs. ''I tried to be mad at you. I
admit I considered fighting you in court. But the more I
saw you and Liddy Bea together, the more I knew I
could never do anything to jeopardize that relationship.
Which isn't to say I don't regret missing her early
years.''

"Oh, Connor, I'm so sorry.''

"Shh! Let me finish. I'll always have a blank where
you have memories. I simply want to start sharing the
steps she'll take from here on out.'' Raising Mallory's
right hand to his lips, Connor pressed a kiss to the fingers
he'd been stroking.

A lump lodged in her throat. His eyes, which could look like storm clouds one moment and the silver skies after a rain in the next, had always left her little more than putty in his hands. When he touched her, Mallory had no resistance to him. Nor was it clear why she *should* resist. Except for the fact that there was so much volatile history behind them. Some of it her fault. Some his. Much more could be attributed to her mother's meddling in their lives. But it all added up to her needing a clear head right now—since they'd be making decisions regarding Connor's role in Liddy Bea's chaotic life. With chronic illness, life could go rapidly into a tailspin.

All those thoughts ran through Mallory's head. Jumbled thoughts and indecision, thanks to Connor's nearness.

She jerked out of his loose grasp more forcefully than either of them might have expected. "That's going to be rule number one, Connor," she said in a shaky voice. "This arrangement—our part, anyway—must remain strictly platonic."

He backed away, raising his palms. "Sure. Whatever you say. I can live with that rule."

Five minutes later, all three of them were seated at the small breakfast table, eating Mallory's whole wheat waffles and fresh fruit. The coffee Connor brought was reheated in the microwave, and Liddy had grape juice. Mallory and Connor sat across from each other, their knees companionably touching, and Connor wondered if he could abide by such a rule. When he used to come upon her studying in their tiny kitchen, her shiny chestnut curls had a way of brushing a spot below her ear that made his toes curl with wanting to kiss the soft, untanned flesh of her neck. In that previous life, he'd answered the call of such yearnings. Now it was going to be pure hell to ignore the blood pounding through his veins.

Leaning his elbows on the table, Connor closed his eyes and dropped his forehead into his splayed hands. How could he ever have been so stupid as to walk away from her in the first place?

Mallory glanced up, thinking she heard him groan. "What's wrong? Is it my waffles or the timetable I drew up?"

Connor opened his eyes to gaze at her between his fingers. "You should've been in the army, Mallory. You have our schedule so regimented, all that's missing is reveille."

She drew back. "It's not that bad."

"No?" He glanced down at the papers spread around them. "You arrive home at five-thirty. I hit the road by five-thirty-three. I come in at two-thirty in the morning and sleep until six, because I'm scheduled in the bathroom to shower and shave from six-o-five to six-twenty-nine. At six-thirty, you have the shower so you can leave the house at seven." He leaned across the table and slammed a hand on the page. "How do we communicate? When? Don't parents—uh…people who raise kids together—need debriefing time?"

Mallory blinked. Moving his hand, she frowned down at her copy of the timetable she'd blocked into *his* and *her* segments. "I don't see any problem. I assume we both have voice mail at work."

"Voice mail? Dammit, Mallory."

Her frown became a scowl. "You promised to watch your language, Connor."

"I did. I'm sorry. You're not going to budge on this schedule, are you?"

"At least let's try it for a week or two. Is that too much to ask?"

"Okay. So, after today, I fix Liddy and me breakfast and lunch. You're on your own. Then you and she have dinner together, and I'm eating at the U's cafeteria. I do morning, noon and four o'clock exchange. You handle the one at night."

Mallory beamed. "See how logically that fits with our work schedules? Except for today and through the weekend. By the way, I've already done Liddy Bea's morning exchange."

"What about weekends?"

"What about them?"

"You've got the same schedule seven days a week. Do you work weekends?"

"Sometimes there are Saturday-night fund-raisers. Typically, Liddy Bea and I save Saturdays for errands. Sundays we meet Dad for church and spend the afternoon and evening at Forrest House. With Dad's busy schedule and my working, it's about his only opportunity to spend time with her."

Connor saw that she'd manipulated the week quite nicely to keep the two of them separated as much as humanly possible and still share quarters. "Since you've sewed up Liddy Bea's Saturdays and Sundays, I guess those are days I can socialize?"

She looked confused, so he spelled it out. "For instance, if I want to invite co-workers in to say, swim or have a barbecue or just hang out, Saturday or Sunday would be the best time for me to do that?"

"I, ah, are you talking about dating?"

Connor hiked a shoulder and his lips quirked in a smile.

Mallory's neck grew blotchy and red. She folded her

hands atop the pages and muttered, "You've repeatedly said that the point of this exercise is so that you can get to know Liddy Bea better. I never factored in more than that, Connor."

"Well, you factored me out of her weekends. Am I supposed to twiddle my thumbs two days a week?"

"No. I assume you'll have laundry, grocery shopping, and…and stuff," she ended lamely.

"I planned to handle domestic chores during the day. Remember, I said we'd be partners in running the house. I know you've had to do it all alone up to now. Part of the reason I suggested a fifty-fifty split was to free up more time for you to have fun. Remember how we used to go to the beach or rent movies and make popcorn at home on a rainy afternoon?"

"I…uh…haven't had time for those things in years."

"Well, you will now. So rework this schedule." He smiled winningly and lightly tapped his finger on her chart. Turning his smile on Liddy Bea, he said, "Come on, kitten. If we're going to visit the U and be back in time for your noon exchange, we'd better rinse our plates and put them in the dishwasher."

"I don't make Liddy Bea clear her dishes, Connor. You go on. I'll clean up."

Connor, who'd risen from his chair, gazed obliquely at the child seated between them. "As long as she's feeling okay, isn't it time she start learning to help around the house?"

Mallory returned a scathing look.

"I wanna help." Liddy Bea jumped from her chair and carefully picked up her plate.

"She's only six," Mallory hissed.

"You want some man to have to teach her how to

cook and sort laundry after she's grown, like I had to do with you?''

Liddy Bea stopped on her way to the sink and turned. ''You taught Mommy to cook? Where was my daddy?''

Mallory kicked Connor's shin.

''Ow.'' He bent and rubbed the spot. ''Sorry, two weeks,'' he mumbled. ''I didn't know she had a mind like a steel trap,'' he mouthed.

''Now you do.'' Mallory stacked her own plate and silverware. ''Liddy Bea. One of these days I'll go to Grandpapa's and dig out a box of old pictures I have stored in his attic. When Connor and I were young, we belonged to the same group of volunteers, who helped people affected by hurricanes. We worked out of tents. Back then, there were a lot of things I wasn't good at. Grandpapa and Grandmother Beatrice employed a cook, a housekeeper and a gardener, in addition to Davis, who drove Uncle Mark and me to school and appointments. I was pretty helpless.''

''Oh. Was my daddy there? Do you have pictures of him, too?''

''Lydia Beatrice. Where has all this preoccupation with your father come from?''

The child went sullen. ''Jordanna and Alexis have pictures of their daddies. Alexis said if I don't have a daddy, maybe I was hatched.''

Connor guffawed. ''Alexis was teasing you, kitten. Some kids are worse than others about that. By the time you start first grade, maybe your mom will have found a picture of your dad in those old photos she has stored in the attic.''

A sunny smile replaced Liddy's pout. ''Okay. Let's go, Connor. Can I carry the box of doughnuts?''

''You may.'' He checked his watch. ''We'll be back

by twelve, Mallory. Use the time we're gone for yourself. Unwind,'' he said, stepping behind her to massage her tight shoulder muscles.

In short order, she all but purred. ''Mmm, I've missed the back rubs you used to give.''

''Yeah? Me, too. Especially the ones in the tub,'' he growled very near her ear.

Her eyes popped wide open. ''Enough,'' she said, briskly ducking out from under his clever fingers. ''Have a good time,'' she rushed on, dropping a quick kiss on her daughter's upturned face. ''Remember, Connor, she has to be buckled into the back seat.''

''I do read,'' he said dryly. ''That was number three on your rule list.''

MIDWAY THROUGH THE SECOND week, Connor thought things were going well in spite of Mallory's growing list of rules. Every time something came up that threw them in close contact with each other, she adjusted the schedule or added a new rule.

He bided his time, figuring everything would change by the end of the week, when she promised to reveal his identity to Liddy Bea.

Meanwhile, he kept busy. His monitors had been delivered, set up and seemed to be functioning normally. His personal things had arrived. Mallory had actually dedicated part of her weekend to helping him find storage space for almost everything.

She'd run across a framed photo of herself in her college cap and gown in a box of items that had come out of his home desk. It did Connor's heart good to see how disconcerted she was, although she insisted he couldn't set the picture on his nightstand. ''Two weeks is nearly up,'' he warned, reminding her of her promise to tell Liddy Bea who he was the following weekend.

Bradford Forrest dropped by unexpectedly on Wednesday, before Mallory got home and before Connor left to work on his project.

"I've gotta admit, my boy. I had plenty of doubts about this arrangement of yours and Mallory's. Can't say I've ever seen Liddy Bea happier. She's slimming down and has some color back in her cheeks.''

Connor poured the senator a brandy, even though it wasn't yet five o'clock. He opened a bottled water for himself. "It's amazing what cutting down on steroids and monitoring food intake will do for a kidney patient. The first few days, holding her to her diet was murder. Nothing against Marta, but I think she gave in to Liddy Bea's cajoling.''

"As did I. Say, off that subject and onto another near your heart. How are the ocean probes operating? I ran into Don Jarvis yesterday at Rotary. He said the young fellow you've taken on as an aide mentioned underwater volcanic activity.''

"That's right. There've been shake-ups off the Venezuela coast this month.''

"Jarvis seems to think your equipment's faulty. He said his South American contacts don't indicate any storm warnings.''

"They wouldn't. That's the beauty of my system. My deep-water probes signal oceanic disruption long before overhead satellites detect anything building.''

"Huh. Jarvis is the local weather guru you've gotta convince if your probes turn up any warnings. With his attitude, I don't envy you. Well, thanks for the update and the brandy. I've got late committee meetings tonight, tomorrow and probably into the weekend if those dunderheads can't decide on appropriations to widen our main evacuation routes. We go through this exercise in futility every year. I'm afraid they'll see the error in their tightfisted ways too late. Liddy Bea? Come kiss Grandpapa goodbye.''

She skipped out of her room, her arms full of Barbie clothes. ''Bye, Grandpapa. We'll see you at church on Sunday.''

Connor followed Brad to the door. ''I don't want to cry wolf, Senator. But I'm concerned by the steady increase of deep-wave activity in the same location. Florida could face a hurricane of the magnitude of Andrew. Your committee may want to set money aside for disaster relief if they aren't willing to facilitate evacuation.''

''You wouldn't be pulling my leg, would you, son?''

''Senator, I never joke about hurricanes. I don't like the data I've seen coming in. And this started before I left Miami. Another meteorologist and I physically checked the monitor I have in the straits. It's operating fine.''

''Huh.'' Bradford tugged at his lower lip. ''I'll pass that on.''

THE FRIDAY MORNING AFTER Bradford's visit, Liddy woke up cross. Nothing Connor did could please her. She refused to eat. ''My tummy hurts, Connor.''

He didn't see anything amiss when they did her morning and noon exchanges. By two, however, she was so cranky, he left a message on Mallory's voice mail, asking her to phone home.

Three o'clock came, and he hadn't heard a word. Liddy Bea's crankiness turned to tears. Unable to calm her, Connor called the hospital and asked for Mallory's secretary.

''Ms. Forrest is out of the office. She's speaking to the women's garden club about doing a children's fair with the hospital. If it's an emergency, I can page her.''

Connor cocked an ear. Liddy Bea had quieted down. He didn't want Mallory to think he couldn't handle a child who'd merely gotten up on the wrong side of the bed. ''Don't interrupt her,'' he said. ''When she checks in, have her phone home, please.''

He gave Liddy Bea a Popsicle and later rocked her while they read her favorite story. She fell asleep halfway through, and he transferred her to her bed. He noticed the juice had stained her face and fingers and also her shirt. But he wasn't about to wake her to wash up.

Connor was somewhat concerned when she hadn't awakened by four. It was a rare day that she slowed down to under ninety miles an hour. Tiptoeing to her bed, he placed a hand on her cheek. She felt warm. On the other hand, she lay in the middle of enough stuffed animals to make anyone sweat. He decided to let her sleep. Maybe she had a touch of the flu. Or maybe this was typical of kids.

Liddy woke up shortly before five, in a better frame of mind. Connor bathed her face and hands with cool water and found her a clean shirt.

''Are you hungry now? You skipped breakfast and lunch.''

She shook her head. ''I want more juice. When's Mommy coming home? My tummy still hurts.''

''It does?'' Connor checked his watch. ''Mom's late. I figure she'll be here any minute. Do you know where the thermometer is? I should take your temperature.''

Again the little girl shook her head.

Connor was rummaging in the medicine cabinet when the doorbell chimed.

Carrying Liddy Bea, he went to the door, peeped out and saw Davis. "Hi," Connor said, after shifting Liddy Bea so he could unchain the door. "To what do we owe this unexpected visit? The senator's not here. Haven't seen him since Wednesday."

"I know. Miss Mallory phoned. She's running late. Rather than detain you, she asked Marta to watch Liddy Bea for a couple of hours."

Connor glanced at the flushed child. "I tried to phone Mallory earlier and we didn't connect. Liddy Bea's complained of a stomachache off and on all day. In fact, I was just hunting for a thermometer."

"Oh? Not feeling well, little lady?" Responding to her droopy shake of the head, Davis looked at Connor. "Bundle her up and I'll scoot right home. Marta has four grandchildren she watches when they're sick. I'm sure she has a thermometer."

"All right, if you think that's what Mallory would want."

"Does Grandpapa have my fav'rite juice in the limo?" Liddy asked, showing a spark of interest.

"You bet." Davis grinned. "After juice she'll probably feel right as rain."

ALL EVENING CONNOR KEPT expecting a call from Mallory. He tried phoning home a few times, but always got her voice mail. Not wanting to appear the nervous dad, he refrained from calling Forrest House. Besides, the reports spitting out of his computer had him and his aide, Jim Kirkpatrick, hopping. A circle of volcanic activity deep in the ocean off Venezuela had increased. Even forecasters had begun to report a tropical depression moving toward the West Indies. Connor and Jim elected to continue monitoring the storm.

Things didn't grow calm until after one in the morning. He couldn't call now and scare Mallory out of ten years' growth. He'd just leave his office in time for his turn in the shower.

By 5:00 a.m., the tremors had totally subsided. Connor stretched. "Go on home, Jim. Thanks for staying. This is the type of early warning we're running this experiment for. I've gotta go take care of Liddy Bea, but she and I will drop back midafternoon to check the readings. Can you pop in later this morning? Call if you need me."

"Sure. No problem. I've got nothing scheduled all day."

Connor barely kept his eyes open long enough to drive home. As he parked his vehicle, the fact that Mallory's car wasn't in her normal spot succeeded in jarring him awake. He tore upstairs. The apartment was dark and quiet. Connor didn't make a habit of bursting into Mallory's bedroom, but that was exactly what he did when he found Liddy Bea's bed empty.

Mallory's hadn't been disturbed, either. There was no note on the kitchen bulletin board and no phone message for him.

Before daylight or not, he punched in the number to Forrest House with a hand that shook.

Marta answered in a sleepy voice.

"This is Connor. I'm sorry to bother you at this hour, but I just got home from work. Well, to the apartment, I mean. Mallory and Liddy Bea aren't here. Did Mallory decide to sleep over at Forrest House?"

He listened to Marta's groggy voice.

"What? The hospital? Liddy Bea's cannula is infected? How? When? Why didn't Mallory notify me?"

Marta couldn't answer his questions.

Bypassing his much-needed shower and oblivious to how badly he needed a shave, Connor raced out of the apartment like a wild man. He bolted down the stairs and just managed to stay under the speed limit en route to Forrest Memorial. Fear had his heart knocking against his ribs.

CHAPTER THIRTEEN

CONNOR REACHED THE HOSPITAL'S front doors, running. He didn't slow as he galloped up the stairs to the pediatric ward. A nurse grabbed his arm as he started past the central station. "May I help you?" she asked pleasantly. However, her hand tightened perceptibly as she spoke.

"I'm looking for Mallory Forrest. I just learned Liddy Bea's been admitted again."

"Are you a relative? It's too early for visiting. The doctors are making their rounds now."

His breath heaved in and out. Connor was tempted to say he didn't give a damn about their rules and yes, he was related. *Her father.* Instead, he forced a calm he didn't feel. "Would you please tell Ms. Forrest that Connor O'Rourke is here?"

The nurse studied his unkempt appearance before slowly releasing him. "Wait right here. I'll give her the message."

Connor watched the woman hurry to a room beyond the one where Liddy had been before. He used the time she was away to tuck his shirt into his pants and to drag a hand though his hair in a futile attempt to look more presentable.

It seemed like forever but was really only moments before she came out again, followed by Mallory.

Connor rushed forward, unprepared for the angry

words Mallory threw at him. "What were you thinking? Letting Liddy Bea go sick all day? You should have phoned me."

"I did! I asked your secretary to have you call. What is it? What's wrong with her? I would've called last evening but I had a crisis at the lab. Jim and I worked all night. When I got home, you weren't there, and no messages anywhere. You scared me to death."

"I spoke with Mandy before she left the office. She didn't tell me you called. I'm sorry I yelled at you. But I thought I'd explained how fast infections can flare up. Oh, Connor, Dr. Dahl had to remove Liddy's shunt and put her back on hemodialysis." Close to tears, Mallory blinked rapidly.

"Aren't there antibiotics to combat infection?"

"She's had so many, her system's resistant to the better antibiotics. Her albumin has soared. He's afraid there was a leak in the shunt. Worse than any of this, though— he got a call last night from the national kidney locators. A really close match came in. And…and…we can't risk a transplant." This time Mallory did dissolve into tears.

Connor pulled her tight against his chest. "God, I'm sorry, Mallory." He found himself blinking, too. "Liddy complained of a stomachache off and on. You'd told me to look for redness or swelling around her cannula. I didn't see anything wrong at her exchange."

"But a fever, Connor! Marta said Liddy's temperature was a hundred and four."

"I couldn't find a thermometer. And she didn't feel warm to me till late afternoon—right before Davis showed up. Uh…can we go somewhere more private to talk?" Connor realized they were drawing the attention of nurses and staff.

Wiping her eyes, Mallory took his hand and led him to an empty lounge.

As they sat, Connor kept one arm looped around her shoulders. Unresisting, she accepted his support.

"About this kidney match. Will the organ keep until Dahl gets her infection under control?"

Tiredly, Mallory shook her head. "Fredric says they're researching a method to extend the life of donor organs. It's still experimental. So...no. This chance is lost." Her voice broke. She patted her pockets looking for a tissue.

Connor spotted a box of them on one of the chairs. He yanked out several and gave them to her, feeling to blame for her tears. "I thought she might have a touch of the flu. I swear, if I'd had any idea—any idea at all— I'd have been pounding at Dahl's door."

Mallory gripped his hand. "I noticed she was whiny when I went in to wake her yesterday morning. I let her sleep in, anyway. My mind was on my meeting with the garden club. Speaking of which, what was your crisis at work?"

"False alarm," he said. "Something that bears keeping an eye on, though. How does hemodialysis differ from what we've been doing?"

"Instead of half an hour three times a day, it takes four hours three times a week, here at the hospital. Hemo is a complete transfer of blood through a machine called a dialyzer. It filters out waste. The clean blood is returned to the body. She now has a fistula in her arm. Did you notice the scars from previous veinal cut downs? She's had so many."

"I just figured all kids have scars from playground mishaps. Can I see her? How's she holding up?"

"She's a trouper. I'm the one who falls apart."

Connor stroked the side of his forefinger along her jaw and suddenly, without warning, dropped a kiss on her trembling lips. "You're entitled, Mal. I wish you'd rousted me. The reason I'm hanging around is so you don't have to shoulder these burdens alone anymore."

She touched her lips where he'd kissed her, her eyes remaining skeptical. "Right. You're as tied up with your work as Dad is with his. He had an early meeting to chair and couldn't be here, either."

Connor picked up both of her hands and held them loosely. "Why can't you accept that I'm in Liddy Bea's life to stay? And yours, too," he said gruffly.

Mallory tugged her hands away. "I wish I could believe you, Connor. Yesterday Alec pointed out that if you had to choose between Liddy Bea or chasing a hurricane, the storm would take precedence."

"He doesn't know me. But you do. Is that what you think?" Connor scrambled to his feet. "If Robinson's so damned concerned about Liddy's and your welfare, why isn't *he* here holding your hand?"

"He's responsible for running the hospital." Mallory leaped up, too. Then she put a hand to her head, and her shoulders bowed. "I can't do this. I can't referee between two grown men. The truth is, Alec, who has older kids, tends to ignore Liddy Bea. And these last two weeks, you've been great with her. I promised I'd tell her who you are this weekend, Connor. I considered begging off, given her present condition. But…I've got no valid reason to postpone it. Would you like to go see her now and watch me flounder through the big revelation?"

Connor's eyes went from bleak to glossy with tears. "I don't know what to say—except th-thank you." His throat worked convulsively as emotion gripped him.

"It's long overdue. I'm just…I don't know how—I mean, what's she going to think of me for hiding the truth?"

"She'll always love you, Mal." Connor shortened his steps to match her reluctant pace. He supported her by placing his palm at the small of her back.

Too soon, in Mallory's estimation, they stood beside Liddy Bea's bed.

"Connor, hi. I knew you'd come. I had a 'fection. That's why I didn't feel good."

"I know, kitten. Your mama told me. If that ever happens again, I'm bringing you straight to the hospital."

"Then you're gonna stay? You're not gonna leave 'cause I'm sick so much?" Liddy Bea sneaked a hand under the palm Connor had placed on her pillow.

Mallory moved forward until her hip rubbed Connor's thigh. "Liddy, uh, I have something to tell you. Something I should've brought up the first day Connor visited you in the hospital. He's…uh…not just an old friend of mine. He's your—ah…" She sawed at her upper lip with even white teeth, glancing quickly at Connor before blurting, "I'm trying to say Connor's your father, Lydia."

It seemed for a moment that they all failed to breathe. Then a sunny smile lifted Liddy Bea's down-turned lips. She grabbed Connor's shirt with the hand not connected to an IV. "I knew! I knew you were my daddy. I knew all along."

"You didn't," Mallory gasped. "How?"

"I just did," Liddy proclaimed with a self-satisfied nod. "He knew about Ellie. And he bought me the frog band. That's when I knew. I don't hafta call you Connor now, do I? I can call you Daddy?" She sank back, wearing the brightest of smiles.

Mallory laughed and cried at the same time. Connor attempted to hug both of them, but it proved too awkward, so he settled for hugging Liddy Bea and throwing his left arm around Mallory, while he grinned like a fool.

"Are we all married now?" Liddy Bea queried innocently.

"Oh, no, baby." Mallory gulped, casting Connor a frantic look. "It's…uh…a long story. One you'll understand better when you're grown-up."

The child's gaze traveled from one adult to the other. "Okay." She gathered the stuffed dog against her cheek. It was the one she always slept with at home.

"There you are!" Fredric Dahl popped his head into the room. "You suddenly disappeared, Mallory. The floor nurse thought perhaps you'd gone home."

"No. Connor came. We had things to discuss, so we went into the lounge."

Liddy Bea peered around her mother. "Dr. Fredric. Connor's my daddy. My real daddy."

Dahl managed enough surprise to appear properly dumbfounded. "Well, I guess I don't have to ask if that makes you happy. Obviously it does. Have you told your grandfather yet?"

"Nope. But I will, and he'll be glad, too." She lay back again.

"Did you need me for something, Fredric?" Mallory looked worried. "The new medication's starting to work, isn't it? She seems perkier already."

"What? Oh, yes, she's responding to treatment. I do want to keep her overnight, though. To be certain we have those bugs on the run." A smile rearranged his somber features. "You and Connor both look like something the cat dragged in. Go home. Get some rest. If she continues to progress, we'll do her first hemo in the morning. I'll release her in the afternoon. Alec just told me you'd come back to work. So, let's say you can pick her up when you finish tomorrow."

Connor, who'd remained silent, moved in behind Mallory and rested his hands on her shoulders. "If she's that improved, what's the chance of retrieving the kidney Mallory said you were notified of?"

The sober expression settled on Fredric's face again. "That one's long gone, I'm afraid. As it turned out, it was only a partial match. I'm confident there'll be another for Liddy Bea when the time's right."

Connor felt Mallory tense in disappointment. He didn't voice his own fears and doubts, but they rode very close to the surface of his weary soul. "The doctor's right about one thing, Mallory. We're both in need of shut-eye. You look ready to drop. Why not let me give you a ride home? You can pick up your car later."

"I won't argue, Connor. Liddy, baby, Mommy's going home for a while. I'll be back this evening. As will Grandpapa. He said so when he phoned to see how you were getting along."

"Daddy? Are you leaving, too?" the child asked around a huge yawn.

Hearing the word fall so easily from her lips sent a warmth stealing through Connor. "I'll stay if you'd rather one of us did."

"No. I'm sorta tired, too." She plucked at Connor's shirt. When he bent over her bed, she said in a loud whisper, "If you're taking Mommy home, will you ask her to let me have a puppy? A real one?"

Mallory ducked her head under the crook of Connor's arm. "I heard that. Just because you have two parents now, little miss, doesn't mean you can play each of us against the other. I'm way ahead of you there. I tried those same tricks when I was your age. They didn't work with my folks, either.''

"Then what about a baby sister? Or a brother? 'Cept I'd rather have a sister.''

Not seeing how flustered Mallory and Connor were, Fredric Dahl, who'd reached the door, turned back with a question. "Have I been out of touch during an elopement or something?''

"No,'' they exclaimed in one voice.

"Not for my lack of asking,'' Connor said belatedly, much to Mallory's chagrin. She grabbed him by the arm and tugged him from the room.

"Let's go before this conversation gets really out of hand. Don't forget hospitals are one big gossip mill. And I work here. Furthermore, if this is a ploy you and Liddy Bea cooked up to get me to agree to a puppy, I say…foiled again.''

"It's no ploy,'' Connor assured her, once they found themselves alone on the elevator. "We belong together, Mallory. There's been a hole in my life for seven years. You're what's been missing, Mal.''

She leveled him a stern sideways look. "You missed me so much you happened to get engaged to another woman.''

He heard the underlying pain in her voice. "I'm not proud of the fact, Mallory. But you're right. Looking back, I see I let Claire drift in to fill a void left by you. Dammit, I'm no good at putting what I feel into words.''

Mallory didn't say anything as they exited the elevator and crossed the hospital lobby. She waved absently to a couple of people who acknowledged her, all the while wondering if Connor was telling her the truth or feeding her a line.

He didn't continue their conversation on the short

drive to the apartment. "Are you hungry?" he asked, rousing himself from a stupor moments before he pulled into the garage.

"I get too keyed up to eat whenever Liddy Bea has one of these crises. And frankly, there's not much in the house. Oh—you're probably starved, aren't you? You worked all night, after tending Liddy Bea all day."

"I could eat. Why don't you go on up? I'll run down to the corner store and pick up the fixings for something easy, like pancakes and eggs."

"Okay. Do you mind getting juice and milk, too? One of us will have to tackle some serious shopping tomorrow."

"No problem." He watched her key in the security code and didn't pull away until the lobby door closed fully behind her.

SHE WAS IN THE KITCHEN, putting a kettle of water on the stove, when he returned. "I figured you'd have gone to bed," he said, sliding the grocery bags across the counter.

"I think I'm running on adrenaline. Maybe herbal tea will settle my nerves."

"I'll take a cup, if you don't mind. I've always had trouble sleeping when it's light."

"Me, too. When the water boils, I'll toss a couple of tea bags into the pot to steep. Meanwhile, let's put away the groceries."

"Sounds good. Did you check for messages?"

She shook her head. "No. Expecting a call?"

"Jim Kirkpatrick promised to read our monitors. He's going to call if they kick up again."

"Oh. I'll bring the tea into the living room when it's ready. You can turn on the TV and check the national weather forecast. Unless you'd rather I start the pancakes.''

''Nope.'' He crushed the last sack and stuffed it behind the cookie jar. ''In fact, I don't feel like eating anymore. Maybe if we both put our feet up, the tea and TV will lull us to sleep.''

''O…kay,'' she said somewhat hesitantly.

''No Jim,'' he called from the hall. ''Your secretary, Mandy, phoned. If you're gonna call her back, maybe I'll grab a quick shave and shower while the tea finishes steeping. I like strong tea.''

''I already poured us some.'' Mallory stepped into the hall, rubbing her neck.

''Sore neck?''

''It hurts when I turn my head. Probably because I carried Liddy Bea from the car to the emergency room. She must weigh sixty pounds.''

''Forty-seven,'' he said. ''We weighed her last week at the pharmacy. You've lost more weight, Mallory. What are you now? A hundred pounds?'' His eyes cruised slowly from her neck to her toes and up again.

''Listen, I get ragged on by Alec all the time about how my clothes hang on me like a sack. One critic is all I need. I weigh one-o-eight, thank you.''

''I'm not being critical. I'm worried, okay? Come here. Sit on the ottoman, and let me massage your neck.''

''I thought you were going to shower and then we were having tea?''

''Yeah, well, I hate seeing you in pain. We aren't running on anyone's timetable but our own today. So, whaddya say?''

''Do you think I'm going to turn down a massage when I hurt? Oh, wait a sec. I need to let Mandy know

I'm not coming in today, so she can tell Alec." Mallory appeared more tense than usual.

"Problems at the office?" Connor jumped up to take the tray she carried, with its steaming pot of tea and two full cups.

"Yes and no. Alec invited Mr. and Mrs. Dorset in for a meeting without telling me. They're a prominent couple he's trying to add to our A-list of contributors. I've told him repeatedly not to set appointments without first checking my calendar. He'll just have to take them to lunch without me today."

He watched her gestures as she talked to Mandy. When she finished, he took a seat on the couch, and she settled onto the low hassock he'd positioned between his knees. "You really like your job at the hospital, don't you?"

"It's perfect when Liddy Bea is well. When I have to juggle a job with her illness, well, no job would be ideal."

Connor took a sip from his cup, then returned it to the tray. "Turn around and let me work on that kink. You're wincing every time you lift your cup."

She complied, but not before setting her cup aside, as well. Bending backward, she rolled her head around her shoulders. At one point, she cringed, then stopped abruptly. "Ow, ow, ow." Reaching back, Mallory dug at her neck. Her fingers tangled with Connor's, as he'd begun to press both thumbs against the tight ball of muscle.

He nipped her ear with his teeth. "Stop messing in," he said huskily. "This is my domain."

"You bit me." She laughed, but hunched a shoulder to her ear. "Oooh. And your face is rough."

"Is this the same woman who used to tell me how cool I looked with a four-o'clock shadow?"

Mallory relaxed and planted her elbows and forearms on his thighs. At his comment, she tensed. "Back then, I was crazy about the rough-hewn look."

"It's in fashion again. Or don't you watch the entertainment channel? All the TV bad boys have dumped their razors." As his low voice rumbled in her ear, Connor's fingers dipped under the collar of her blouse, widening the small circles on her skin.

She let her head loll against his hands. "Ah, that feels like heaven. If you only knew how much I've missed your magic hands."

He drew her closer. "Just my hands?" Looming over her, he feathered kisses on her closed eyelids.

She caught her breath as his lips moved onto her cheekbones. The instant his warm breath and soft lips whorled around her left ear, her breath sighed out. She felt heat gather low in her stomach. A very small part of her brain pulsed a distant warning; a tiny voice cautioned her to call a halt. She knew where this kind of activity led. However, it had been so very long since she'd indulged her feminine yearnings. She allowed herself a passing thought: What would it hurt to enjoy the prelude to lovemaking?

Connor eased her higher on his right leg, which gave him fuller access to her lush mouth. Since moving in with her, he'd snatched a few harmless kisses. Until now, he hadn't realized how badly he wanted to kiss her in passion and be kissed back.

"You taste like berries," he murmured.

"The tea, it's a mix of raspberry and honey." Her lips formed an O around the word, *honey*. Connor took advantage of the moment, plunging his tongue into the hot interior of her mouth.

Straining against him to ease the new tension winding tight in her belly, Mallory grabbed the points of his collar and pressed her breasts to his chest.

Connor moaned low in his throat and slid sideways on the couch, turning her at the same time so that her full weight rested on the length of his body. He loved the way their lips were welded together, and barely noticed that he and Mallory were frantically tearing at each other's buttons until he felt one fly off his shirt, and air cooled his damp skin.

In no time at all, he divested Mallory of her blouse. The lacy edges of her bra scraped against the hair on his chest. Heat raged in his groin.

Far back in his hazy brain lurked a bit of reason. Reason called him names for taking advantage of Mallory when her defenses were low. Reason reminded he had, without forewarning her, prepared for the inevitability of where this was headed. But, in his own defense, he hadn't gone to the store with any idea of buying condoms. The shelf happened to be right next to the checkout.

Connor might have listened to those objections—except his control snapped the instant Mallory's hand closed over a rigid part of his anatomy that had come to life the minute she kissed him back.

"Wait. I, uh, need to get something." Untangling their limbs, he raced to the kitchen and unearthed his stash from its temporary hiding place behind the cookie jar. He returned almost before she'd struggled upright, and he dumped a handful of condoms on the coffee table.

Her eyes widened at his sheepish grin. Then, driven

beyond reason, Connor toppled fully onto his back, allowing her an opportunity to take the lead if she wanted to.

She did.

Things reheated quickly. Mallory ran her lips from his navel to his pectorals and back again as she dispensed with his belt buckle. When he squirmed to help her, she shoved his jeans and shorts down around his ankles.

Time disappeared for both of them. Once more they were hot-blooded kids, making out on Mallory's narrow dorm bed. Clothing posed few barriers.

Connor rucked up Mallory's skirt. Babbling nonsense, he tore away the thin fabric of her lace bikini panties. At the moment it didn't matter that the panties matched the bra one of them had flung over the lampshade. The only significant thing was pleasing each other. Fumbling only slightly, she sheathed him with a condom he handed her.

Connor lifted her slight weight so that she could settle over him.

She realized he'd encountered resistance. Things were moving too fast; after all, she hadn't experienced a sexual relationship in almost seven years. "Sorry," she panted, looking into his unfocused silvery eyes. "It's been a long time for me."

"And me. Slow down. Come here and kiss me."

She stiffened. "No more lies, Connor. Not now. How could it be a long time for *you?* I heard Claire ask for one room at my dad's. And I know how long you spent in hers later."

"I'm not lying." He stroked his hands up her sides and cupped her breasts, reveling in the way they still fit his palms nicely in spite of the weight she'd lost. "About the time I learned about Liddy Bea, the fact that

I'd never slept with Claire became an issue for her. A big issue. That's all I'm going to say about our relationship. I should have realized a lot sooner. You stood between us. Always.''

''Really?'' Mallory smiled, shook back her hair and took all of him inside her.

From then on, she gave, he took. He gave, she accepted. Until sweat poured off them both, and her chin and breasts were tender from the scrape of his shadowy beard. They climaxed in a merging of flesh that left them both limp and clinging weakly together.

Slowly the air from the overhead fan cooled their exposed limbs and Mallory's backside. ''Um,'' she murmured, lazily outlining each of Connor's ribs. ''Oddly enough, my neck doesn't hurt anymore.''

His deep chuckle jiggled her body where she lay sprawled on top of him.

''Don't laugh. I wasn't finished. I was about to say my face feels as if I've undergone a dermabrasion. In case you aren't familiar with the term, it's also known as a face peel.''

Connor lifted his head and inspected her skin. ''Ouch. Jeez, Mal, I'm sorry. I should've shaved first.''

''I'll heal.''

''Not before people out in the world guess what you've been up to.''

''Regrets, Connor?'' She levered herself off him and began to collect her garments that were strewn about.

He sat up. ''I regret marking up your skin. If not for that and one other detail, I'd be happy to spend the rest of the day on this couch with you.''

She glanced up from a critical examination of her useless panties. ''What's the second detail?''

Swinging his legs off the couch, Connor slid into his jeans. "The fact that we still aren't married."

For an instant a look of panic crossed her face. Then she shrugged. "There's no need to rush."

"We have a child. Why not do what we should've done seven years ago? We're compatible on all the levels that count. We both love Liddy Bea. Why not quietly tie the knot? Or if you want to make a big splash at a church wedding, that's okay, too."

Mallory wadded her undies in one hand and pulled her blouse together with the other. She seemed to want to speak, but no words were forthcoming.

Connor approached her hesitantly and lightly trailed his fingers down her cheek. "I love you, Mallory. I think I always have. I sense that you want something more from me than I've given up to this point. Tell me what. I'm trying my best not to blame your mother for stealing seven years of our lives. I've relocated to be near you and Liddy. Now she knows I'm her dad, and she's comfortable with it. What more can I do?"

"I don't know, Connor. It's like I'm all wound up inside, waiting for the other shoe to drop. Maybe it's because I've loved you forever. For me, there's never been any doubt. But you did leave."

"Yes, I did. I had a problem with who you were, compared to me. I was also set on fulfilling a promise I made when my mom died, to keep other people from needlessly losing their lives the way she did. I don't care about the difference in our backgrounds anymore, and I'm close to realizing my promise. You and Liddy Bea are important to me, Mallory. Why can't you see that?"

"How important?"

"Very. Very, very," he added when her eyes reflected unmistakable cynicism.

"Maybe this is too soon for me, Connor. My life these past seven years has inched forward a day at a time. There were weeks I longed for you so much, I felt physically ill. And when I found out you'd come back to the States, I waited for you to phone. You didn't. I grew to accept that. Then circumstances forced me to go to you. And…and I discovered you were engaged."

"I've explained how my engagement to Claire came about. As for not contacting you when I reached Miami—" He raked a hand through hair that was already awry. "I honestly assumed you'd gotten on with your life. When I pictured you, which I tried not to do because it hurt, I saw you married to some political type with a mansion not unlike Forrest House."

"You hurt. I hurt. Wounds take time to heal. Maybe that's what I mean. I don't know what more I need. I only know I can't make any kind of commitment."

"I'm sorry. I'd reach back and change our lives if I could. Since that's not an option, I'll just wait until you're ready to marry me."

"All right." Turning, she walked toward the door that led to the hall. "And another thing," she said over her shoulder. "This…today…just now…was a fluke. No matter how enjoyable, it can't happen again until we do get our lives sorted out."

Connor followed her, pressing so close, Mallory stumbled. "I'm glad you didn't try to insinuate it was unpleasant. You may be sure of your control, Mal. Mine is rocky at best. And nonexistent when we're in the same room. Oh, a word of warning. If I see Alec Robinson sniffing around you, I won't be responsible for my actions."

Eyes nearly navy in the dim hall light, Mallory blinked once, then turned and fled to her room.

Still too on edge to think of sleeping, Connor walked more slowly. Though their bathrooms were separated by Liddy Bea's bedroom, he heard Mallory's shower running when he stepped into his. His imagination ran wild. Connor wondered if she remembered the many times they'd taken a shower together, usually after they'd both come home from hard days at work. Bracing his hands on the tile wall, Connor gnashed his teeth and let the hot spray wash away taunting memories. He used all the hot water in the tank before he felt in control enough to shave with the blade he preferred over an electric razor.

It was a new man who reentered their shared living space. Hearing Mallory rummaging in the kitchen, he went to investigate.

She glanced up, surprised when his long shadow blocked the sun streaming into the breakfast nook. "Oh, I assumed you'd gone to bed. I tried lying down. I'm afraid I'm beyond tired." Blushing faintly, she gestured to the teakettle on one of the stove burners. "At the risk of repeating the process during which we first went astray, I'm brewing a new pot of tea."

He remained standing in the doorway. "I'd argue the point about going astray. But there are certain drawbacks to getting older. Power surges are fewer and farther between. If you'll trust me on that, I wouldn't mind sharing a cup. I may even have a piece of the banana bread Marta sent over with your dad on Wednesday." As if underscoring his hunger, Connor's stomach growled.

That broke whatever tension still lingered between them. Their combined laughter, however, was cut short by a ringing phone.

"Do you want to get it, or shall I?" he asked, cocking his head to one side.

"You. If it's for me but not about Liddy, please fib. Say I'm asleep."

"Okay." Stepping to the wall phone, he snatched up the receiver before the voice mail kicked in. "O'Rourke, here. Oh, James, hi. What's up?"

Mallory moved quietly about the kitchen, pouring tea and slicing generous slabs of Marta's bread. She pursed her lips nervously as she watched the range of emotions that flickered across Connor's handsome face.

"I'll be there in ten minutes," he said. "Fifteen, tops." Hanging up, he started out of the room.

Mallory called his name twice before he glanced back. His eyes roamed over her for a moment without really seeing, and then he seemed to connect with her again. She wasn't sure if he'd totally blanked her out, or if he was surprised to see she'd cut the bread and set two places at the table.

"I've gotta dash to the lab. Jim has odd feedback coming in from a unit I have in the deep water off Brazil. The tracking station in Venezuela reports calm."

"Oh." She shrugged. "You're going back in with no sleep or food? Can't your tech store the readouts?"

"I don't know why there's a discrepancy. And it *is* my system. My neck on the line. You go ahead and eat, and catch some Zs. If this blows over, I'll meet you at the hospital in time to pick up Liddy Bea. Or I'll be at the lab if you need me sooner."

With that, he banged out the front door.

Mallory sank down in the chair across from Connor's steaming cup of tea. It took a while to wade through all her fears and worries, all her memories, both sad and good. In the end, she had her answer as to why she'd hesitated about saying yes to Connor's proposal. He'd told her she was important to him, and that Liddy Bea was, too. But the truth was obvious—they weren't as important as his project. Maybe it was an unreasonable expectation, but dammit, she wanted to be the top priority to the man she married. Crossing her arms on the table, she put down her head and wept for all that might have been.

CHAPTER FOURTEEN

"I PROBABLY BOTHERED YOU for nothing." Jim Kirk-patrick greeted Connor with a long face.

"Show me what you have."

James picked up a stack of computer printouts. "These ran over three hours. The velocity readings are to the edge of the chart. Using the calibrations you set up, I thought we were in for a huge blow. So I called you. Almost immediately the activity stopped. Boom. Gone."

Connor flipped through the stack, repeating Jim's calculations. At the end, he threw down his pen. "Weird. My formulas extend out exactly the same as yours. If the impulses hadn't stopped, I would've said we were looking at two, three days at the most to batten down the hatches all along the coast."

"Lucky for them the ocean earthquakes quit shaking."

"Yes. But the question is, why? All the studies I performed in the South Pacific showed that if the underwater plate activity reached these levels, it always triggered a destructive tsunami or a stage-four hurricane."

"Maybe we're looking at the proverbial calm before the storm. Could these intermittent rumblings be a prelude to the big one?"

"Don't even whisper that, Jim. It's still early for big hurricanes." Connor flipped pages on a desk calendar.

"Maybe sharks or some curious fish batted my probes around. The inconsistency, though, has me baffled. That's what I have to be able to explain to the powers that be."

"Which reminds me. You had a phone call from the man himself."

Connor raised an eyebrow as he waited for Kirkpatrick to produce the message he was looking for. "And who would that be? I'm the new guy in town, remember."

"Don Jarvis is Tallahassee's weather guru. He's the director of Gulf atmospheric dynamics, appointed by the governor. He rules. Jarvis began the conversation by saying he'd spoken with Senator Forrest. And he went on to ask in his arrogant way if you'd been holding on to data he seems to think it's his right to have."

Connor groaned. "Brad Forrest mentioned Jarvis. Projects like mine threaten guys like Jarvis, who can't imagine prediction possibilities beyond the tried-and-true methods of satellite-produced data."

"Yeah. Jarvis lectured at a few of my advanced meteorology classes. The guy grew up on the cutting edge of satellite weather transmission. You'd think someone like that would embrace new possibilities for research."

"If you're okay here by yourself, I probably ought to pay him a visit. I've wanted to tour the new weather information center, anyway. In the seven years I've been away, the state's pumped a lot of money into upgrading the site, or so Senator Forrest claims."

"How did you get in so tight with a senator, if I may be so nosy as to ask?"

"Have you missed the rumors? Brad Forrest is my daughter's grandfather."

"Zowie. That would be Mallory Forrest's kid? Ms.

Forrest is hot. A real babe. Uh…jeez, sorry for thinking out loud." James backed off. "I've never met her, only seen her on TV. On the news—at fund-raisers. But how come, if it's your kid, her last name is still Forrest?"

"Long story, James. Someday, if we have time on our hands, I'll tell you. Maybe by then I'll be lucky enough to have rectified that oversight." Hoisting himself out of his chair, Connor slid the data sheets together, folded and pocketed them. He left the office with a smile and a wave.

MALLORY HADN'T THOUGHT she'd fall asleep after Connor left. But she did. Awakening much later, she felt totally refreshed and relaxed for the first time in a long while. For the latter, she had to credit Connor. Good sex had a way of stripping away tension. And good sleep had a way of restoring perspective. Once again she experienced a sense of hope about her future with the man she loved.

As she prepared to go visit Liddy Bea, Mallory caught herself smiling foolishly. Busy though her life had become over the last few years, she decided it was a shame she had to be so discriminating about the lovers she chose. Well…lover. There'd been only one. Certainly, over the years, she'd had other offers. Unfortunately, none of them were from Connor O'Rourke. And after today, Mallory understood why she'd held out for him. With Connor, she wasn't a prominent senator's daughter, the social catch of the year or any of the other labels attached to having been born a Forrest. With Connor, she could be herself. And that was nice. Very, very nice.

Half an hour later, feeling as if a glow still surrounded her, Mallory slipped into Liddy Bea's room.

"Hi, Mommy. You just missed Daddy."

"Connor was here?" Mallory had expected him to phone sometime during the afternoon. She was disappointed he hadn't, and she'd checked for messages again right before leaving the house. Only Alec had called.

"Guess what? Daddy talked to Dr. Fredric. If I get to go home tomorrow afternoon, Daddy said he'll bring me a s'prise." The child's gray eyes sparkled like the sun filtering through rain-laden clouds.

"A surprise? What kind of a surprise?"

"Oh, Mommy! If he told me, it wouldn't be a s'prise."

Mallory didn't know why the news annoyed her, but it did. "Well, you're certainly looking more chipper. The hemodialysis must be doing its job, baby."

"I'm a big girl, Mommy. Not a baby. I'm six, going on second grade."

For no reason, tears sprang to Mallory's eyes. She dragged a chair closer to Liddy's raised bed, and sat, giving the lump in her throat time to go down. "I guess you will be in second grade come September." Mallory linked hands with Liddy's. Gently she stroked the angry black-and-blue marks where nurses had repeatedly drawn blood. In the years since Liddy Bea had been first diagnosed with kidney failure, Mallory had seen holes poked in nearly all of the child's tiny veins and arteries. She'd found that so painful. Watching your child suffer and being unable to do anything about it was worse than being in pain yourself.

Where had Connor been, then? Off pursuing his dream career was where.

That was probably why Mallory harbored resentments over him waltzing in now, stealing Liddy Bea's affections with blithe promises of surprises.

Sighing, Mallory kissed the dimples in the small hand.

Her assessment was unfair to Connor, who'd said time and again that things would've been different if he'd had any idea he'd gotten her pregnant.

"What's wrong, Mommy? Are you mad at Daddy?"

"No. It's just different for me, having him around."

Liddy squeezed Mallory's fingers. "A nice different. I think Daddy's been lonesome for a long time. He needs us, Mommy."

"Really? What makes you say that?"

"The other day, him and me went and put flowers on Grandmama Lydia's and Grandmama Beatrice's special places. Daddy looked real sad."

"You didn't tell me you'd gone to the cemetery." Mallory's brow wrinkled. "I realize I've been lax about taking flowers since we moved, but…you're saying Connor bought flowers for *both* grandmothers?"

Liddy Bea bobbed her head. "Pretty ones."

"I had no idea he remembered where his mother was buried. And for him to remember my mom…well, that's nice." Mallory felt a chunk of ice fall away from her heart.

Even when they'd been in high school, Connor was thoughtful and sensitive, while other boys she'd dated were self-centered. Those qualities, coupled with Connor's sense of humor, were what initially attracted her to him. Well, if you discounted the fact that her pheromones went wacko whenever he appeared.

"Mommy, I'm tired of watching TV. Will you read me a story? Nurse Susy let me bring two new books back to my room after dialysis. Daddy read one, but he said I should save the other for you. He said it'd take my mind off my s'prise."

Mallory laughed. "He's learning."

"Learning what?"

"To be a parent." Her voice sounded happy when she said it. And she retained warm thoughts toward Connor—until she got home several hours later and found he'd left a message informing her that he and Jim Kirkpatrick were flying to Jamaica to check on a probe off the coast of someplace called Pedro Cay. "I'll do my best," he said, "to be home by the time you check Liddy Bea out of the hospital tomorrow. Fredric said she'd be ready to leave sometime around five."

"That's great," Mallory mumbled. "What do I tell her about that damned surprise if you don't get back?"

NEXT DAY, AS LUCK WOULD have it, the apartment was dark and empty when Mallory and Liddy Bea swept in at six-ten.

They'd eaten, and Mallory's nerves were stretched thin listening to Liddy Bea wonder aloud at the top of her voice what was keeping her daddy and thus her anticipated surprise.

Mallory was wiping down kitchen counters with angry swipes when she heard a key in the lock, followed by a thunk, a bump and scratching sounds as if a dozen mice had scampered across the entry tile. Before she could rinse her sponge and wipe her hands, Liddy Bea squealed delightedly and began to laugh.

Mallory hurried toward the hallway, rounded the corner—and fell back in shock. Her daughter's promised surprise pounced on Mallory's bare feet, licking them with a warm tongue.

"A puppy?" She hopped about to avoid the wet nose of the wiggling, squirming ball of white fur. "Connor, you bought Liddy a *puppy* without consulting me?"

"Surprise!" His cocky grin drove the indignation straight out of Mallory's lungs. Striding across the hall, he caught her up in a bear hug and swung her feet clear off the ground. For a man who couldn't have had an hour's sleep in the last forty-eight, he seemed frightfully energetic to Mallory, whose own energy had waned.

"The pup's name is Boo Boo. He's an eight-week-old West Highland terrier that got dumped outside the humane society the day I went there just to have a look. The staff needed time to check him over and give him his shots. Mal, don't look at me like that. Tell me honestly, can you resist that ball of fluff?"

Once Connor had set her back on her feet, Mallory managed to stave off the dog's onslaught. "It's not the shots, Connor, it's the day-to-day care."

"I told Liddy Bea he's largely her responsibility. I bought a bed, puppy food and grooming tools. Oh, and a leash. She and I will walk him during the day."

"But what about our carpets? Who'll take him outside to pee at night? Not Liddy Bea. And you'll be at work."

Connor scratched his stubbed chin and looked sheepish. "Give him a chance, Mal. Kids and dogs go together. I never had a pet, nor did you. Remember how we used to wonder if we hadn't missed something important?"

"No." The protest sounded feeble even to Mallory. Because Liddy Bea held the pup close, and both girl and dog gazed up at her from large, anxious eyes. "All right. We'll give him a try. But I'm warning you, Connor, this had better be your last earthshaking surprise."

That statement seemed to make him hesitate. A guilty expression crossed his face two seconds before he dug a small square box out of his pocket. "Bear with me through one more," he begged, more or less pinning Mallory to the wall.

Liddy Bea hauled her new puppy over to have a look.

"I bet he's brought you something to keep Ellie Elephant comp'ny," she hooted.

Mallory felt her color drain and her heart start to flutter. She raised half-frightened eyes to lock with Connor's unwavering stare. "Not a figurine, Liddy Bea. It…uh…looks suspiciously like a r-ring box."

She didn't take the box, so Connor popped it open. "I saw this in the window of a Kingston jewelry store this morning. "I intended to offer you my grandmother's ring. The one I have in a vault. But I thought we'd save it for Liddy Bea, for when she's older. This ring is you, Mal. It has fire."

She dragged her eyes away from his. The ceiling light reflected off a many-faceted pink center diamond, surrounded by a cluster of rubies. A matching wedding band was a tangle of smaller pink and red stones that blazed in the light.

"Aren't rubies bad luck?" she ventured, watching Connor push the engagement portion of the set onto the third finger of her boneless left hand.

"Old wives' tale," he assured her, bestowing a kiss on the back of her hand. "I love you, Mallory Forrest. Will you be my wife?"

The ring's sparkle was refracted through the tears that suddenly filled her eyes. Mallory found herself tongue-tied. The objections she'd had to their marrying paled in light of the hope she saw on Connor and Liddy Bea's faces, and Mallory stammered out her consent.

Following two additional trips to the car, Connor prepared a celebration he'd hatched while on his unplanned Jamaican trip. A cake, balloons, a small bottle of champagne, even a special chewy toy for Boo Boo. Also newspapers. A whole stack, which Connor distributed three-deep across the kitchen tile. The last item he carried up to the apartment was a child gate. He attached it to the kitchen door. "We'll pen Boo Boo in here at night for a while, to save the carpet."

"Why can't he sleep with me?" Liddy Bea wailed.

"When he's older and house-trained, kitten." Connor brushed away her copious tears. "We've gotta train the little guy. It might upset Mom if he had an accident in your room."

The ring, the smooth way Connor dispensed with Liddy's tantrum, the easy way he called her Mom, coupled with his passionate kiss before they all trundled off to bed, lulled Mallory into thinking everything was going to be storybook perfect.

And life was idyllic for two weeks. During that time, she set an August first wedding date, blithely ignoring Alec's dire predictions of doom. Her brother, Mark, could get leave for the big event and had agreed to serve as Connor's best man. Bradford, though surprised, said he'd certainly be proud to walk Mallory down the aisle.

But then, sometime during the night of July 28, everything changed. A phone call from James Kirkpatrick rousted Connor before dawn. It was one of the rare times he was able to spend in Mallory's bed. He wasn't totally cognizant when he grabbed the phone. He and Mallory had indulged in passionate lovemaking more than once throughout the night—thanks to Fredric Dahl's opting to keep Liddy Bea in the hospital after her regular dialysis to run a series of routine lab tests.

Mallory, slower to wake from love-sated sleep, didn't realize it was Connor's student aide on the phone. Flying out of bed, she began to dress. "Oh, my God, what's happened to Liddy Bea? Fredric said this was just routine."

Connor, naked as a jaybird, rolled out on her side of

the bed and took Mallory's arm. "Shh," he warned, giving her arm a shake. "It's not the hospital, Mal. It's Jim Kirkpatrick. He says all our sensors along the Caribbean corridor have gone crazy. He's afraid this is the storm warning we've been expecting.

Mallory clutched an unbuttoned blouse to her breasts. Connor saw it was the one she'd haphazardly discarded several hours earlier while in the throes of desire.

"Connor?" Her eyes remained wide and still unfocused. "Connor," she repeated. "Mark's due to fly in to Pensacola tomorrow. We're getting married Saturday. Tell me those readings are a mistake," she pleaded. "You aren't going to let a storm ruin our wedding, are you?"

"Mal, honey, calm down." Connor tried to console her by pulling her into his arms. But he was stopped by the tether of a short telephone cord. "What, James? No, I wasn't telling you to calm down. I hear the computers spitting reports like crazy. I'll be there in ten minutes. Maybe twenty." He'd been watching Mallory's eyes grow more horrified, so he adjusted his arrival time.

Hanging up, Connor turned the lamp up a notch to see where his own shirt and pants had landed. He spoke evenly and quietly as he began to pull on the wrinkled clothes. "My system has recorded erratic readings for over a month in that region, Mallory. There's nothing I'd like more than to dismiss this volatility as more of the same inconsistent underwater tremors we've been documenting. I hope that's all it'll turn out to be."

Mallory sank back onto the bed. She hunched over her knees. "But you suspect not. I hear the worry in your voice, Connor."

He knelt in front of her and gathered both her cold hands in one of his warmer ones. "It's barely 4:00 a.m.,

Mal. Go back to bed and get some sleep. I'll phone you at six—or before, if the shaking stops.''

''But what if it doesn't? What about Liddy Bea? She's due to be released at ten. I have that fund-raiser breakfast buffet with the Lady Lions. I have to attend. We agreed you'd collect Liddy Bea.''

Connor chewed on the side of his upper lip. ''If this blows over like the other warnings, there won't be a problem. If not, I'll figure out something else. But Jim's not the one who's supposed to call outlying weather stations if this escalates. It's my job to do that.''

''And Liddy Bea's your daughter,'' Mallory reminded him in a chilly voice.

''Yes, she is. What's one fact got to do with the other?''

Shaking off his hands, Mallory pulled the tangled sheet up around her like a toga. ''I should've listened when people told me you'd put your job before your family.''

''People? What people?'' Connor, who'd reached for his socks and boots, stopped to glare at her through narrowed eyes.

A guilty expression crossed her face.

''Oh, I get it. Alec Robinson's still feeding you lies.''

''Not just him. Dad had reservations when I announced our plans to marry. Anyway, does it really matter who cautioned me? You're proving them right. You're ready to foist Liddy Bea's care onto someone else at a mere hint that your precious machines are acting up. What this says to me is that once again, your career supersedes our relationship, Connor.''

''Supersedes…? That's not fair, Mallory! Listen to me. I've poured my heart and soul into seven years of research to develop an early-hurricane-detection system.

Not for any personal fame or glory, which is what your tone implies. I thought the storm that killed my mom had the same kind of impact on you as it did on me. If these readings are on target, Mal, I have the potential to save lives. A lot of lives.''

"You know what, Connor? That's noble of you." She pounded her heaving chest. "I have a daughter to care about. She's sick and she's not used to being shuffled around to accommodate a job. You spit out Alec's name like it's a dirty word. He may not take Liddy Bea to play in the park, or...or...buy her a puppy. But he's been understanding enough of my concerns to give me time away from work to look after her properly.''

"Good. Great. I have a potential crisis. Why can't you cancel out on today's fund-raiser to pick her up from the hospital? You talk about *my* job interfering. What about yours?'' He sighed, a frustrated sound. ''I'd intended, if necessary, to call on Marta. She could sign Liddy out. But if that's not good enough for you, Mallory, do it your way.'' Shoving his sockless feet into his boots, Connor stomped out of the bedroom.

Dragging the satin top sheet off the bed, Mallory chased him into the hall. ''Fine, Connor,'' she shouted. ''Maybe if you can't leave your stupid equipment, you'd like someone to stand in for you at our wedding, too.''

He stood at the front door, with the pale light of a new morning filtering through the lace curtains that covered the living-room windows. As he scooped up his keys and wallet from the hall credenza, his eyes glittered dangerously. ''If these reports are for real, and Jim thinks they are, the grandmother of all hurricanes could reach our shores before Saturday. Instead of decorating the church, Mallory, you may be organizing volunteers to carry evacuees...refugees...to places like it. As I said,

I'll call and keep you posted.'' Reaching behind him, he wrenched open the front door.

''Are you telling me to postpone our wedding?'' Mallory's voice faltered.

His face a harsh mask, Connor answered through gritted teeth. ''Maybe. I don't know yet. But our wedding won't be the only thing disrupted. Houses and businesses will be boarded up to withstand eighty- to one-hundred-mile-an-hour winds. Shipping will be suspended due to massive swells. Even with early warning, boats will probably be lost and air traffic grounded. That's a worst-case scenario, Mallory. I've got to go. So are you handling Liddy Bea's hospital release? I repeat, it's entirely possible that this is another false alarm, and I can go get her and take her back to my office. She loves stapling reports and playing computer solitaire.''

Mallory barely had time to croak out her consent, adding that Connor should phone Mandy and ask the secretary to page Mallory, before Connor slammed out of the apartment. He left her with satin pooled around her feet like the train on her wedding dress. A dress she might never get to wear.

Their entire exchange seemed impossibly surreal, especially after the fantastic night they'd spent together. What just happened was a lot like a replay of the argument that resulted in their first breakup.

Crumpling, Mallory sat in the puddle of satin, waiting for the tears burning the backs of her eyes to fall. They didn't, though. Perhaps she'd shed all her tears over Connor O'Rourke. All she felt was a big, empty hole in the place her heart ought to be.

Minutes ticked by. At last, when it became patently clear that Connor wasn't going to have second thoughts and come back, she rose with as much dignity as possible and stalked to the bathroom. Mallory went in to shower—to cool off and to prepare the explanation she'd have to give Alec for not staying until the end of the breakfast fund-raiser she'd worked so hard to pull together.

If Connor's crisis proved to be real...

JAMES KIRKPATRICK GLANCED up from a desk overflowing with computer printouts. "Jeez, Professor O'Rourke, pardon me for saying so, but you look like something that crawled out from under a rock."

"What do you expect? You jerked me out of bed. I'm not a night owl, James. Tell me, has anything changed since you phoned?"

"The surges appear to travel in waves. Is that good or bad?"

Connor went to stand behind his aide. He peered over James's shoulder at the dancing graph. "Let me rerun the calculations. From what I can see, the activity doesn't appear to be increasing. On the other hand, this time there's some type of deep ocean disturbance from off the coast of Brazil, all the way to Cuba. Why don't you take a break? Go grab us coffee and muffins or something." Connor dug a twenty-dollar bill out of his jeans pocket and tossed it on the desk.

"Gosh almighty, I hate to leave if all hell's gonna break loose."

Connor managed a smile for the eager young meteorologist. One he really didn't feel. Yet he wasn't so old that he didn't remember his student days. Too often all they dealt with was routine weather; aberrations were welcome. No longer an eager student, Connor would rather the weather stayed balmy and bright.

"You won't be gone ten minutes, Jim. Even if something is building in the lower Atlantic, the point of my system is *early* warning. That means we can calculate the direction and magnitude before any of the satellites even register a tropical depression. If this is big, there'll be a day or two, not merely minutes, to add to your education.''

''I guess so.'' The young man snapped up the twenty and headed out.

''By the way, Jim, my daughter's getting out of the hospital at ten. I've set my watch alarm for eight-thirty. If this storm remains steady, I'll slip out for a bit, check her out and bring her back to the office. Otherwise, if it blows up in our faces, I need to notify Mallory in enough time so she can leave some big do she's in charge of.''

''Oh. Is Liddy Bea sick again?''

Connor shook his head. ''Routine tests. Dr. Dahl says she's looking so good, he wanted to redo all the blood tests to see if there's a decrease in her antibodies. An elevated antibody count ruined her opportunity to get a kidney last time.''

''That's too bad. She's a sharp little kid. And cute as a bug. I hope these tests show an improvement. She deserves a break. Her mom, too. Oh, and you, Prof.''

''Amen. Only, according to Mallory, perfect kidney matches don't grow on trees. The list is miles long. Lydia may have missed her chance.''

James went quietly out. But really, Connor thought, what else was there to say? At times, *sorry* didn't cut it. Still, at times *sorry* went a long way. Looking back on his rift with Mallory, he realized he'd acted like an idiot because of his jealousy over Alec Robinson's attempts to turn her against him. Connor reminded himself that she'd said stuff, too. Still, when he phoned Mallory, he'd have to apologize.

He'd plowed through all the old data and half of the new that rolled in by the time James returned from a nearby coffeehouse. He'd set down two steaming cups of chicory coffee and piping-hot muffins.

"Hey, Prof. You have sort of a frantic look. Something big brewing?"

"Could be." Grabbing one of the coffees, Connor wrenched off the lid and swore after taking a hot swallow. "Pull up a chair and give me your take on these latest readings. There are chips imbedded in the devices to measure noise levels along the corridor, and they've come to life in the last few minutes. They have a high threshold. I think if this doesn't stop in another half hour, I'm going to start notifying weather stations from here to the West Indies."

"That's sticking your neck out, isn't it? I'm here to tell you the sun is out and there's not a cloud in the sky. I have a broadband in my car that gives weather reports from Puerto Rico, Haiti and the Bahamas. What I heard is they've all got the same conditions. Sun, blue skies, slight breeze. Perfect beach weather."

"Yeah, well, last year the national weather guys hosted me at a seminar for all the heads of the major weather stations. They're aware of my system. Most of 'em were pretty interested in the documentation I handed out from my South Pacific research. I think they'll listen. After all, this baby is breathing down their back door."

"I see what you mean." James tried to whistle through his bite of muffin. "All the checkpoints have risen in intensity since I left." He pulled off two new data sheets. "Wow, take a gander at *this* jump."

Connor did a quick survey, set aside his coffee cup and reached for the phone just as his watch alarm sounded. "Damn, I hate asking Mallory to interrupt her work to go after Liddy Bea. But I predict things are going to get crazy for us real soon. Too crazy to bring my daughter here. I'd hate to frighten her.'' Connor started dialing Mallory's secretary.

''Mandy, Connor O'Rourke here. Will you page Mallory at her breakfast and have her call me ASAP? It's really important that I talk to her. I'll wait to make sure she gets the message.'' Breaking off a cap of the tempting muffin, Connor tucked the receiver between his shoulder and ear, planning to eat a bite while he waited for Mandy to come back on the line. When she did, he dropped the muffin, spreading crumbs all over his charts. ''What do you mean, she left the Lady Lion's breakfast? Dr. Dahl phoned at eight? What for?''

Straightening, Connor rubbed at a furrow between his brows. ''Why would Fredric need her at the hospital ASAP? Dammit, didn't he say *why* he wanted you to interrupt her?'' Connor stood up and began edging around the desk. ''I'm sorry, I'm not yelling at you, Mandy. I'm concerned. If something's happened to Liddy Bea, I don't understand why Mallory didn't notify me.''

He held the phone away from his ear as Mandy's voice grew hysterical.

''Okay, okay, don't worry about it. Do me a favor, please. If Mallory checks in with you, tell her to stay put at Forrest Memorial. I'm on my way.'' He slammed down the phone and raced toward the door.

''Wait!'' James called. ''You're not leaving me with this mess, are you?''

Indecision crossed Connor's face. Then he blew out a breath and loped back to the desk to snap up his cell phone.

''Write down this number and put me on speed dial.

Hand me that list of weather-station numbers. I'll start phoning directors on my way to the hospital. If for any reason this activity eases up in the next thirty minutes, you and I can split up the list and cancel our warning. I don't think we'll have to, though. I promise, Jim, as soon as I find out what's going on with Liddy Bea, I'll scoot right back here. I'm afraid things'll be getting real rough over the next day or so.''

''That's for sure. Say, you'd better take your java along, Prof. In fact, I think I'll call my mom and have her bring us a big thermos of coffee.''

''You do that, Jim, and thanks.''

Connor tried calling the pediatric ward as he hurried to his car. The only number he remembered was busy on two tries. Cursing, he backed out of the college parking lot and began phoning the heads of the larger weather stations along the corridor from the Florida Keys to Panama.

He was completely unprepared for their skepticism. Which was putting it mildly. The last director he phoned, his old nemesis in Miami, Jay Durham, laughed outright.

''O'Rourke, you've been smoking funny stuff. I'm looking out my office window at one of the most beautiful, sunny days we've had all year. If you think I'm gonna put hurricane preparations in motion on the basis of your say-so, you're nuts.''

The crack of Jay's receiver practically deafened Connor. He entered the driveway at Forrest Memorial, unable to appreciate the beauty of the place. He was sick with worry over Liddy Bea, and mad as hell that his years of tedious research were being sloughed off by colleagues.

His queasy stomach tightened ominously when he spotted Mallory's vehicle. Pulling in beside her, he ran all the way to the lobby, walked across it fast and dashed up the stairs. He burst onto the ward, gasping for air. The first person he saw was Liddy Bea. She wore a smile that bloomed tenfold the minute she noticed her dad.

"Daddy, Daddy! Mommy said you couldn't come. She said you hadda work."

Mallory whirled, her eyes traveling quickly over Connor's disheveled appearance. "What are you doing here, Connor?"

"I phoned you to beg off. But Mandy said you'd received a call from Dr. Dahl and that you'd left the breakfast early. Hearing that scared me to death."

"I'm sorry. Fredric wanted me to see the results of the latest lab work. Compared to last month, it's fantastic. Her antibodies are virtually nonexistent. She's been returned to the top of the national donor list. And since Fredric explained that he doesn't know how long this chance will last, they've promised to double-screen her for every kidney they get."

"Hey, that's great." Connor lifted Liddy Bea into his arms and gave her a kiss on the cheek.

"If you were planning to ask me to pick her up, Connor, things must not be going well for you."

"You don't know the half of it," he said grimly. "My system indicates we're about to be pummeled by a huge storm. Not one weather station I've phoned will give me the time of day."

"Connor, that's awful." Mallory's gaze was drawn to the window. "It is hard to imagine, though, with the sun shining like this. I guess I wouldn't blame them, except that I saw your TV appearance. The data you presented was very convincing."

"Thanks. Mal, I want to apologize for my behavior this morning. It was uncalled-for."

She shrugged off his words. "If what you're saying is true, I was wrong for making such a big stink. I'll take Liddy Bea home and let Alec know I'm taking the rest of the day off. How long do you expect the storm to last? Will it blow out by Saturday?"

Connor wished he could assure her that their wedding could go on as scheduled. "Only time will tell, Mallory. Until this plays out one way or the other, I probably won't be home. My advice is stick close to a TV. And keep it tuned to a local weather channel." Wrapping her in his free arm, he kissed her hard on the mouth.

Liddy Bea giggled as she watched them. "Everything's gonna be all right, Daddy. On Saturday Mrs. Sun will shine. And before Mr. Moon comes out, you, me, Mommy and Boo Boo are gonna be a real family."

The nursing staff standing around them clapped. But as Connor walked Mallory and Liddy Bea out to their car, he only wished he could be as optimistic as his daughter.

CHAPTER FIFTEEN

A DAY INTO THE STORM VIGIL, Mallory brought sandwiches to the men. And a razor and clean shirt for Connor. "How's it look?" she asked worriedly, taking care not to let Liddy Bea overhear. "Local forecasters are downplaying the urgency, even though they've upgraded the depression to a tropical storm."

James snorted and said something like "Those fools!"

Liddy Bea ran over to hug her dad. Hoisting her up in his arms, Connor danced with her to where Mallory stood. "You two are a glad sight for weary eyes." He kissed them both.

Liddy wriggled out of his arms and ran off to inspect something that caught her attention. Connor sorted out a series of graphs and showed them to Mallory. "Just look at this obvious buildup. The satellites in Panama have finally come to life. Havana's calling it a deep trough. They've projected heavy wind and rain. But it's more than that. Way more, Mal. Why won't the forecasters listen to me? It hasn't even been a year since they all reviewed my studies from the South Pacific."

She nodded. "I know. By the way, Mark landed at Pensacola last night, and he said the final leg of his flight was pretty turbulent. This hurricane's really going to happen. And it's going to wreck our wedding, isn't it?"

she lamented. "Telling me to cancel had nothing to do with you getting cold feet, did it?"

"Not cancel, postpone. And God, *no!* How could you think that of me?"

"I just did," she said bluntly. "Well, I'd better call the church and the florist and everyone, and then start phoning the people we've invited. Fortunately we kept the list to close friends—only fifty of them." Grinning helplessly, she shook her head.

For Connor, the scene was déjà vu. Maybe he wasn't destined to get married.

"I brought the guest list and my cell phone. May I use an empty desk? When I'm done, I'll find out if anyone's organizing hurricane-relief volunteers," she muttered.

"I'd like you and Liddy Bea to stay. Depending on how the storm breaks after it passes Cuba, we'll know in a matter of hours if it's coming at us."

James rocked back in his chair. "We don't think it'll veer off. Dr. O'Rourke's probes in the Gulf have begun to trip. It's as if the hurricane's traveling along an underwater fault line."

Liddy Bea sat on a quilted bed sack her mom spread on the floor, coloring. "Mommy, we should've brought Boo Boo. If it's gonna storm, he'll be scared."

"Uncle Mark is driving up from the base. Even though he's staying with Grandpapa, I'll ask him to swing by the apartment to pick up Boo Boo. Mark still has a door key," she informed Connor.

He stepped up behind the chair in which she sat and massaged her shoulders. "I'm sorry I foisted off the pup's full care on you these last few days. This wasn't my original plan." Swinging her chair to face him, he curved her ring hand around his. Once her eyes lifted to meet his, Connor pressed his lips to the ring he'd placed on her finger the night he brought home the dog. "I'm sorry about having to shift the wedding, too. Shove it ahead a week. Two, max. Luckily, Mark has a full thirty-day leave."

"I'll ask the church secretary if we can put a tentative hold on a new date. By the way—this building is safe, isn't it? And Dad's office? God, Connor, have you phoned him and stressed how critical your early warning could be to coastal residents? He's in a position to rattle a few cages."

"Meteorologists ought to take my word."

"But they're not," James declared from across the room. "If Senator Forrest has more clout, why not let him use it?"

"You're right. It's stupid to let ego stand in the way of possibly helping thousands." He picked up the phone and punched in his future father-in-law's private number. Mallory began making her own calls.

"Senator? Connor here. I hope I'm not interrupting, but I have an issue I need to discuss with you." Practically hoarse from having talked so hard and fast to colleagues, Connor nevertheless managed to bring Brad up to date.

"What's wrong with Jarvis and the others?" the senator barked. "Dammit, I'll phone that knucklehead and have him meet me at your office. See you in ten minutes."

In the interim ten minutes, clouds blanketed the sky, leaving Jarvis more prone to listen to Connor's dire predictions when he arrived. "I've gotta admit, I don't like the looks of these indicators, O'Rourke. It's just...I've always relied on satellites. Hell, if those shadows on your video probe are an actual path, the storm's racing toward St. George and Dog Island even as we speak.''

''I've been trying to tell you that for two days. This sucker's taking on legs your satellite can't see. Here, check this latest report. The wind velocity's picked up from sixty to seventy miles per hour just since I phoned the senator.''

''I'm sorry I doubted you, Connor.'' Jarvis paced the perimeter of the office, nervously punching numbers into his cell phone. ''What's your guess as to an ETA for this tropical storm hitting our coast?''

''Hurricane, Donald,'' Connor said, taking the liberty of using the top weather bureaucrat's first name. ''Our whole coast's already at risk, as are the boot heels of Alabama, Mississippi and, of course, lower Louisiana.''

''No time to waste,'' Brad insisted. ''I'll use my phone to notify Beatrice's former hurricane volunteers. Mallory, what are you doing? If Jan Long needs help rounding up supplies or organizing evacuees, are you able to lend a hand?''

''I'm canceling wedding guests. Thus far, most of them think I'm being a total flake.'' Her lower lip trembled. ''Not that I blame them. It's only in the last few minutes that our sun's gone into hiding.''

''I'm sorry, honey,'' Brad said, placing a hand over the mouthpiece of his phone. ''But if you don't trust Connor on this, what does that say for your future together?''

''I trust him,'' she said emphatically. ''I'm just disappointed. I've waited such a long time…and, well, given our previous mishap, I'm beginning to wonder if we're jinxed or something.''

''No way,'' Connor insisted from where he sat phoning his original list of weather directors a second time.

"Once we get past this storm, our family will have clear sailing. All the weather forecasters will be begging for my system. From then on, I guarantee you won't be able to pry me out of your bed. Not even if the roof falls on us." He winked, finally forcing a smile out of Mallory.

"You expect me to believe that because—" She broke off teasing him when her phone rang. Everyone in the room automatically lunged for their own instruments at the sound.

"Fredric," Mallory exclaimed. "Wow, is that telepathy, or what? You and Betty were next on my list. Connor's storm-warning system shows Florida's inner gulf, including Tallahassee, is in for a hurricane. We're postponing our wedding for two weeks."

Connor, whose eyes were always on either Liddy Bea or Mallory, saw a tremor suddenly course through her too-thin frame. Since he'd completed his last call, he cocked an ear toward hers.

"Fredric, is this for real? Yes. Yes! Oh, thank you! Lord, it's a miracle. When?" She tipped the phone away from her mouth and beckoned her dad and Connor to come closer. "You guys won't believe this," she whispered. "The national donor list has another organ match for Liddy Bea. In Maine. Bangor, I think Fredric said. A teen in a boating accident. His parents have decided to donate his organs so that his death won't seem quite so senseless. Isn't that wonderful of them? And courageous."

"It must be a tough call," her father murmured. "Fredric's sure of the match? I don't think we could take another false alarm."

"He said it's a ninety-eight percent match. They don't get much closer. Physicians in Bangor are making arrangements to fly us the kidney." Tears filmed her eyes, and the hand that held her phone began to shake. "Maybe our tide is turning."

"Wait," Connor cautioned, "let me speak to him. Depending on when the flight takes off, they might not be permitted to land here."

Mallory looked ashen. "Oh, no! This can't happen to Liddy Bea. Not again."

"Are you licensed to practice in any other state?" Connor was asking Fredric. "In Boston? Good." Sliding a hand over the mouthpiece, he spoke softly to the senator. "Do you know of anyone with a corporate jet who might rent it to us ASAP? I have a pilot's license, and so does Mark. If Dr. Dahl can get clearance at his old hospital in Boston to operate there, we could fly Liddy Bea out of the approaching storm more easily than having them try to land the kidney here. But we'd have to make that decision immediately."

"Yeah, like now," Jim reiterated from a space between the computers. He also wore earphones connected to a battery radio hooked to his belt. "If the whole south coast isn't already broadcasting warnings, they should be. She just plowed across Havana without losing steam. National forecasters have now named our storm Hurricane Annalisa."

Connor and Brad grew still. Jarvis turned shades of green.

First to recover, Connor punched a fist in the air. "It's about damned time. We've been telling them this for hours."

James smiled grimly. "National is taking major flak for not listening to you earlier. As well they should."

"I'm glad my system's working, but personal recognition isn't what concerns me at the moment. Jim, please run those calculations again, based on where Annalisa is now. See how fast she's moving. I need to know how much time we've got to reach the airport and ready a plane.''

"It's two o'clock.'' James fed figures into a program Connor had loaded on his computer. When the young tech looked up from his keypad, his eyes were worried. ''She's smoking. If you're not off the ground by five, gale-force winds could keep you grounded until this time tomorrow. That's provided she doesn't hit us and stall. In that case, we could be looking at two days of taking a beating.''

Connor thrust the phone back at Mallory. "It's not that I don't trust you, James, but I need to calculate this for myself. Mallory, tell Dahl to collect whatever supplies he needs and meet us at the airport no later than three-thirty. Senator, can you lay hands on a plane by then?''

"I think so.''

Mallory relayed Connor's message. When she hung up, she went to Liddy Bea, who'd fallen asleep on the bed sack. Wrapping the child and lifting her, Mallory went to stand by Connor. "Would you really leave in the middle of this mess and fly us to Boston?''

He glanced up, frowning. "Do you imagine I'd send you two off alone to face something as critical as a transplant?''

She raised one shoulder in a negligent shrug. "After we…argued the other day and you charged out of the house, I did think you'd put your work before anything. And now that your predictions are actually coming to pass…''

"First of all, you and Liddy Bea will always be the number-one priority in my life. The other day, I didn't see a problem with having Marta, who's essentially family, watch her for a few hours. As for dealing with the hurricane, my system did its job. I tried my best to get the attention of weather-station directors. Now Annalisa is the mayor's problem and the governor's."

Mallory leaned over and kissed Connor's mouth, even though it was awkward to do while holding a sleeping child.

His hands came up to caress her face. Their kiss continued until Bradford cleared his throat. Even then Mallory pulled back, but Connor rose from his chair to follow her lips.

"Knock it off, you two lovebirds," the senator growled. "I got us a plane, son. A nice six-seater. It'll be gassed up and air-ready by the time we drive out there."

Jarvis joined their circle. "Reaching the airport may be more of a task than you think, Brad. A lot of businesses have closed early to let workers go home and board up their houses. The roads are clogged. Damn! The mayor should've organized a more orderly dismissal."

"I'll handle getting us to the airport," Bradford said. "Davis drives this city like he owns it."

Connor began stowing his reports in a drawer. "James. You've done a bang-up job. It's up to you whether you want to stay and record Annalisa's progress. Or you can leave now to be with your family. Before the phone lines get bogged down, you'd better let your mom know one way or the other."

"Thanks, Professor O'Rourke. I'd kinda like to see this through. I'm already thinking it'll make great report material for my advanced statistical weather prediction course."

Connor and the other men laughed, which awakened

Liddy Bea. She roused and rubbed her eyes. "What's funny, Daddy?"

"We're happy, kitten," Connor said, scooping her out of Mallory's arms. Then, as she caught his eye and gave a small shake of her head, he realized Mallory would rather he didn't tell Liddy Bea about the kidney. Probably in case their plans went awry. So he quickly switched gears. "We're excited because Daddy's invention worked like a charm. You're too young to understand the importance of patents, but believe me, one day you'll appreciate the benefits."

Mallory telegraphed him a grateful smile. "We're going to take a ride on an airplane, Liddy Bea. You, me, Daddy, Grandpapa and Dr. Dahl."

"Not Uncle Mark, and Boo Boo?"

"Maybe Uncle Mark, if Grandpapa asks Davis to bring him. Marta will have to take care of Boo Boo until we return, though." Mallory addressed her dad. "Will you break that news to Marta when you phone Davis? Or better yet, let me talk to Marta myself. I need her to finish calling our wedding guests."

The old man rolled his eyes, but he did as she asked.

ALL THE ADULTS WERE ANXIOUS because it took Davis so long to reach the campus office. Part of the reason he was late was that Mark had asked him to swing by the apartment to grab Liddy Bea's favorite stuffed dog.

"Thanks," Connor and Mallory exclaimed in unison.

Their ride to the airport was slow. Lines of cars and pickups loaded with plywood to board up house windows blocked major through streets. Wind gusts drove torrents of rain over the limo's broad windshield. Thankfully, Liddy Bea snuggled down in Connor's arms with her stuffed dog and drifted back to sleep.

The uglier the sky grew, the more Mallory fussed and fidgeted. "Connor, I feel rotten for doubting you, even for a second. But...are you positive you shouldn't stay here?"

"Yeah, Connor." Brad, sitting beside Davis, looked over his shoulder. "Mark and I have been through a transplant procedure. No reason we can't provide Mallory total support."

Connor tightened his hold on Mallory's hand. "There's a big reason. I'm here for my child and her mother. I wasn't before."

The senator tugged at an earlobe. "That you are. If I didn't apologize earlier for Beatrice's behavior toward you, I'd like to rectify that, Connor."

"Not necessary. All things happen for a reason. For instance, sure the streets are mobbed. But there's a good chance none of these folks will perish in Annalisa. Maybe if Beatrice *hadn't* arranged for my first grant, I wouldn't have been able to design the system."

Bradford relaxed, looking relieved. Mark reached over and slapped Connor's shoulder. "Thanks, Connor. It's time to put all that behind us and concentrate on getting Liddy Bea through this operation."

Dr. Dahl, who sat next to Mark, half turned in his seat. "Do you two pilots actually believe they'll let us fly in this weather? If not, Mallory, you know I'll have to call and release the kidney."

"No," she cried brokenly. "If Liddy misses this opportunity, it's not fair."

"We're going to Boston if we have to steal an amphibious vehicle from the navy and drive up there," Connor told her with deadly calm. "How many hours do we have to claim the organ?"

"It's not merely a matter of laying claim to it," Dahl

said worriedly. "I need time to prep Liddy Bea. To repeat the critical match testing and also lower her body temperature to match the organ that's been iced down for travel. The kidney's already been checked and found to be in good condition. By the way, I asked Rhonda to send a note of appreciation to the young victim's family. On edge as we all are, our situation is nothing compared to theirs."

"They are being totally generous. I hope we get a chance to really thank them. But this weather..." Mallory shuddered and burrowed into Connor's side.

"There's the airport," Davis announced abruptly. "What's the hangar number, Senator?"

Brad rattled it. Through a cascade of rain coating the windows, the car's occupants strained to see the large numbers painted on the buildings they passed.

Finding the correct one at last, they made haste piling out of the car. Accepting Davis's best wishes, all of them except Connor and Mark boarded the aircraft warming on the tarmac.

A mechanic stood nearby. "If you're lucky, you may have a ten-to-fifteen minute window to taxi down the runway and get off the ground," he hollered. "If you'd been five minutes later, I'd have shut her down and gone home myself."

Connor shook the man's hand. He and Mark lost no time in starting down the preflight checklist. The radio crackled. "NT-four, niner, seven, seven, you haven't filed a flight plan. Request to take off denied."

"Control tower, this is NT-four, niner, seven, seven. Time is of the essence. We seek clearance to transport a child to Boston Hospital to receive a kidney delivered there today. Request permission to take off as soon as you have a runway clear.'' Connor sounded calm. Inside, his guts were churning. *What if they still refused?*

He signaled the mechanic to pull the block. As he taxied forward, a blast of wind rocked them wildly. ''Make sure our passengers are all buckled in,'' he told Mark.

''Roger.'' Removing his earphones, Mark took a quick turn through the cabin. He returned in time to hear the tower authorize clearance.

They rolled down the runway, gathering speed. The plane soared aloft, only to be buffeted left, then right and left again by the greedy wind. Pulling back on the stick, Connor cleared the required space and at once went into a steep climb, in spite of knowing he must be scaring his passengers half to death.

Bullet-size hailstones hammered the craft. Thick black clouds swallowed them, plunging them into darkness. For what seemed like an eternity, the flailing plane bucked and moaned. Then, with what seemed a massive push from behind, they emerged above the angry, swirling layers of the storm.

Mark relaxed in his seat as soon as they shook off the ominous clouds.

Connor remained on edge until well after he'd passed Atlanta and turned to follow the unseen coastline to Boston. He didn't breathe freely until Logan Airport controllers acknowledged entry into their airspace.

Bradford and Dr. Dahl hadn't been idle during the flight. They'd orchestrated everything on the ground. A limousine waited to whisk them off to the hospital the moment they touched down. Oddly enough, the weather in the northeast was normal for early August. They stepped out into a crisp, sunshiny afternoon.

Liddy Bea awakened toward the end of the flight. Wide-eyed, she huddled close to her mother.

Mallory followed Connor to where he stood consulting with the hangar staff in charge of storing and refueling the plane. "Liddy Bea is asking a gazillion questions. What shall I tell her? I hate to get her hopes up until she's checked over again and Fredric has his hands on that kidney."

"We have to prepare her, sweetheart. I know kids are adaptable, but she deserves time to prepare mentally."

"What if we get her hopes up, only to have them dashed if something goes wrong?"

"We're out of the storm. The hospital verified the organ's already here. The rest of the operating team's been alerted. Please, stop worrying."

Mallory let him cuddle her a bit before they entered the limo. She mustered a stoic face for their daughter, in spite of the fact that she remained a bundle of nerves.

Even after Liddy had been poked and prodded by the assembled team, and hugged and kissed by her family, Mallory continued to fret. She paced the hall after Liddy's anesthesia had been administered, and she was wheeled into the operating room. "Maybe I shouldn't have been so quick to accept this kidney on her behalf. Perhaps the storm hitting Tallahassee was a warning to back off. What if I was wrong? What if I was just being selfish, Connor? What if something goes terribly wrong? She's been through so much already."

Fully embracing her, Connor rocked her and kissed the top of her head. "Come and sit in the waiting room with Mark and your dad. Do you think Dr. Dahl would have recommended surgery if Liddy Bea wasn't ready? Not five minutes ago, he said her immune-system levels still measured zero percent."

Tears squeezed from under Mallory's tightly closed eyelids. "I know. I must seem an ungrateful wretch to you. It's just...she's so little, and I wonder how much trauma one body can stand. Maybe I've set too much store in wanting her to have a normal life. Maybe I should be thanking God I have her at all."

"Does this self-flagellation have to do with my reappearance in your life, Mal?"

"I don't know. Maybe." She turned in his arms, saying earnestly, "Is it so crazy to fear that Liddy Bea is somehow being punished because I spent seven years wanting you so much?"

"Is that what's bugging you?" Connor used his thumbs to dry the tears glistening on her pale cheeks. "My mom said God doesn't punish people. I can't believe he let me find you and my child, only to rip away our plans of becoming a family."

"So, we're really what you want, Connor? Liddy Bea and me? You don't have a single regret that we screwed up your engagement to Claire?"

"I told you, no. You're the woman who's haunted my sleep. I hooked up with Claire because I was sure I'd lost you. Like I told you, Mallory, if I'd known about Liddy Bea, you couldn't have blasted me out of your life."

"Ok-ay," she sighed. "Let's go wait with the rest of our family."

Mark shifted on a leather couch to make room for them. "Dad went down for coffee. Mallory, we couldn't remember how long the surgery takes. Last time, wasn't it three hours or so? But we had both of you to worry about then, so maybe my recollection's foggy."

Connor drew Mallory into the curve of his arm. "Before they wheeled Liddy Bea away, Dr. Dahl said he figured four hours in surgery and another three in recovery, give or take. Mallory and I get to visit her in recovery. You and Brad will have to wait until they move her to a room.''

''Last time, Dad and I went home to sleep at night. The thing about being here in Boston is that we'll have to find a hotel. I'll go make reservations. How long do you think we'll need rooms?''

Mallory squeezed Connor's knee. ''Fredric said she'd be hospitalized for at least six days. He said Connor and I could get married next Saturday if we'd like. But we'd already decided to wait until the following weekend— and that way, she'll still be able to serve as our flower girl. I'll phone our church secretary right after we see Liddy in recovery and ask Barb to confirm that date, provided the storm hasn't done too much damage.''

''I phoned James while you met with the transplant team, Mal. Early reports suggest less-than-normal damage.''

''Hey, that's great.'' Mark gripped Connor's hand and then hugged his sister. ''When Dad said you'd put off the wedding, I assumed I'd come home for nothing. I had no hope of getting leave again if you'd had to reschedule it a few months from now.''

''What's all the hugging for?'' Bradford asked, walking slowly into the room, carrying a tray filled with cups.

Connor jumped up to assist him. ''We were just telling Mark that if everything goes as we hope with Liddy Bea's surgery, he won't miss our wedding. We've booked the service for a week from next Saturday.''

''Well, that is good news.'' He beamed at them both. ''I phoned to make sure Davis made it home. So far, property damage is minimal, and there've only been three or four reported injuries. No loss of life. And Forrest House stood up well.''

Mallory accepted a cup of coffee. "I'm glad. So, does that mean we can still have our wedding reception there?''

Bradford grinned. "You'd better. Marta's tickled as a pig in slop that you asked her to feed the folks at your reception. You know," he said casually, "what would you all think, if after the wedding dust settles, I put the home place on the market?''

Mark and Mallory looked stunned for a moment. But after the initial shock wore off, they all started talking about possibilities. Discussing how to dispose of the mansion and where Brad would move occupied their time. The hours slipped away unnoticed, except for the fact that Connor and Mallory jumped from their seats every time they heard footsteps in the hall.

"I looked at a condominium near the capitol," Brad told them. "The unit I like has enough space that I'd still need Marta's help. And there's quarters for Davis. I just won't have the pool and grounds to worry about, or all those stairs. But there's extra bedrooms, so Liddy Bea can spend the night. Or Mark, until he finds a good woman to take him off my hands.''

Mark blushed. Fortunately, his father's teasing was interrupted by Dr. Dahl, who stepped into the waiting room, still wearing his scrubs.

"The surgery went like clockwork," he announced, half muffled by the mask he hadn't quite pulled off. "Mallory, you and Connor can go suit up anytime. I told the nurse to let you into recovery for a few minutes. Output from the new kidney is excellent—far better than the first transplant. Barring any unforeseen complications, I think this is a good, solid implant.''

"Thank God." Mallory slumped against Connor. He rained kisses all over her face before standing and pulling her off the couch.

"Come on, let's go see our girl."

Almost giddy in their initial relief, they nevertheless followed hospital rules to the letter as they hurriedly slipped into sterile gear.

Fredric cracked open the door to the recovery room. He pointed out Liddy Bea's crib, then backed out and let her parents tiptoe forward alone.

As if sensing their presence, Liddy Bea groggily opened one eye. A slow smile spread across her face. "Mommy. Daddy. You know what? This time ev'rything's gonna be jus' perfect."

"Yes." Mallory and Connor both spoke. A sheen of tears glossed both sets of eyes. "Dr. Dahl told us your surgery went well," Mallory said, clutching Liddy's hand.

"That's not why I know," Liddy Bea confided through a sleepy yawn. "I know 'cause two angels said so in my dream. An' I believe 'em, 'cause one looked 'xactly like our picture of Grandma Beatrice and the other like Grandmama Lydia." Still smiling softly, she let her eyelids close and went back to sleep.

Standing with their arms locked tightly around each other, Connor gazed down into Mallory's blue eyes and she stared dazedly back. "Why not?" he whispered, feeling a profound contentment creep over him.

"Hmm. And you a scientist."

"Yep. Come on, Mallory. Is it so hard to believe that you and I have turned a corner, headed toward the rosy future we talked about when we were young?"

"No. It feels right. *We* feel right. I love you, Connor. I never stopped loving you."

"I love you, too, Mal. And I will forevermore." Drawing her quietly from the room, Connor put every emotion they were both feeling into a long-overdue, promise-filled kiss.

HARLEQUIN *Super*ROMANCE®

CREATURE COMFORT

A heartwarming new series by
Carolyn McSparren

Creature Comfort, the largest veterinary clinic in Tennessee, treats animals of all sizes—horses and cattle as well as family pets. Meet the patients—and their owners. And share the laughter and the tears with the men and women who love and care for all creatures great and small.

#996 THE MONEY MAN
(July 2001)

#1011 THE PAYBACK MAN
(September 2001)

Look for these Harlequin Superromance titles coming soon to your favorite retail outlet.

HARLEQUIN®
Makes any time special ®

Princes...Princesses...
London Castles...New York Mansions...
To live the life of a royal!

In 2002, Harlequin Books lets you escape to a
world of royalty with these royally themed titles:

Temptation:
January 2002—*A Prince of a Guy* (#861)
February 2002—*A Noble Pursuit* (#865)

American Romance:
The Carradignes: American Royalty (Editorially linked series)
March 2002—*The Improperly Pregnant Princess* (#913)
April 2002—*The Unlawfully Wedded Princess* (#917)
May 2002—*The Simply Scandalous Princess* (#921)
November 2002—*The Inconveniently Engaged Prince* (#945)

Intrigue:
The Carradignes: A Royal Mystery (Editorially linked series)
June 2002—*The Duke's Covert Mission* (#666)

Chicago Confidential
September 2002—*Prince Under Cover* (#678)

The Crown Affair
October 2002—*Royal Target* (#682)
November 2002—*Royal Ransom* (#686)
December 2002—*Royal Pursuit* (#690)

Harlequin Romance:
June 2002—*His Majesty's Marriage* (#3703)
July 2002—*The Prince's Proposal* (#3709)

Harlequin Presents:
August 2002—*Society Weddings* (#2268)
September 2002—*The Prince's Pleasure* (#2274)

Duets:
September 2002—*Once Upon a Tiara/Henry Ever After* (#83)
October 2002—*Natalia's Story/Andrea's Story* (#85)

Celebrate a year of royalty with
Harlequin Books!

Available at your favorite retail outlet.

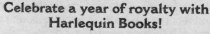

HARLEQUIN®
Makes any time special ®

Visit us at www.eHarlequin.com

HSROY02

Harlequin invites you to experience the charm and delight of

COOPER'S CORNER

A brand-new continuity starting in August 2002

HIS BROTHER'S BRIDE
by *USA Today* bestselling author
Tara Taylor Quinn

Check-in: TV reporter Laurel London and noted travel writer William Byrd are guests at the new Twin Oaks Bed and Breakfast in Cooper's Corner.

Checkout: William Byrd suddenly vanishes and while investigating, Laurel finds herself face-to-face with policeman Scott Hunter. Scott and Laurel face a painful past. Can cop and reporter mend their heartbreak and get to the bottom of William's mysterious disappearance?

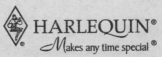

HARLEQUIN®
Makes any time special ®

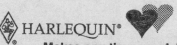

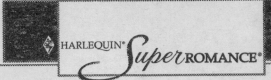